PSYCHO
HOUSE

PSYCHO HOUSE

• Robert Bloch •

TOR
HORROR

A TOM DOHERTY ASSOCIATES BOOK
NEW YORK

This is a work of fiction. All the characters and events portrayed in this book are fictitious, and any resemblance to real people or events is purely coincidental.

Psycho House

A TOR BOOK
Published by Tom Doherty Associates, Inc.
49 West 24 Street
New York, NY 10010

Library of Congress Cataloging-in-Publication Data

Bloch, Robert, 1917–
    Psycho house / Robert Bloch. — 1st ed.
        p.   cm. — (Tor horror)
    "A Tor book"—T.p. verso.
    ISBN 0-312-93217-0
    I. Title.
PS3503.L718P75   1990
813'.54—dc20   89-39881
                                                            CIP

First edition: February 1990
0   9   8   7   6   5   4   3   2   1

This book is for

Kirby McCauley

*just in case he has
nothing to read*

·1·

WHEN Terry and Mick got to the front door the moon went behind the clouds.

"See?" Mick whispered. "Now you know why I said to bring flashlights."

"What are you whispering for?" Terry said. "There ain't nobody here." But Terry's flashlight switched on just as fast as Mick's.

"Don't be too sure." Mick located the smallest key on the loop chain and inserted it in the lock, then hesitated.

"Scared?" Terry said.

"Not me." The key turned in the lock and the door opened. "Anybody coming?"

Terry glanced toward the road. "All clear."

Mick nodded. "Good. Let's go in and see what's shaking."

The two slight-height, short-haired, blue-jeaned figures moved over the open threshold into the office. Here a pungent odor of fresh paint filled the darkness that their flashlights' beams did little to dispel. Blinking, Terry followed Mick to the reception desk, then halted abruptly at the sight of the shadowed shape looming up behind the counter. Only its back was visible.

Now it was Mick who whispered. "See? What did I tell you? It's him!"

Terry gulped. "Can't be."

"No?" Mick reached out to press the silver nipple of the circular bell on the countertop.

There was no sound—but now, slowly, the figure in the shadows turned, and they stared into the face of Norman Bates.

"Welcome to the Bates Motel," he said. "Your room is ready."

His eyes were glassy and his grin was fixed, but only the shrillness of his voice betrayed him.

"Sheesh! How'd they do that?"

"Easy. Ain't no real bell. It's 'lectronic. They got the dummy on a pivot like. You press the bell and it turns on some kinda tape recording."

Terry jumped as the wax figure swung back to its former position. Concealing concern wasn't easy. "So that's ol' Norman! You really think he looked that way?"

Mick shrugged. "They say Fatso Otto wants ever'thing to look, you know, like real."

Terry inhaled, conscious of the paint odor. "Sure musta cost a bundle to build this place."

Mick nodded. "My dad says Fatso Otto borryed it from the bank. Case anythin' goes wrong he ain't going down the tube."

Terry ran the flashlight beam over the office walls, then glanced toward the window. "You're the one who's gonna go down the tube if your dad finds out you borryed his keys."

"Don't worry. Now he's finished up all the painting he won't need to come back here. He just stuck 'em up on a hook in the garage—that's how I got hold of 'em last night and he never seen they was gone, so why should he notice now? All he does is sit there with his six-pack watchin' that scuzzy ballgame."

"Where does he think you are now?" Terry asked.

"Over at the lieberry, doing homework."

"Bet I know what kinda homework you'd really like to be doing," Terry said.

"Shut up! Lieberry closes at nine. We better get moving, you wanna see the rest of this joint."

Turning, Mick led the way to the door on the far wall. It opened without the necessity of using a key. "That's funny," Terry said. "I thought the only way you'd get into the rooms was from outside."

"There ain't any more rooms 'cepting this one, dummy! All the rest is just fake walls made so's it looks like it was the whole motel. Dad says Fatso Otto will maybe add on some rooms later if business is good."

"You think people are gonna come and pay money just to see where ol' Norman did his thing?"

Mick grinned. "We're here, ain't we?"

"Yeah, on a freebie. But so far I don't see why anybody would want to buy tickets to look at a fake."

"Would you like it better if the real Norman was around to come at you with a real knife?"

"He's dead—ever'body knows that."

"What about ghosts?"

"What about cutting out all that crap? You can't scare me."

Which was true. Terry wasn't scared, not even here, as they entered the bedroom beyond the open doorway. That's all it was, just a motel bedroom; nothing different about it except the paint smell. Staring at the bed through the flashlight beam Terry admitted it might be a little more scary if the real reason for coming here was that Mick wanted to Do It To Her.

But sheesh, sooner or later somebody was gonna Do It To Her and it was nothing to worry about; Nila Putnam said she'd been Doing It with Harry for almost a year now and it was great right from the start. Of course who could believe Nila Putnam, she was such a liar, and super-ugly; a hunk like Harry wouldn't touch her with a ten-foot pole.

And let's face it, Mick wouldn't touch Terry, either, because Mick was a girl too. Even though she didn't look any more like Michelle than Terry looked like Theresa. Not in jeans and sweatshirts, anyway. Maybe she'd let her hair grow out over the summer so's it would look better when it came time to start busing over to Montrose High School in the fall.

"What're you standing there for?" Mick said. "Move it."

Terry's flashlight beam paralleled Mick's as they came through the doorway of the bathroom and up to the shower stall.

"Are you ready for this?" Mick said. There was something funny about the way she sounded and Terry realized what it was: a combination of whispering and echo. Voices always have echoes in the bathroom, that she could understand, but why was Mick whispering?

Unless she was getting scared. But hadn't she kept telling her there was nothing to be scared about? Ol' Norman really was dead, and there was nobody here but the two of them.

Then Mick ripped the shower curtain back and there were three.

The naked woman in the shower stall peered up at them, wide-eyed and fearful, her hands raised, open-palmed and pressing outward to ward off the slash of an invisible knife.

There was no blood, but even with her eyes closed Terry could see it; there was no sound, but she could hear the silent screams.

She turned away to face Mick before opening her eyes and forcing a grin. "Hey, that's some statue!"

"Ain't no such thing. That's a dummy, dummy—my dad said Fatso Otto had it made special back east someplace. Sent 'em a picture of that bimbo who got killed and my dad says it looks just like her."

"How'd he know—he ever ball her or somethin'?" Terry giggled.

"Don't be funny!" It was obvious from the way she said it that Mick wasn't mistaking Terry for another Whoopi Goldberg. "My dad was only a kid when this all happened here."

Terry nodded, but she didn't like the here part. Because even if this was a fake bathroom and the frightened figure in the shower stall was merely wax, there had been a real Norman, a real knife, a real murder, and here was just too gross. Here at night, in the dark, listening to the sound of the door opening in the other room.

"What's that noise?" Terry grabbed Mick's arm.

"I don't hear anything."

Terry's grip tightened. "Shut up and listen!"

For a moment they stood in silence, then Mick pulled her arm free, then turned. "Nobody out there," she murmured.

"Where you going?"

"Where you think?" Mick started back into the bedroom. "You coming, or are you chicken?"

Terry knew the answer to that one; she *was* chicken, but she moved up to join her companion anyway. No matter who or what might be creeping around out there in the office, she felt safer with Mick than she did with that wax lady in the shower stall—that naked lady waiting for the bare blade to come down.

As Mick reached out to open the bedroom door, Terry tapped her on the shoulder. Her whisper came quickly and urgently. "Wait—turn off your flashlight first. What if he sees us?"

"Nobody out there!" Mick sounded disgusted, but Terry noticed that she did keep her voice down and she did switch off her flashlight before easing the bedroom door open.

It moved forward, fanning the warm, fume-filled darkness of the office. Somewhere in the far reaches of the room the figure of Norman Bates still stood behind the shadowed counter of the reception desk. Still stood and stood still, for there was no sound of movement, no stir of shape or shadow.

Together the girls inched their way from the bedroom to the office door. It too was opened slowly and cautiously; only when it swung wide to reveal the deserted roadway beyond did it seem safe to switch their flashlights on again.

The night air was warm too, but it bore no hint of the acrid paint odors and Terry took a deep breath as Mick led her along the walk bordering the office, then stepped off onto the path arching upward against the hillside where the dark house loomed.

"Hey."

Mick halted, glancing back as Terry spoke. "Now what?"

"Do we hafta go up there?"

"No, chicken. If you like, I'll take you right home and put you back in the coop." There was disgust on Mick's face as well as in her voice. "Wasn't for you we wouldn't be here in the first place. When I tole you about sneaking in here last night you wanted to see it so bad you almost peed your pants."

"Sheesh, you think I'm scared or somethin'?" Terry made a production out of lifting her left wrist and squinting at her watch. "If I don't get home when I said, Mom'll have a hemmrage."

Now it was Mick's turn to glance at her own watch and top Terry's production by adding a scowl as she replied. "We still got plenty of time. It'll only take like ten, fifteen minutes to look around. Unless you're too chicken—"

That did it. "Who's chicken?" Terry said. "Let's go, turkey."

So it was like the old song Aunt Marcella used to sing—"Over the river and through the woods to grandmother's house we go." Only there wasn't any river or woods, just the walk leading up to the porch stairs of the house on the top of the hillside. Not grandmother's house, but Mother's. Norman's, really, because his mother was dead. And he was dead too. It was the house that was alive—this *new* house.

Terry felt better when she reminded herself of that. If there was such a thing as ghosts they'd be in the old house, but this place was brand-new, just like the motel. Fatso Otto built it at the same time and for the same reason, to make money off tourists. Which he sure as hell wouldn't do in a place that had ghosts hanging out in it.

So there was nothing to be scared of and besides she was getting like a free preview, right?

It all sounded good inside Terry's head, but the sound of the porch steps' protest beneath their feet was almost a screech, and the grating of the key turning in the lock of the front door sent a harsh echo across the hillside.

Of course there was no one there on the hill to hear except the two of them, no one listening in the deep, dark hallway of the house as they entered.

Flashlight beams chased shadows from the corners. *Too bad nobody invented a gismo that can light up your mind the way a flashlight can light up a hallway.* Terry snuffed out the thought, wishing it could be that easy to snuff out what else she was thinking about the dark and the shadows here.

But it wasn't, even with the fresh paint smell rising all around to remind her that this wasn't the *real* house, the murder house, the place where that detective died and Norman's mother lived even though she was dead too. Or was she?

Terry gulped. *She'd damn well better be, or else.* But *else* wasn't a word Terry wanted to think about, any more than she'd wanted to think about *here*.

The neat thing to do right now was just take like a real fast look-around to show that smartass Mick she wasn't chicken, then hightail it for home before Mom busted her behind for her.

Mick was already focusing her flashlight beam at the stairway just ahead on the right side of the hall. "Let's go upstairs first," she whispered.

Whispering again. Terry didn't like the sound of it, any more than she had when she was the one who whispered in the motel. Whispering means you're scared, and if Mick was scared now, maybe there was a reason. And if the reason was upstairs—

Again it was time for a fast either-or. Either go upstairs with Mick or stay down in that dark, spooky hallway all alone.

Terry tilted her flashlight upward, toward the bobbing blue-jeaned butt of her guide. The stairs creaked, she reminded herself, only because they were new.

The thing is, they didn't look new, and neither did anything up above. Whoever built this place must of done it from photographs, just like they used to make those wax dummies. Or maybe they just guessed at how it must of looked in the olden days and bought up a lot of junk to furnish it with. Like here in the bathroom where Mick was beaming over a kind of bathtub she'd never seen before, one with legs on it. And the toilet was something else, it had an overhead tank and a pull chain. That she remembered seeing once before someplace, maybe in a book about pioneer days.

But she was grateful for one thing—there was no shower stall in this bathroom.

Maybe ol' Norman didn't believe in taking showers. Or maybe showers hadn't even been invented way back then. Terry was a little fuzzy when it came to the details of American history; sometimes she couldn't even remember the date when Elvis died.

The idea of thinking about that right now in a place like this took her by surprise; she turned to share her reaction with Mick and had another surprise.

Mick was gone.

"The fruit cellar. Down here."

Mick angled her way behind the basement steps and
y followed. It seemed to her that the flashlight beam
getting weaker while her urge was getting stronger.
re sure as hell wasn't going to be any john in the
t cellar but maybe Fatso Otto had one put in on the
floor. If she knew him, it was probably a pay toilet.
it now she didn't much care; all she wanted to do
take a fast look down here in the fruit cellar and
i go upstairs and take a fast leak.

"Hey!" Mick's voice jolted her. "What's happened
our light?"

Terry blinked down at the dim outline of her hand
ching the metal cylinder. She rattled it, her thumb
king the projecting switch. "Batteries must be dead,"
said.

"Mine's okay." Mick brandished her beam in her
t hand. With the left she gripped the handle of the
r beneath the bottom of the stairs.

"Why don't you open it?" Terry said. "Whatcha
ing for?"

"Promise me one thing first," Mick told her. "No
aming."

"You got to be putting me on. I ain't gonna scream."

"Maybe not," Mick said. "But I sure let out a good
when I come down here last night. 'Course I heard
hose stories about how Norman Bates' *real* mother
ed like when they found her down here, but it still
ne to makin' and shakin' because the dummy is so—
—yucky."

"Won't scare me none," Terry said. "It's just a statue
n old lady."

"That's what I thought." Mick's shadow nodded on
wall at the base of the stairwell. "But I forgot all the
gs Norman did to her."

"Like what?"

"Like killing her, for starters. Giving her and her
riend some kinda poison in their drinks, I forget just

"Hey!" she yelled.

And echoing along the dark and empty hall corridor
a dozen voices yelled back.

The echoes were still dying down as she hurried out
into the hallway. "Mick—where are you?"

"In here."

The sound of Mick's voice and the beam of her
flashlight guided Terry into the surprisingly small room
across the hall. Here Mick's flashlight had taken control,
playing across the walls and furnishings. Terry followed
the progress of the beam, and from what it revealed she
quickly realized that they must be standing in Norman
Bates' bedroom. Had to be, because there was an old-
fashioned bureau instead of a vanity, and a plain cot for
a bed with no spread. It sure as hell didn't look like one
of those fancy layouts at the Holiday Inn.

It didn't really look like a man's bedroom either;
this was the kind of place you'd fix up for a kid to sleep
in. But once upon a time Norman Bates *had* been a kid.

Terry wondered about that. What was ol' Norman
like before he grew up and turned into a creep?

Looking around the room gave her part of the answer. There was no jock stuff here, no balls, bats, helmets or even a baseball cap, and there weren't any
pennants hanging on the walls over the two bookshelves
in the far corner. The shelves were almost filled; he must
have done a lot of reading. That didn't prove he was a
freak, Terry reminded herself—lotsa people used to read
books in the days before TV was invented. So this still
didn't tell her very much about what Norman Bates was
really like.

It was Mick's flashlight that gave the best answer as
it fanned across the wall opposite the closet door and
halted on a picture.

"Here he is!" Mick said.

And there he was, the smiling little boy in overalls,
sitting on a pony, captured on film and confined by
frame. Not that Terry thought of him that way. Staring at

the faded photo all that crossed her mind was a question. How could such a neat little kid grow up to be a monster?

There was no sense asking Mick; she wouldn't understand a thing like that. Besides, Mick was doing one of her disappearing acts again, and if Terry hadn't turned around just in time she wouldn't even have noticed her edging back out into the hallway.

"What's with you?" she said. "Always sneaking off on me. You gotta use the john or somethin'?"

"Won't catch me using any john around here," Mick told her. She started down the hall, moving to a dark door that opened easily with a push instead of a key.

Mick swept the flashlight beam forward in a gesture of invitation. "Mother's bedroom," she said.

The paint smell was definitely out of place here. That's the way Terry felt in this room—out of place. Talk about ancient history, Mother's bedroom was a real Golden Oldie, just crammed full of stuff, kinda junk you'd find like in a museum. But there was nothing here that interested her except the big bed, and that turned out to be a disappointment too because it was empty.

She frowned at Mick through the flashlight's glow. "Thought you said you're gonna show me Mother."

"That's right," Mick nodded.

"Well, where *is* she?"

"Hold your water, will ya?" Mick started toward the doorway. Then, stepping out into the hallway, she halted so suddenly that Terry almost bumped into her from behind. "Wait!" she murmured. "I think I hear somethin'."

They stood unmoving for a moment, two small figures frozen in shadowed silence. But that's all it was; shadows rising around them and silence settling down below.

No sounds. Nothing to be afraid of. The creaking noise came directly from their own Reeboks as they came down the corridor and descended the stairs. Mick

paused as they reached the lower land[...] see the first floor?" she asked.

"Is Mother here?"

Mick shook her head. "No, but she[...]

"Where?"

"In the cellar."

So that's where they went, Mick an[...] Terry a reluctant rear guard. She kept te[...] she wasn't chicken but that was a lie[...] than chicken, she was a pigeon too, f[...] hype about how exciting it all was. [...] turned on because she put something [...] man but as far as Terry was concerned [...] around in the dark and sniffing up all th[...] paint fumes was no big deal. Okay, that [...] the motel office was a pretty cutesy ide[...] the shower stall that didn't move was ki[...] that's all there was to see then ol' F[...] likely to end up on *Lifestyles of the R*[...] just from selling tickets. He'd have t[...] more than that. Or come down with [...] cellar.

Trouble was when they got there th[...] a basement; a bare-walled, painted-o[...] didn't even have one of those big furna[...] shovel coal into in the olden days; mus[...] heating system upstairs instead if they [...] ing open in wintertime. Not that Terry [...] damn one way or the other; that was F[...] lem, not hers. Her problem was that sh[...] to feel she had to go to the john and wha[...] futzing around down here in the first p[...]

"Okay," she said. "We're here. I stil[...] thing."

Mick turned, her head bobbing in [...] halo. "That's on account of this is only [...] said she was in the *cellar*, remember?"

"What cellar?"

what they said it was, but it must of been an awful way to die, because you can see it in her face. Or what's left of her face."

"I thought ol' Norman fixed her back up again," Terry said.

"He had to *dig* her back up first."

Mick sounded as if she was having a ball telling her about this but Terry wished she would have waited until they were outside again. It was too hot down here, too stuffy, too dark, too closed-in; too damned much like the place ol' Norman dug up his mother from.

"That must of been a couple a months afterward," Mick said. "So by the time he got his hands on her again she could of been, like you know—"

"Do you *have* to talk about it?" Terry didn't give Mick a chance to reply. "Besides, I know what he did to her then. Taxdermy."

"Taxidermy, dummy!"

"So who cares? Bottom line is ol' Norman stuffed her."

"That ain't the way he told it. He thought she was still alive. They used to talk to each other all the time— only he was talking to himself, of course. But after that detective started snooping around, Norman put his mother down here in the fruit cellar so's nobody would hear her. Or see her."

"Okay, okay! Let's just look at the old bat and get outta here," Terry said.

Mick let out a snicker. "Scared you, didn't I?" Her left hand moved to the doorknob and her right hand tilted the flashlight so that when the door opened the beam would fall directly upon what waited within.

"Get ready for the gross-out!" she said.

And opened the door.

The muscles of Terry's neck constricted preparatory to vocalizing her reaction at what she saw. But strangely enough no sound issued from Terry's throat and it was

Mick who screamed at the sight of what was in the cellar.

Or what wasn't.

Because the fruit cellar was empty.

Terry peered through the open doorway, then turned to her companion. "Mick—"

Mick didn't look at her; she was still staring straight ahead, but now her scream modified into intelligible response. "She's gone!"

"So?"

Mick turned, shoulders shaking. "She was here last night, I know it because I saw her! You believe me, don't you?"

Terry nodded. "All right, she's gone. Do you have to get so uptight about it?"

"You don't understand, do you?"

Terry thought she did. "This is a put-on, right? You want me to think you're flaking out because Mother all of a sudden came alive and walked out of here?"

"That's just it!" Mick could prevent herself from screaming now, but the hand holding the flashlight was shaking. And in the shimmer of its glow Terry saw a face contorted with fear. "She didn't walk. Somebody *took* her! Maybe you were right when you said you heard somethin'. Maybe somebody came to snatch her up, maybe they saw us—"

Now Mick's control of her voice seemed only momentary and Terry reached out to put a reassuring hand on her shoulder. Mick wheeled, shaking her head. "Come on, we gotta get outta here!" Her feet stumbled toward the stairs, then pistoned as she raced upward. The fringes of her flashlight beam faded away abruptly into the confines of the staircase above, leaving Terry trapped in the deepening darkness below.

"Wait—wait for me!"

But the frightened footsteps did not halt or heed. Terry floundered up the stairs, her left hand groping for a railing that wasn't there, meanwhile thumbing fran-

"Hey!" she yelled.

And echoing along the dark and empty hall corridor a dozen voices yelled back.

The echoes were still dying down as she hurried out into the hallway. "Mick—where are you?"

"In here."

The sound of Mick's voice and the beam of her flashlight guided Terry into the surprisingly small room across the hall. Here Mick's flashlight had taken control, playing across the walls and furnishings. Terry followed the progress of the beam, and from what it revealed she quickly realized that they must be standing in Norman Bates' bedroom. Had to be, because there was an old-fashioned bureau instead of a vanity, and a plain cot for a bed with no spread. It sure as hell didn't look like one of those fancy layouts at the Holiday Inn.

It didn't really look like a man's bedroom either; this was the kind of place you'd fix up for a kid to sleep in. But once upon a time Norman Bates *had* been a kid.

Terry wondered about that. What was ol' Norman like before he grew up and turned into a creep?

Looking around the room gave her part of the answer. There was no jock stuff here, no balls, bats, helmets or even a baseball cap, and there weren't any pennants hanging on the walls over the two bookshelves in the far corner. The shelves were almost filled; he must have done a lot of reading. That didn't prove he was a freak, Terry reminded herself—lotsa people used to read books in the days before TV was invented. So this still didn't tell her very much about what Norman Bates was really like.

It was Mick's flashlight that gave the best answer as it fanned across the wall opposite the closet door and halted on a picture.

"Here he is!" Mick said.

And there he was, the smiling little boy in overalls, sitting on a pony, captured on film and confined by frame. Not that Terry thought of him that way. Staring at the faded photo all that crossed her mind was a question. How could such a neat little kid grow up to be a monster?

There was no sense asking Mick; she wouldn't understand a thing like that. Besides, Mick was doing one of her disappearing acts again, and if Terry hadn't turned around just in time she wouldn't even have noticed her edging back out into the hallway.

"What's with you?" she said. "Always sneaking off on me. You gotta use the john or somethin'?"

"Won't catch me using any john around here," Mick told her. She started down the hall, moving to a dark door that opened easily with a push instead of a key.

Mick swept the flashlight beam forward in a gesture of invitation. "Mother's bedroom," she said.

The paint smell was definitely out of place here. That's the way Terry felt in this room—out of place. Talk about ancient history, Mother's bedroom was a real Golden Oldie, just crammed full of stuff, kinda junk you'd find like in a museum. But there was nothing here that interested her except the big bed, and that turned out to be a disappointment too because it was empty.

She frowned at Mick through the flashlight's glow. "Thought you said you're gonna show me Mother."

"That's right," Mick nodded.

"Well, where is she?"

"Hold your water, will ya?" Mick started toward the doorway. Then, stepping out into the hallway, she halted so suddenly that Terry almost bumped into her from behind. "Wait!" she murmured. "I think I hear somethin'."

They stood unmoving for a moment, two small figures frozen in shadowed silence. But that's all it was; shadows rising around them and silence settling down below.

No sounds. Nothing to be afraid of. The creaking noise came directly from their own Reeboks as they came down the corridor and descended the stairs. Mick paused as they reached the lower landing. "You wanna see the first floor?" she asked.

"Is Mother here?"

Mick shook her head. "No, but she's waitin' for us."

"Where?"

"In the cellar."

So that's where they went, Mick an eager leader and Terry a reluctant rear guard. She kept telling herself that she wasn't chicken but that was a lie. She was worse than chicken, she was a pigeon too, falling for Mick's hype about how exciting it all was. Maybe Mick got turned on because she put something over on her old man but as far as Terry was concerned forget it. Banging around in the dark and sniffing up all that stink from the paint fumes was no big deal. Okay, that moving statue in the motel office was a pretty cutesy idea and the one in the shower stall that didn't move was kinda scary. But if that's all there was to see then ol' Fatso Otto wasn't likely to end up on *Lifestyles of the Rich and Famous* just from selling tickets. He'd have to come up with more than that. Or come down with it, there in the cellar.

Trouble was when they got there the cellar was only a basement; a bare-walled, painted-over basement. It didn't even have one of those big furnaces they used to shovel coal into in the olden days; must have a built-in heating system upstairs instead if they figured on keeping open in wintertime. Not that Terry gave a diddly-damn one way or the other; that was Fatso Otto's problem, not hers. Her problem was that she was beginning to feel she had to go to the john and what was she doing futzing around down here in the first place?

"Okay," she said. "We're here. I still don't see anything."

Mick turned, her head bobbing in the flashlight's halo. "That's on account of this is only the basement. I said she was in the *cellar*, remember?"

"What cellar?"

"The fruit cellar. Down here."

Mick angled her way behind the basement steps and Terry followed. It seemed to her that the flashlight beam was getting weaker while her urge was getting stronger. There sure as hell wasn't going to be any john in the fruit cellar but maybe Fatso Otto had one put in on the first floor. If she knew him, it was probably a pay toilet. Right now she didn't much care; all she wanted to do was take a fast look down here in the fruit cellar and then go upstairs and take a fast leak.

"Hey!" Mick's voice jolted her. "What's happened to your light?"

Terry blinked down at the dim outline of her hand clutching the metal cylinder. She rattled it, her thumb working the projecting switch. "Batteries must be dead," she said.

"Mine's okay." Mick brandished her beam in her right hand. With the left she gripped the handle of the door beneath the bottom of the stairs.

"Why don't you open it?" Terry said. "Whatcha waiting for?"

"Promise me one thing first," Mick told her. "No screaming."

"You got to be putting me on. I ain't gonna scream."

"Maybe not," Mick said. "But I sure let out a good one when I come down here last night. 'Course I heard all those stories about how Norman Bates' *real* mother looked like when they found her down here, but it still got me to makin' and shakin' because the dummy is so— like—yucky."

"Won't scare me none," Terry said. "It's just a statue of an old lady."

"That's what I thought." Mick's shadow nodded on the wall at the base of the stairwell. "But I forgot all the things Norman did to her."

"Like what?"

"Like killing her, for starters. Giving her and her boyfriend some kinda poison in their drinks, I forget just what they said it was, but it must of been an awful way to die, because you can see it in her face. Or what's left of her face."

"I thought ol' Norman fixed her back up again," Terry said.

"He had to *dig* her back up first."

Mick sounded as if she was having a ball telling her about this but Terry wished she would have waited until they were outside again. It was too hot down here, too stuffy, too dark, too closed-in; too damned much like the place ol' Norman dug up his mother from.

"That must of been a couple a months afterward," Mick said. "So by the time he got his hands on her again she could of been, like you know—"

"Do you *have* to talk about it?" Terry didn't give Mick a chance to reply. "Besides, I know what he did to her then. Taxdermy."

"Taxidermy, dummy!"

"So who cares? Bottom line is ol' Norman stuffed her."

"That ain't the way he told it. He thought she was still alive. They used to talk to each other all the time—only he was talking to himself, of course. But after that detective started snooping around, Norman put his mother down here in the fruit cellar so's nobody would hear her. Or see her."

"Okay, okay! Let's just look at the old bat and get outta here," Terry said.

Mick let out a snicker. "Scared you, didn't I?" Her left hand moved to the doorknob and her right hand tilted the flashlight so that when the door opened the beam would fall directly upon what waited within.

"Get ready for the gross-out!" she said.

And opened the door.

The muscles of Terry's neck constricted preparatory to vocalizing her reaction at what she saw. But strangely enough no sound issued from Terry's throat and it was

Mick who screamed at the sight of what was in the cellar.

Or what wasn't.

Because the fruit cellar was empty.

Terry peered through the open doorway, then turned to her companion. "Mick—"

Mick didn't look at her; she was still staring straight ahead, but now her scream modified into intelligible response. "She's gone!"

"So?"

Mick turned, shoulders shaking. "She was here last night, I know it because I saw her! You believe me, don't you?"

Terry nodded. "All right, she's gone. Do you have to get so uptight about it?"

"You don't understand, do you?"

Terry thought she did. "This is a put-on, right? You want me to think you're flaking out because Mother all of a sudden came alive and walked out of here?"

"That's just it!" Mick could prevent herself from screaming now, but the hand holding the flashlight was shaking. And in the shimmer of its glow Terry saw a face contorted with fear. "She didn't walk. Somebody *took* her! Maybe you were right when you said you heard somethin'. Maybe somebody came to snatch her up, maybe they saw us—"

Now Mick's control of her voice seemed only momentary and Terry reached out to put a reassuring hand on her shoulder. Mick wheeled, shaking her head. "Come on, we gotta get outta here!" Her feet stumbled toward the stairs, then pistoned as she raced upward. The fringes of her flashlight beam faded away abruptly into the confines of the staircase above, leaving Terry trapped in the deepening darkness below.

"Wait—wait for me!"

But the frightened footsteps did not halt or heed. Terry floundered up the stairs, her left hand groping for a railing that wasn't there, meanwhile thumbing frantically at the flashlight switch but without results. Except for one. As the hand holding the flashlight flailed forward, her knuckles struck the sidewall and the momentary twinge of pain relaxed her grip so that the flashlight fell.

The flashlight fell, and then the pain was no longer a momentary twinge. The pain, the *new* pain, lanced through her leg as the metal cylinder struck her ankle, then bounced off with a momentum gained from the force of the blow.

Terry gasped, wincing as her weight came down upon the injured ankle. Placing the palm of her left hand against the unseen wall of the stairwell, she stooped cautiously to run the fingers of her right hand across the swelling that was already beginning to bulge below the top of her Reebok. Her groping fingers loosened the lacing but could not ease the pain.

Gritting her teeth she reached the basement landing. Pain stabbed at a different angle here on the flat surface, but there was no sense moaning. No sense calling out, either, because she didn't hear Mick's footsteps on the stairs leading up to the first floor. Sure must of gotten out of here in one holy hell of a hurry; putting on about how brave she was, but underneath it had been Mick who was really chicken all the time. So what if somebody *did* bust in and steal that crummy dummy? They wouldn't have any reason to stick around afterward.

Or would they?

Maybe Mick knew something she hadn't talked about, maybe she had a real reason to be scared and that's why she hooted out of here in such a hurry. It wouldn't hurt for her to do the same, Terry told herself, only she couldn't because it *did* hurt. Moving up the basement stairs, she wondered if that damn flashlight had busted her ankle. Whatever, it sure hurt like hell. And groping her way down the dark corridor was like walking on a bed of hot coals.

Twice she had to stop, and the only thing that kept

her going as she came around the edge of the upper staircase was the sight of the open front door ahead, with
Mick standing in the corner beside it. Despite the increased intensity of the pain Terry increased her pace.
As she did so the front door started to swing shut.

"Hey, grab the door!" Terry called.

Automatically her right hand reached forward to
carry out her own command, but by now the door had
already closed and Mick was turning in the shadows.

Only the figure emerging into the hallway wasn't
Mick. And the silvery thing in its upraised hand wasn't
a flashlight.

· 2 ·

AMY Haines hit the last stretch around six
o'clock but the sky was already dark as midnight.

It had been three days since she had left Chicago,
two days since leaving Ft. Worth to start the drive back
up again. What had impressed her the most during the
first two nights had been the sight of a skyful of stars—
something that long exposure to urban illumination had
obliterated from her vision and her memory. Tonight, of
course, there were no stars above, but on the pavement
ahead the raindrops sparkled and glittered before her
looming headlights.

The rain was heavier now, pelting the pavement and
splattering static across the signal band of the car radio.
Amy switched it off with a sigh and concentrated on

coping with the rush-hour traffic flow. The six o'clock peak load here was less than she'd expect to encounter at two A.M. on any Chicago expressway. And rain or no rain, she was making progress. Sometimes the long way around is the shortest way home.

At least that's what she kept telling herself. There had to be some excuse for doing what she did; it would have been so much easier just to drive her own car straight down from Chicago instead of taking a flight all the way down to Ft. Worth, on the slim chance that there still might be something of interest there.

But Ft. Worth had been a disaster area, and aside from the star-studded spectacle of the previous nights' skies there hadn't been all that much to see during the long, exhausting hours spent on the road. And what she'd secretly hoped for hadn't happened. She didn't feel a bit like Mary Crane at all.

"Secretly"? "Foolishly" was a better word. How could she possibly expect to identify with someone dead and gone all these years? The world she'd lived in was dead and gone too; Amy found that out in Ft. Worth when she tried to find an entry point into the past. Her trip in the rented car followed the same route Mary Crane had taken, or as much of it as anyone had ever been able to determine, but over the passage of years the landscape, even the freeways themselves, had changed.

Besides, there was no resemblance between Mary Crane and herself. She hadn't ripped off a bundle of cash from her employer and fled town, switching cars en route to avoid detection. Most importantly she had not stopped off to spend a night at the Bates Motel. Part of a night, really—a night that ended with the splashing of a shower and the slashing of a knife.

There were only two things she had in common with the unfortunate girl who had died before she herself had been born. Like Mary Crane on her last evening of existence, she was driving through a rainstorm—and she was on her way to Fairvale.

But she was on the freeway, not on a side road leading to the Bates Motel. And both the actual motel and
the house above it were long gone, as was the trans-
vestite who murdered the girl and, later, the detective
who came seeking her.

Gone, but not forgotten. And there were things that
she'd better not forget. The off-ramps, for example; here
was a sign announcing the location of an upcoming exit
for Montrose and Rock Center. Fairvale would be next,
or so she guessed.

And correctly.

As the car spinned and spiraled down the ramp
Amy's sigh of relief was drowned in thunder. Turning
right onto the county highway leading into town, relief
gave way to anticipation, underscored by a flash of lightning that slashed across the sky the way Norman Bates'
knife had slashed across the—

But what put *that* into her head? This was no time
for such thoughts, now that she was entering Fairvale
itself. Rain and darkness dampened and dulled her first
impressions of the town; at first glimpse and first glance
it seemed no different from a thousand other small com-
munities scattered throughout the heartland of midwest
America.

Which, of course, was what made it so fascinating,
she reminded herself. So many similarities between
Fairvale and all the others, with only one significant difference—it had happened here. *Here was where the
knife slashed down.*

Hard to believe and, of course, strictly speaking, the
actual murders took place some seventeen miles away
from Fairvale's main street. But Norman Bates had gone
to school in this town, he had walked these streets as an
adult. Local citizens knew him as a friend and neighbor.
He'd probably visited some of them in their homes here,
done business in the local stores. From the looks of
them, most of the residences and shops had been around

back then. Fairvale itself was like something preserved in a time capsule.

Self-preservation, the first law of nature. Norman Bates had gone a step farther—he'd preserved his mother in himself. Which made him a time bomb, not capsule, a bomb that had long since exploded.

But now was not the time to think of that. Now was the time to peer ahead at oncoming local traffic and thank God that the windshield wipers were still working. Outside of a few drivers inside their cars there was no one to take note of Amy's arrival at the courthouse square. She recognized it from photographs: the granite shaft of the World War II memorial, the Spanish-American War trench mortar and the Civil War statue of a Union veteran flanking it on either side of the block. Preservation was Fairvale's way of life.

But the annex adjoining the main courthouse was comparatively new and so was the Fairvale Hotel in the next block on the opposite side of the street. The parking lot next to the building was almost empty and Amy slid into a space close to the overhang above the entrance. Even so, she wished she'd brought an umbrella, because just lugging her bag from the car to the shelter of the overhang was enough to expose her to the chill of the undiminished downpour.

But the lobby was warm and dry and, somewhat to her surprise, comfortably well furnished. There were no other guests visible in the area at this moment and no sign of a bellhop or porter waiting to relieve her of the overnight bag. But there was a clerk on duty behind the reception counter; a tall, gangling young man with a sallow complexion, green eyes, and hair the color of used kitty litter.

Placing his comic book to one side, he devoted his full attention to the needs and welfare of the arriving guest.

"Looking for somebody?" he asked.

"I'm Amelia Haines. I believe you have a reservation for me."

"Oh." The greenish eyes slipped sideways toward the discarded comic book, but only for a moment. "What did you say that that name was again?"

"Haines." She spelled it for him as he consulted a register which apparently rested on a lower level beneath the countertop. Obviously the Fairvale Hotel was no more into computers than its clerk was into neckties.

But he did find her reservation and she had no problem signing in, except for the fact that she couldn't fill out the space assigned to *Name Of Company*. When she pushed the completed form across the counter the clerk glanced down at the card and noted the omission. "You're not working for anybody, lady?"

"Self-employed," Amy said. "Not that it's any of your goddamned business."

At least that's what she would like to have said, but due to the somewhat delicate nature of her situation, she merely nodded. No sense making waves or even reaching across the counter to give this nosy young jerk a slight belt across the chops. She even managed a smile of pseudo-gratitude as she accepted the key to room 205.

No mention was made of bellboy assistance and she didn't bother to ask; long before she crossed the lobby and reached the single elevator, the green eyes behind the counter were again eagerly attempting to decipher the lettering inside the balloons above the heads of the comic's characters.

Room 205 was state-of-the-art, if one considers plastic *decor* an art form. But at least it contained the feminine essentials—a mirror, a closet, and a telephone. Amy glanced out of the window at the flat rooftop, wondering if it covered a restaurant or kitchen area below. She hadn't bothered to ask if the hotel had a coffee shop and/or dining room, but she hoped so; the last thing in the world she wanted right now was to expose herself to what was happening beyond the windowpane. Closing the drapes obscured the sight but did little to muffle the sound of the rain drumming down on the adjacent roof.

The thing now was to get out of her travel-creased and still slightly dampened clothes, but what she really wanted to do this very moment was find out about food. Her watch told her it was eight o'clock and her stomach added as a postscript that it had received no consideration whatsoever since she'd stopped the car to gas up during the noon hour.

She picked up the phone and called the hotel operator. At least that was her intention, but his voice on the other end of the line was that of the comic book reader behind the reception counter. Restraining herself from apologizing for interrupting his studies, she asked about the dining situation.

"We don't have a dining room here," he told her. "Coffee shop's open until nine."

"Thank you." Amy hung up without bothering to ask about room service; this being state-of-the-art she was willing to settle for the serendipity of a small supply of toilet paper instead of those little squares from the dispenser. Such are the hopes and dreams of the seasoned traveler.

In that capacity Amy had no great expectations of what she might encounter when she entered the downstairs coffee shop through a side entrance off the lobby. It proved to be the usual fast-food setup; stools closely aligning the three-sided counter so that each bite-grabber could get a good view of the fry-cook's activities through the rectangular opening in the rear wall. Small booths offered imitation-leather seats, imitation comfort, and outside-window views. Tonight, however, the drapes were drawn; nobody wanted to look out at the rain. Apparently nobody wanted to eat either because when Amy entered she saw no other customers. Booths and stools were empty and so were the expressionless eyes of the waitress-cashier who plodded out from the kitchen area to plunk a glass of ice water down on the table mat of the corner booth that Amy selected.

"Evening." The word could be construed either as a greeting or a statement of fact; the waitress' voice was expressionless. "Menu?"

"Please." Amy could be monosyllabic too. Not out of rudeness, but because she sensed that the weary woman with the wilted uniform and hairdo wasn't in the mood for idle conversation; all she really wanted was nine o'clock closing and a chance to kick her shoes off.

So Amy gave her order—*pot roast of beef w. choice of 2 vegs* was usually a safe bet in light of previous experiences—and quickly added, "Coffee, now."

Then she relaxed as the waitress headed kitchenward. At least fry-cooks can't do too much damage to a pot roast, and when it came to coffee she'd learned that wherever you dined you'd just have to take a chance.

Amy sipped her water and settled back in her seat. Her feet didn't hurt, but now, at the end of the long day's driving, she could empathize with the waitress. At best, waiting on tables in a place like this must be a boring occupation, almost as boring as being a customer.

Outside the rain thudded down but here there was no source of sound, not even from the kitchen where the waitress and the fry-cook were presumably puzzling over the order, since Amy had forgotten to specify her choice of vegies. Oh well, sometimes you've got to resign yourself to living dangerously. Let it be their decision and her surprise. She just hoped they wouldn't be trying to get rid of yesterday's squash or creamed rutabagas.

A pity she couldn't hear their conversation. At the moment she felt the need for some distraction, and gazing at the glass-coffined slices of embalmed pies and pastries really did nothing for her. Alone in the bleak, forlorn flare of the fluorescence she scanned the booths nearby, hoping to catch sight of a discarded newspaper. Fairvale wouldn't have a daily, of course, but perhaps some salesman out of Springfield might have discarded one after his meal.

No such luck. Amy abandoned her efforts with a sigh of resignation. In cases like this there was nothing one could do except read the menu.

Two events spared her that fate. The first was the return of the waitress, coffeepot in one hand, cup and saucer in the other. The second was the arrival of additional customers, a male trio clad in rainwear. By the time Amy announced and received her choice of cream and sugar the three men had seated themselves on stools at the end of the counter. As the waitress departed to serve them, Amy creamed, sugared, and sipped her coffee. A trifle too hot, but the addition of an ice cube from her water glass solved that problem.

Satisfied, she turned her attention to the newcomers. From where she sat all she could see were two backs and a semiprofile. The backs were broad and burly, the heads above them surmounted by the inevitable baseball caps. The semiprofile sat beside them at the angle closest to Amy's observation post. He was a small man, sharp-featured, his mustache a grey wisp beneath a beaked nose. His headgear was traditional, immediately identifying him as a lawman—a member of the local constabulary, the Sheriff's Department, perhaps State Highway Patrol. Then Amy glanced down, saw the black boots with their pointed toes, and made her ID. Only the Sheriff's Department would indulge in this form of foot-fetishism, and any man this small could bypass departmental qualifications solely through election. This had to be the Sheriff himself.

And his name was Engstrom. Milt Engstrom, to be exact. This information was relayed in the conversation between the counter customers, along with the announcement that they too wanted coffee and yeah, it sure as hell was coming down cats and dogs outside.

It was at this point that the waitress returned with Amy's dinner platter and set it down on the mat before her. The 2 vegs. turned out to be peas and carrots, neither of them fried, creamed, scalloped, or the victims of any other unnatural practices. And the pot roast was good.

So was the distraction. Like many of those accustomed to solitary dining, Amy had consciously or unconsciously perfected the art of people-watching and eavesdropping. And while in this instance the watching was nothing to write home about, what she was hearing might definitely be worth putting down on paper. In the absence of pen and pad she made a mental note of the conversation at the counter.

Reduced to its essentials, the Sheriff and his two anonymous companions were talking about Terry Dowson's murder last week and Mick Sontag's alibi.

Amy paid little heed to the exact phrasing of the questions but she paid strict attention to Sheriff Engstrom's answers.

No, he didn't mind talking, now that the goddamned reporters had cleared out. Hank would be running most of the stuff in this week's paper anyhow.

Way it added up, Joe Sontag went out to the garage for something and found out his keys were missing. According to him, he guessed right away where his kid must have gone and went after her in his pickup. When he got to the Bates place she was already running up the road. He pulled up alongside her and she was just climbing in when they both heard what sounded like screams coming from the house. Not all that loud and clear, understand, because when he backed up to park and started running to the porch he saw that the front door was closed.

"The kid didn't come with him?" one of the baseball caps asked.

"He told her to stay in the truck, and a damn good thing he did too, considering what he found in the hall when he yanked that door open."

"Pretty bad," said the other baseball cap.

The Sheriff nodded. That in itself told Amy nothing, but the *way* he nodded was eloquent.

"You say he didn't see anybody?"

"*He* says." Again the Sheriff nodded. "And I believe him. According to his story he went straight back to the pickup and drove down to the Fawcett place, which was the closest he could find a phone. Irene took the call and got hold of me just as I was heading out to check Crosby Corners. Only took me another three, four minutes to get there, but by then young Mick was really having hysterics—which was only natural after that damfool father of hers blabbed about what he'd found up at the house. When the ambulance from Montrose Hospital got there, Mick was the one who needed attention. It was too late to do anything for Terry."

"You don't think—"

"That Mick could have had anything to do with it?" The Sheriff shook his head quickly. "No way either she or Joe Sontag could have pulled off something like that. No way, no motive, no weapon that we could locate."

"Suppose they stashed the knife someplace first before Sontag went to call you?"

Engstrom shrugged. "Just doing that wouldn't have gotten them off the hook. They'd both need a complete change of clothing. The way Terry was put down, whoever did the job was bound to get splashed. Neither Mick or her father had a drop of blood on their clothes or shoes, even though there was a big pool around the body. Just to make sure we sent what they were wearing that night over to Montrose for labwork."

"If they didn't do it, then who did? Don't you have any clues?"

"Just what I put out in the press statements. The only fingerprints we came up with were the girls'. The killer didn't touch anything inside the house and motel, or else he or she was wearing gloves."

One of the Sheriff's companions glanced toward him quickly. "He *or* she?"

"Who knows? Besides, I don't want any of those women's libbers to feel left out."

"Come on, level with us. You must have some kind of theory."

"I don't have much use for theories." The Sheriff paused long enough to swallow the remaining contents of his coffee cup. "Captain Banning put two of his men from the State Highway Patrol on full-time duty, just to see if they could come up with anything. Main thing they looked for was someplace nearby where a car might have been parked on the night of the murder. Couldn't locate so much as a tire tread to show for it. Which means that whoever committed the murder was probably a transient."

"Meaning you don't think you're going to find anyone?"

"Don't be too sure of that. We're still working on it." The Sheriff's coffee cup rattled down into the cradle of its saucer. "Now, if you boys will excuse me, I'm heading out for a little fresh air and sunshine."

That was when Amy tuned out; she didn't wait to hear which of the trio was paying for the coffee or whether they were going Dutch. In the end the three men left together and Amy did her best to down the rest of her pot roast before it got any colder. The waitress appeared to warm the coffee and stoically endured rejection of her dessert offers. When Amy paid, tipped, and left, the pie slices still lay in state, awaiting either a further viewing or decent burial tomorrow.

The clerk at the reception counter was obviously not into speed-reading; his eyes and lips were still moving over the final pages of his comic as Amy crossed the lobby. But as she entered the elevator he must have glanced up, because she sensed his eyeballs boring into her back.

Or was she just edgy? The chance conversation she had overheard could be a godsend, but there was a hint of the diabolic in its details. Lack of details, rather; it was Amy's own imagination that had supplied them and was still going about its grisly business now. *Pool of blood*. It was all too easy to expand that simple phrase into a full and explicitly gory story.

But was the story complete in itself, or merely a continuation? As Amy left the lonely elevator, moved down the lonely hall, and unlocked the door of her lonely room, questions were her only companions.

Once she switched on the lights she settled down in a chair and eased her feet out of their shoes. Had that weary waitress downstairs been able to kick off her shoes yet?

Amy shrugged the question off. It was the other questions that demanded an answer. Questions about connections. Somewhere in her yet-to-be-unpacked overnight bag was the collection of notes and data she'd carefully prepared and assembled but there was no need to consult them for details. All she needed now were the links in the chain of events.

It was more than thirty years ago that Norman Bates had been confined in the State Hospital for the Criminally Insane and it was almost a decade ago that he'd murdered two visiting nuns and escaped, only to be killed in a struggle with a hitchhiker he'd picked up in a van stolen from the nuns. The charred body found in the burned van was mistakenly identified as that of the hitchhiker and Norman Bates was still sought as an escapee.

There were more killings. Mary Crane's sister Lila and her husband, Sam Loomis, died in Fairvale on the night following Norman Bates' escape. His physician at State Hospital, Dr. Adam Claiborne, undertook a search on his own that led him all the way to Hollywood where a film about Norman was being prepared. Both the film's producer and its director died violent deaths and the actress playing Mary Crane narrowly averted the same fate.

Dr. Claiborne returned to State Hospital as an inmate rather than an attending physician. When his prized personal patient crashed out he'd apparently flipped in a similar fashion—Norman's other persona was his mother, and Claiborne's was Norman Bates.

Obviously Claiborne had not gone over the wall of the asylum to kill poor Terry Dowson so there was no connection there; at least none that would be obvious. On the other hand people had not suspected the connection between Norman and his dead mother. And years later, after all that continuing intensive therapy, no one at the hospital seemed to have realized he was still potentially dangerous. Certainly Dr. Claiborne didn't recognize his own schizoid disorder. And the murder victims out in California had no inkling that death was traveling in their direction from almost two thousand miles away.

But there was an overall connection, the apparently unrelated events did form a continuing chain, and somehow Amy sensed that last week's tragedy was the last link.

At least she fervently hoped it was the last—although there was always a possibility that it was only the latest.

Latest. Amy glanced at her watch. Almost nine, so there was probably still time. Reluctantly abandoning her cushioned comfort she rose and crossed to the bedstand on which the telephone rested. Reaching down into the shelf opening below, her fingers groped empty air. They repeated the exercise, when, one by one, she opened the drawers of the bureau. Either the hotel didn't provide guests with the local phone directory or there was no such animal.

Amy picked up the phone and informed the desk clerk of her predicament. He must have finished his pursuit of literature for the evening, because he sounded a bit more friendly.

"I can get the number for you from down here," he said. "Who do you wanta call?"

When she told him his voice did a double take.

"State Hospital?"

"That's right," Amy said. "Person-to-person, for Dr. Nicholas Steiner."

There was momentary hesitation at the other end of the line. "Pretty late."

Doing her good deed for the day, Amy resisted the impulse to inform him that she wasn't calling for a time signal. "He's expecting to hear from me."

"Okay, lady. Just hang on and I'll get him for you."

A few minutes later she was talking to a nurse, and after another minute or so to Steiner himself.

"Dr. Steiner speaking." The voice of an elderly man resonating through well-worn vocal cords. "I take it you're calling from town?"

"That's right. I'll be staying here at the Fairvale Motel."

"Please—it's *hotel*. They don't like to mention motels in Fairvale."

"Sorry," Amy said. "It must have been a Freudian slip."

His response was a dry chuckle and as she listened it seemed to have an echo. Either the rain was creating problems with the connection or there was somebody else on the line.

Amy chose her words carefully. "I was hoping it might be convenient for me to come out sometime tomorrow."

Steiner cleared his throat. "I'll have to ask."

"You haven't told him? Or shown him my letter?"

"Not yet. In view of what happened, I thought it best to wait for a more opportune moment."

"Are you saying there might be a problem?"

"I hope not. I'll know more after I talk to him tomorrow morning."

"I was planning to spend a little time at the courthouse before noon, but I can get out to the hospital by two o'clock if you're available. Of course I'll give you a call first."

"That won't be necessary. If he refuses to allow you to invade his privacy, feel free to invade mine."

His chuckle, her thanks, and the click of the receiver sounded simultaneously. All three conveyed a hollow quality and once again Amy wondered about the possibility of eavesdropping.

But who was she to talk—wasn't that what she was doing at dinner? It was something to think about, one consideration among many. But right now the priority was to unpack the overnight bag and distribute its contents wherever appropriate in the room, its closet, or the adjoining bath.

As she solved these problems in logistics Amy found herself stifling a yawn. Kicking off her shoes had eased foot-fatigue, but her body felt tired all over, and its encasement of skin and sinew could not be as easily removed.

Not that Amy really wanted to part with her body under any circumstances. She surveyed it with a touch of pride as she removed her makeup and stripped in the bathroom; for someone who would never see twenty-six again there really weren't too many grounds for complaint. At least her legs were good and as long as she took it easy on the french fries her hips didn't constitute a problem. She noted a tiny hint of sag in her left breast, but in a way it only contributed to the natural look. Nobody would mistake her cleavage for Silicon Valley.

No one had been in a position to make such a mistake recently, worse luck. She dismissed the thought; this was neither the time nor the place for such activity. Outside, the cold rain was still coming down. But here in the shower stall the water was warm. The only chill came from a sudden, unexpected comparison of what she was presently doing and what Mary Crane had done those many long years ago or, more precisely, what had been done *to* her under the same circumstances.

How old was the Crane girl when she died? Amy withdrew a number from her memory-bank. Twenty-nine. In order to reach that age she'd have to stay here under the spray for an additional two years. In any case, enough of this shower-stalling.

Time to towel-dry her hair—there just wasn't enough room to bring everything, which meant either she needed a larger bag or a smaller hair dryer. Time for powder, deodorant, and a fresh nightie for a wilted bod. Time to snuggle under the sheets and cast a final sidelong glance at the face of the wristwatch resting on the nightstand. Time to tell time.

It was exactly ten P.M. No need to ask for a wakeup call; her eyes would open automatically at seven A.M.

Amy switched the lamp off. Somehow the rain sounded louder in the darkness. Perhaps it would stop before morning. Sunshine makes no sound.

No sound, nothing to disturb her, not even raindrops now. For a moment inner vision behind closed eyelids gave flickering glimpses of highways stretching ahead; it was as though she was reenacting the hours of driving today, editing them visually, then miniaturizing them on a microchip of memory.

Now both sound and vision had vanished, together with sensation. No rain, no pain, no Crane. Because Mary Crane was two years older, she'd died before Amy was born, so what was the point in bringing her back to life? Points were for knives and knives were for killing and nothing would happen as long as she remembered that, remembered next time to bring a bigger bag, buy a smaller dryer, stay out of the shower.

But she was in the shower again, because all at once she heard the water running, opened her eyes to see the shower curtain waving.

Only the water wasn't coming from the showerhead and the curtain wasn't flapping in the stall. Amy sat up quickly, switching on the lamp beside her. What she heard was the rain and what she saw flapping was the curtain before the window opening outward.

Open. Amy was out of bed and halfway across the

room before she fully realized the potential significance of the term. The window had been closed when she went to bed; although she remembered glancing out of it after her initial arrival, she couldn't recall opening it then. Considering that there was a storm going on outside, there'd be no point.

She halted in midstride. Suppose there *was* a point? That's what she'd been thinking about when she fell asleep, the point of a knife.

Amy glanced around the room. She'd left the closet open and its contents were plainly visible. The clothing on the hangers stirred slightly in the draft from the open window but the spaces between and behind the garments revealed nothing but their shadows.

The bathroom door was open too, and Amy tried to remember if it was poised at the same angle when she retired. Not that this would really make any difference; if the opening had been wide enough for her to exit, it was wide enough for someone else to enter.

Amy edged up to the bathroom doorway as quietly and cautiously as she could. Anyone lurking inside wouldn't hear her barefoot passage across the room or the sudden thudding of her heart beneath the slight sag of her left breast.

All of which was stupid, she reminded herself, because she'd switched the lamp on and that would be signal enough for anyone in the bathroom to stop lurking and start—

Forget it. There was nobody in that bathroom. Amy quickened her pace, peered around the edge of the doorway, and slowed her heartbeat as she saw that the room and shower held nothing to be afraid of.

Except the *nothing* itself.

Turning, she made her way to the flapping curtain and the open window. The curtain billowed inward, giving her a glimpse of the rain pelting down on the bare expanse of the flat one-story roof directly below. Someone could have come to the window by way of that rooftop, clambered to the ledge, pushed the window up to enter.

Again she reminded herself there was no point, none that she could see and none—thank God—that she had felt. The explanation was simple; she'd forgotten to lock the window and it blew open.

Too simple. Amy pulled the window shut, adjusted the curtains, returned to bed, and—after a surprisingly short interval—fell asleep once again.

So it wasn't until seven o'clock the following morning that she realized how easy it would have been to determine whether or not there had been a visitor.

But by then it was too late. There were no visible markings and the carpet was dry.

·3·

DR. Nicholas Steiner awoke that morning at five forty-five, beating the clock by a full fifteen minutes.

He reached out to switch off the alarm, then settled back again on his pillow with a self-congratulatory smile imposing itself upon his wrinkled face. At this point in time beating the clock was always an occasion for a victory celebration. Or, in this instance, at least an excuse to lounge in bed for another fifteen minutes until his official rising time.

Glancing toward the window he noted that the rain had stopped and the clouds were clearing. That was something to be grateful for; meteorologists, psychologists, and all the other -ologists might dispute him, but Steiner knew from his own experience that weather patterns affected the behavior patterns of his patients. Wind, moisture, barometric pressure, sunspots perhaps, but above all the moon. Just because they didn't call them "lunatics" today didn't change the facts. Tides, menses, and cerebral stimulation were still governed by the goddess when her shining countenance came fully into view.

Now what brought that on? There was enough to think about without wasting his time mooning around. At his age he could no longer afford such musings; his poetic license had been revoked. Forget the lunar flights, the fancies, come down to earth, rejoin the human race.

But not just yet. Steiner cocked an eye at the clock. He still had another eight minutes and until then there was no need to enter the human race or the rat race it was forever running.

Once up and dressed, once shaved and breakfasted, it was necessary for Dr. Steiner to assume his professional posture as a humanitarian and, hopefully, a healer. But right now during those eight precious minutes still left to him, his posture would remain recumbent and his private opinion unchanged.

Simply stated, Steiner had come to the conclusion, after long years of observation, that his mentally disturbed charges were less disturbing than the concept of the so-called normal person roaming unconfined in our society. Except for cases involving physiological damage, the problems of the average mental patient might be construed as symptoms of sensitivity. The problems of the so-called normal person were usually symptomatic of mere stupidity.

The majority of the normal population cannot draw a map of the world in which they live. Most of the citizens of this country can't tell you its history. They are unable to identify quotations from the Bill of Rights, the Constitution, or its amendments. They can't list the Ten

Commandments. They can't even tell you the number of bones in their own bodies or accurately locate the principal organs, let alone describe their functions.

The average person doesn't know the earth is moving as well as revolving; he can't name the planets of our solar system. Ask him to identify some great men and he'll rattle off a variety of Johns, depending on his age— John Wayne, Johnny Carson, John Lennon, John Belushi. Inside his head is a gaggle of jocks, rock performers, and "media personalities" including talk-show hosts and currently popular guest bimbos. He cannot name two Nobel Prize winners. Don't expect him to explain the workings of the electoral college or the function of photosynthesis. Nevertheless, he's a mine of information— and misinformation—about cars, sexual practices, and other sports.

But the eight minutes were up now and so was Steiner. Dr. Nicholas Steiner, the caring, sympathetic, understanding, empathizing and consoling counselor whose lifelong career was dedicated to restoring the mentally ill to the ranks of normal society.

In addition to attendance upon his bodily needs and functions Dr. Steiner had certain diurnal duties to perform, and it was a good two hours before he was able to see Adam Claiborne.

But out of sight doesn't necessarily mean out of mind, and the problem of Claiborne occupied Steiner's thoughts for some while prior to their actual meeting.

For that matter, Steiner's mind had never really been free since Claiborne had been confined. It's not easy to deal with the fact that a former professional colleague is now a patient in the same institution where he once served as your assistant.

Not easy to deal, not easy to heal. But at least some progress had been made in the years since Claiborne had been undergoing therapy. According to Steiner's evaluation he seemed to be making significant gains. At least he was able to talk about himself *as* himself again—

there was no longer any evidence of that "Norman Bates will never die" delusion. Odd, Steiner parenthetically observed to himself, how many patients suffering from psychotic disorders seemed to identify with Norman over the years. It was as though he had somehow touched a nerve, as the saying goes.

The saying went, because it was meaningless in this situation. The problem confronting Dr. Steiner this morning was how to confront Claiborne with what was going to happen this afternoon. And he'd better come to grips with it and quit stalling. A man his age could no longer afford the luxury of delay. Don't waste time or time will waste you.

Sound advice, but it didn't solve his problem and he found himself reaching Claiborne's room before reaching a solution.

At least what Claiborne occupied could legitimately be described as a room, in contrast with the quarters to which most patients were assigned. Perhaps the State Board would take a dim view of the matter, but thus far none of its members had ever set eyes on Claiborne's room. Except for the presence of the standard bunk bed occupying the far corner and the security bars crisscrossing the window, Claiborne's quarters might be mistaken for a small private office. Once his initial disorientation vanished and the possibility of violent reaction or over-reaction gave way to abreaction, Steiner had furnished him with the desk, swivel lamp, bookshelves, and the volumes he requested with which to fill them. A final aesthetic touch was the rug on the floor, something to which any inspector from the State Board would object. That had been Steiner's own idea; at least it lent a hint of comfort to the surroundings in which his old colleague was destined to live out the rest of his days, poor devil. There was no television set in the room; Claiborne had never been *that* crazy.

Male nurse Lloyd Semple accompanied Steiner to

the door, then halted, keys dangling, as Steiner took a precautionary squint through the peephole.

Claiborne had apparently been lying on the lower level of the bunk bed, but now as the keys clinked, he swung his legs over the side and eased himself into a sitting position. A quick glance reassured Steiner that his reaction indicated alertness, not alarm, though it was still difficult to reconcile himself to the evidence of how Claiborne had aged. Over the past few years he'd gone quite grey and his forehead seemed permanently furrowed in a frown. But there was nothing out of the ordinary about his manner and Steiner, satisfied, knocked on the door.

"Adam, I'd like to talk to you. Mind if I come in?"

"By all means, Nick. My house is yours."

Steiner turned, signaling to the male nurse. As Semple selected the proper key, the doctor issued his instructions in a low murmur. "I don't think we have any problems, but I'd like you to stand by outside, just on the off-chance."

Nodding, Semple unlocked the door, pushing it open far enough for Dr. Steiner to enter the room, then closed and relocked it behind him.

Claiborne, on his feet now, advanced and extended his hand in greeting. "Good to see you," he said. "Thanks for stopping by."

Steiner noted that his patient seemed bright, cheerful, and loquacious. As for himself at this moment, he wished to hell he hadn't given up smoking. He didn't know what to do with his hands because he had a problem on them.

"Sit down," Claiborne said, indicating the swivel chair before the desk. Turning, he moved to the bunk bed and again seated himself on the side, leaning forward to keep his head clear of the upper level.

"Sure you'll be comfortable there?" Steiner asked.

"No sweat."

No sweat, just small talk, Steiner told himself. He still hadn't figured out a way of leading up to what he wanted to say. Had to say, rather; given a preference, he wouldn't discuss the matter at all. But since it concerned a patient's interest, there was no choice.

Sometimes intimacy involves actions rather than words. Steiner wondered if he should draw his chair back from the desk and bring it closer to the bunkside. Hesitation vanished as he reminded himself that Claiborne's right hand had been partially but permanently crippled when a shot in the wrist put an end to his rampage out there on the coast. Since then the injury had rendered him comparatively harmless. Steiner suddenly remembered that Maurice Ravel had once written a *Piano Concerto for the Left Hand Alone*. Not to worry—Claiborne didn't play piano.

Telling himself to relax, he swiveled around and propelled himself into position close beside Claiborne.

"What's on your mind?" Claiborne said.

Steiner smiled. "Isn't that supposed to be my line?"

It was Claiborne's turn to smile now. "I forgot."

"Frankly, so did I." Dr. Steiner nodded. "Just between us, you've made remarkable progress."

"Thanks to your help." For a moment Adam Claiborne's smile twisted wryly. "Or maybe I'm just undergoing temporary remission."

Steiner shrugged. "There are times I wonder if all of what passes for sanity isn't just a form of remission from our natural state. What was it Norman Bates used to say? Something like 'everybody goes a little crazy at times.'"

"I remember," Claiborne said softly. "He said a lot of things that made sense. Come to think of it, between the two of us, you and I probably know more about Norman than anyone else still alive."

Steiner breathed a silent sigh of relief. This was the opening he'd been hoping for. "That could change," he said.

"In what way?"

"I don't suppose you're familiar with the work of Amelia Haines," he said.

"Should I be?"

"Not necessarily, but under the circumstances I wish you were. Two years ago she published a book titled *Tricks or Treats,* about the Walton case."

Claiborne's reaction was a puzzled frown and Steiner reminded himself that without access to television or newspapers it was unlikely that his patient could keep abreast of recent or current crime waves.

"The case itself goes back about five years or so," Steiner said. "Bonnie Walton was a prostitute who committed the serial murders of eight clients before she was apprehended. As I understand it, Miss Haines was commissioned to do a magazine article on the case, but what she learned led to a book-length, thoroughly researched study. For some reason or other, the publishers sent me a copy when it first came out; I thought it was an honest, objective job, without the usual sensationalism you might expect."

Claiborne's smile had vanished. "Why are you giving me a book review?"

"I'm not giving a review," Steiner told him. "I'm offering you an option." He leaned forward. "Miss Haines contacted me recently to request an interview. Because of the success of *Tricks or Treats,* her publishers are interested in having her do a similar book about Norman Bates."

"Similar?" Claiborne's voice was strident. "But there's no comparison. Norman wasn't a serial killer, not if you stop to analyze the circumstances—"

Dr. Steiner gestured quickly. "That's exactly it. What Miss Haines wants to do is analyze the circumstances rather than conduct a postmortem on Norman himself. She's already accumulated quite a bit of material. As a matter of fact, she happens to be in Fairvale right now. I got a call from her last night, asking if she might come out and talk to me this afternoon."

He paused, waiting for a response, but none came. "Would you have any objection if I discussed Norman Bates with her?"

"That's your privilege."

Steiner took a deep breath. "Yours also. Would you like to speak to her yourself?"

"Why should I?"

"I can't presume to provide you with reasons. Mine are simple enough; I think it could help give her a greater insight into what really happened, make it a better book. I believe she's sincere about finding the truth. That's why she came here, because she'd like to contact everyone left who might still have some connection with the case."

"Case?" Claiborne echoed.

Steiner cursed himself silently for making the slip; he might have known it was a mistake to use that word in this connotation. But it was too late now. The best he could do was to try concealing any outward sign of reaction as Claiborne voiced his paranoia.

"How can you say that? You make it sound as though there were some kind of criminal proceedings. Norman never stood trial. There's no such thing as a Bates 'case'!"

"I'm afraid there is now," said Steiner softly. "At least that's what they're calling it."

"What are you talking about?"

"A child was murdered last week, a little girl named Terry Dowson."

Claiborne's eyes widened in surprise, then slitted in angry accusation. "And you're accusing me?"

Steiner shook his head quickly. "Of course not."

If Claiborne heard the demur he didn't heed it. "You've had me here under lock and key for damn near seven years now! For God's sake, Nick, what makes you think I could sneak off and kill some kid I've never even heard of?"

"Nobody's saying you're involved."

The anger in Claiborne's eyes gave way to a glint of suspicion. "Oh no? Don't think I'm not aware of how people talk about me, ever since—"

Steiner broke in, gesturing. "There's nothing to worry about. If you must know, I did get an inquiry on the day following the murder. Because of what I told them, it's now a matter of official record that security checks show you were here in this room before, during, and after the time the girl was stabbed to death."

"Stabbed?"

Steiner nodded. "They haven't found the weapon, but they think it was probably some sort of butcher knife."

Anger glinted once more in Claiborne's eyes. "Just because the murderer used a knife, those miserable bastards think that's enough to drag Norman's name into the mud again." Now scorn joined anger. "The Bates case—"

Steiner shook his head. "They're not calling it that because of the weapon," he said. "It's the location."

Claiborne's frown furrows deepened. "Where did you say this happened?"

Steiner hesitated. He hadn't said where, he didn't want to say where, but there was no way out now. And perhaps paranoia required puncturing rather than reassurance. "They found the girl's body in the Bates house," he said.

Claiborne stared at him. "What are you trying to tell me? The Bates house burned down years ago."

"True. We both know about it. But what you don't know is that the house has recently been rebuilt."

"That's impossible!"

Steiner nodded again. "Rebuilt and restored," he said. "Apparently someone located an old photograph album with pictures taken against the background of various interiors, plus enough exterior shots to guide reconstruction. Of course there was no way to duplicate furnishings exactly, but I understand they managed to come pretty close to the originals.''

Claiborne had continued to stare and now he spoke in a shocked whisper. "How could they do a thing like that? And why?"

Try as he would, Steiner could not bring himself to maintain eye contact. And it didn't matter now, because he was flying blind. Flying into the face of misfortune, into the face of a patient whom he should have protected, not traumatized.

And while he was at it, he'd better rid his mind of all this nonsense about traps, flying blind, and putting a face on misfortune. What he really needed was a security lock on his tongue, but it was too late for silence now. And come to think of it, this security lock business was just another example of what he'd promised himself to avoid. It was time to choose his words carefully—very carefully.

"There's one obvious reason for rebuilding the Bates house," he said. "Profit."

"Are you trying to tell me that anyone would want to buy the place and live there? It doesn't make sense!"

"It wasn't built as a permanent residence," Steiner said. "Just for visitors."

"They can't do that." Something was happening to Claiborne's voice. "Making a hotel out of the house? They must be insane!"

"It's not supposed to be used as a hotel." Steiner softened his tone, hoping Claiborne would follow suit. "Neither is the motel, for that matter."

"They rebuilt *that* too?" If anything, Claiborne's response was louder than before.

"Only the office and one room," Steiner told him. "The rest of the building is just a shell."

"Then where's the profit coming from?"

Steiner pitched his own voice lower. "Tourism," he said.

"You mean they're turning the property into a tourist attraction?"

Steiner shrugged. "So I'm told."

Claiborne leaned forward, his features distorted. "What are they going to do, charge people so much a head to take a look at the murder mansion? Will they have tour guides give a canned speech about what happened? Are they going to offer family rates or let the kiddies in for free?"

"Take it easy," Steiner said. "It's not that bad." But it was. He'd been an idiot not to anticipate the problem. Ordinarily he went counter to today's trend of substituting sedation for solutions, but right now he wished he'd relaxed his opinions and his patient.

Claiborne stared at him. "Why didn't you stop them?"

"I think you know the answer to that question, Adam. We're twenty miles away from Fairvale. I'm not a resident, I have no say-so in community affairs. For that matter, when you get right down to it, it's not even a question of Fairvale's choice. From what I understand, the Bates property comes under the jurisdiction of the County Board of Supervisors."

Claiborne's scowl was deep-set. "Don't you think I know that? You could have talked to Joe Gunderson."

Steiner shook his head. "I don't know anybody by that name." And yet, very faintly, it rang a bell.

"Don't give me that! Everybody knows Joe Gunderson. He runs this county. Mother went to him about a permit before she started building—"

This time the bell clanged loud and clear. Gunderson, the county's political boss, famous throughout the area for twenty years. And dead for ten.

Steiner took a deep breath. "Adam, I want you to listen to me now very carefully."

Claiborne wasn't listening to anything but the sound of his own voice. Or was it his own? "You're not fooling me. The reason you didn't talk to Gunderson is because you don't care what happens, nobody cares what happens, you're going to let them go ahead and do anything they like, turn the motel into some kind of carnival sideshow!"

"I've told you, there's nothing I can do—"

"You've told me a lot of things, haven't you, about who I am and what *I* should do. But I don't believe you anymore. I *know* who I am."

The bell inside Steiner's head clanged again, this time in warning. Its tone changed as Claiborne's voice was changing. And now, incredibly, his distorted features were changing too.

Steiner pushed his chair back.

"Stop it, Adam! Calm down now, and relax."

"I know who I am and what I must do!" Adam Claiborne shouted.

But it was not Adam's face that Steiner saw before him now as Claiborne rose; nor was it himself that Claiborne got hold of as the long fingers found his visitor's throat.

Dr. Steiner gasped, clawing at his attacker. Gasp became gurgle, gurgle trickling into silence as the pressure tightened, cutting off the blood supply to the brain.

Steiner's last conscious thought came as a simple observation. Perhaps Claiborne didn't play the piano but he'd certainly learned how to use his left hand.

·4·

MORNING sunshine filtered through the bathroom blinds as Amy finished applying minimal makeup in the fluorescence illuminating the mirror above the washstand. That would suffice while she was indoors; this afternoon, before leaving, she'd subject herself to natural light from outside the window and do a more thorough job. What she did now would serve her purpose—which was to go downstairs and have someone serve her breakfast.

Why was she so hungry? Must be all this fresh air. Thinking of air brought back the memory of her fleeting panic upon awakening last night to confront that open window. Once again she reassured herself that it must have been unlocked, blowing open when the wind did its work. In any case, nothing had happened and it seemed silly to be uptight about it.

Nevertheless she started at the sound of the phone jangling in the bedroom beyond. She picked it up after the fourth ring, but hesitated for a fraction of a second before speaking.

For some reason or other, answering the phone had always presented problems. "Hello" seemed meaningless; ritualism, like asking "How are you?" when opening conversation with a total stranger whose welfare was really not a matter for concern at the moment. "Amy Haines speaking" or "Amy Haines here" both sounded superfluous; of course she *was* the one who was speaking and since she was not a machine she certainly had to be here in order to do so. Which really left her with little choice but to say, "Yes?"

So, of course, she said "Hi!" instead.

"Miss Haines?" A man's voice, deep and resonant. "Hope I didn't wake you up."

"You didn't." Amy flicked her left forefinger at the lower lash of her left eye; apparently a speck of mascara was causing a problem there. "Who is this?"

"Hank Gibbs—*Fairvale Weekly Herald*. I'm calling from the lobby. Thought maybe if you were free I could invite you to come down and have breakfast."

Amy hadn't put on her watch yet; it still lay on the nightstand. Twisting her neck, she glanced down to read the time. Nine A.M. Apparently her finger had done a good job because her eye was clear, with no further feeling of discomfort. And if Fairvale was like most of the other small towns she knew, the courthouse wouldn't be opening until ten o'clock.

"Thank you, Mr. Gibbs," she said. "I'll be down in five minutes."

After hanging up Amy went to retrieve the larger of the two plastic-bound notebooks she'd placed on the bureau while unpacking last night. Opening it she scanned the contents of the second page until she found what she was looking for. Yes, here he was on the list—Hank Gibbs, nwspr. ed., Fairvale. The fact he'd sought her out instead of vice versa might be a good omen. In any case, she wanted to see him.

By the same token, it might be a good idea if nobody saw the list, or for that matter, the rest of the contents of this particular notebook. Carrying it over to the closet, she opened her overnight case and placed it under lock and key. When she crossed the room again she slipped the smaller notebook into her bag. One last reassurance from the mirror and she was off.

The elevator was empty when it arrived and she was the sole passenger when it descended. All of which made for a meeting that was quick and easy because

Hank Gibbs was the sole occupant of the lobby when she stepped forth into it.

At first glance Gibbs appeared to be a man pushing forty, and forty was pushing back. About five-eight, Amy judged, with the mesomorphic build of a former football player who has allowed himself to go out of training and into McDonald's. He wore tan slacks, a blue-and-white checked shirt open at the collar, and a brown jacket with the leather elbows popular a dozen or more years ago. His blond hair was cut short in a manner that clearly indicated that the local barber wasn't much for all that newfangled hairstyling. But somehow Gibbs, with his tanned face and surprisingly vivid blue eyes, seemed quite appropriate to the setting in which she was encountering him. Amy's first impression was that he might have stepped out of one of those old-time Norman Rockwell cover illustrations for *The Saturday Evening Post.*

"Pleased to meet you." Apparently Amy's first impression was correct; Hank Gibbs accompanied his statement by shaking hands—a custom she tended to believe had gone out of fashion around the time Gloria Steinem reached puberty.

His hand was warm, his grip firm; body language reinforcing his greeting. For a moment she regretted not having taken a little more time on her makeup, then pushed the thought aside. This was business.

But breakfast itself was pleasure. Their waitress was tall, angular, bespectacled, and briskly efficient; the coffee was stronger, the service prompt and unobtrusive. Even so, Amy was aware that the young woman who served her, together with the waitress assigned to counter-trade, checked Hank Gibbs and herself whenever their eyes were free to do so. The eyes of other patrons also searched out the activities of what they presumably regarded as the odd couple. Apparently Amy and her companion were considered an item; but if Gibbs didn't seem concerned about the possibility of gossip, why should she?

His eggs were fried, with a side order of ham; hers were scrambled, with bacon. Both had toast and passed on the fried potatoes. But before their orders arrived Amy had already removed the small notebook from her purse.

"I hope you don't mind if I ask you a few questions," she said.

"Not at all." Hank Gibbs smiled. "Matter of fact, you took the words right out of my mouth." His smile broadened. "I guess the first thing we'll have to decide is just who is interviewing who."

Amy peeked at her watch. "To be perfectly frank, I think it will help if you'd let me interview you first. Maybe we could set up another meeting later, at your convenience. I've got to check some things out this morning over at the courthouse, and perhaps you'll have some information to assist me."

"What's your hurry?" Gibbs sipped his coffee, then held out the half-empty cup to the waitress as she approached. "I take it you expect to be here all day."

"Not really. I have an early afternoon appointment."

Gibbs nodded. "At State Hospital."

"How did you know?"

"I stopped by Sheriff Engstrom's office on my way over here. His secretary told me." Gibbs rescued his refilled coffee cup from the waitress. "In case you're wondering, she got the information from the desk clerk here."

"Since when—"

"Since time immemorial." Gibbs reached for the sugar. "This is a small town, Miss Haines. Word gets around. The desk clerk is Les Chambers; his father used to be the sheriff here when Engstrom just started out as a deputy. Les and Engstrom are almost like family, you could say, so whenever anything happens over here at the hotel it gets back to the Sheriff's office right away."

"All I did was place a phone call," Amy said. "But nothing happened."

"Not until about half an hour ago." Gibbs stirred the sugar in his cup. "Word came through while I was still at the Sheriff's office." He hesitated for a moment, frowning. "Guess I should have told you earlier."

"Told me what?"

"Dr. Steiner won't be seeing you this afternoon. He's in Montrose Hospital." Gibbs lifted his spoon from the coffee cup in a quick gesture of response to Amy's sudden look of alarm. "Far as they know, it's not all that serious but he's going to need a couple of days' rest. It's Claiborne who's in a bad way."

"What happened?"

"No details yet. It seems Dr. Steiner was talking to Claiborne in his room; there was some kind of flare-up, and Claiborne tried to strangle him. By the time the male nurse broke in Steiner had passed out. Nobody's given the straight story about how Claiborne was pulled off but somewhere along the line he suffered what they're calling a coronary embolism. He's at the hospital too, listed in critical condition."

"My fault," Amy murmured.

"What did you say?"

"It's my fault that it happened. When I called Dr. Steiner last night I asked about the possibility of seeing Adam Claiborne when I came out and he said he'd speak to him this morning. According to what you tell me, I should have left well enough alone."

"Wrong. First of all you can't judge anything on the basis of what I have told you because there's not enough information to go on. Secondly, you don't strike me as the type who'd ever settle for leaving well enough alone. If you did, you wouldn't be a journalist. Any more than I would." Gibbs shook his head. "But the bottom line is, don't blame yourself for what you think may have happened or what did happen. There's no need for a rush to judgment."

True enough, Amy told herself. It doesn't pay to be judgmental about anything without getting sufficient input first. She glanced up at Hank Gibbs; his appearance hadn't changed since their meeting, but he was a perfect illustration of misjudgment, because he no longer looked like a Norman Rockwell illustration at all.

"Relax," Gibbs said. "Steiner's going to be okay and Claiborne will probably make it too. Point is you don't have to be in such a hurry to get over to the courthouse because now you have all day. But if you want to ask any questions, feel free."

Amy did relax enough to take another sip of her coffee, and while she didn't feel entirely free, at least what he'd said lifted some of the burden from her conscience. Enough so that she was able to accept his invitation.

"How long have you been editing the paper?" she asked.

"Nine years. Why?"

"I was wondering about the files. Would there be anything going back about thirty years ago?"

"Not that I know of." Gibbs smiled. "Believe me, I looked. Then I asked around, trying to find out if some of the older folks happened to save copies from back in those days. If anyone did, they won't admit it; people here didn't want to talk about Norman Bates back then and chances are they didn't want to read about him either. Most of them still don't seem to want to know the details." He leaned forward. "Why do you?"

"Because he's become a symbol," she said. "In some ways he seems to be more alive today than he was thirty years ago. Or is it just that we've turned into a violent society?"

"I think our society has always been violent," Gibbs said. "The only difference is that now we're beginning to admit it. And we've still got a long way to go. People fool themselves into thinking that reading about it or watching it on screen is 'facing reality.' But actually what they see or read is preselected. I think that we turn our backs on violence in its worst and most com- monplace forms—penning and butchering fowl and live- stock, death on the highways, crime in the streets." Gibbs shook his head. "But who am I to get on a soap- box? Isn't that what your book was all about?"

Amy nodded. "I started to tell the story of Bonnie Walton, try to find out why her grungy life as a common hooker could lead to committing a series of cold-blooded murders. But *Tricks or Treats* ended up dealing more with her johns than with herself. When I researched their past histories it seemed to me that all of them were victims of society before they became victims of murder. A couple of them turned out to be just kids sampling what they thought would be more sophisticated sex, the same way they'd experiment with designer drugs in preference to pot."

Hank Gibbs arched his eyebrows. "That's a pretty heavy way to describe it," he said.

"Caught me out?" Amy smiled as she spoke. "Most of what I just said is a direct quote from the book. I don't usually talk that way."

"Why not?"

"No audience, I suppose."

"Try me." Gibbs reached for his coffee cup. "You were saying about the johns—"

"All they seemed to be looking for was a little excite- ment to ease the monotony of a dull existence. In the case of the three middle-aged men you could strike out the word 'existence' and substitute 'marriage.' The older men weren't looking for great sex—from what I was able to find out, they weren't looking for sex at all. A little con- versation, a little sympathy, the temporary illusion of being the center of attention; that's what they were buy- ing. But they got more than they bargained for. Sad."

"I agree." Gibbs finished his coffee and centered his cup in the saucer. "I'm glad you don't sound like one of those feminists."

"I believe in equal rights," she told him, "but that

means looking at both sides of the question. There's no doubt that Bonnie Walton was also a victim; forces in her early life drove her into prostitution, and prostitution drove her into mental illness. You might say that her psyche, as well as her body, was bedridden.''

"I might, but I'll bet you beat me to it." Gibbs smiled. "Something tells me that's a line from your book too.''

"Right." Amy glanced down at her notebook for a moment as she continued. "But what I'm leading up to is that it seems possible Norman Bates might have been a victim if we had all the facts to go on.''

Gibbs nodded. "Problem is, there's not too many people around who knew him.''

"And some of those who did had a very short acquaintance," Amy said. "That insurance investigator, Arbogast, probably saw him for only a few moments. With the Crane girl it might have been a matter of several hours, but of course there's no way of telling. And now with her sister dead, Sam Loomis dead, Sheriff Chambers and his wife both gone, there doesn't seem to be anyone left who had a direct connection with the case. I'd been counting on Dr. Steiner and Claiborne but it looks like that will have to wait. Meanwhile—''

"Meanwhile, what?''

"I have a secondary list." Amy opened the notebook. "There's this man who's responsible for putting up that replica of the house and motel.''

"Otto Remsbach? Might be a good idea if you found out what that's all about.''

"Don't you know?''

"Not very much." Gibbs shrugged. "You'll probably get more out of him than I could. You're prettier.''

Amy ignored the lead, if it was a lead; as far as she was concerned pleasure ended with breakfast. This was business. "Then there's a Dr. Rawson. Also Bob Peterson, and of course I want to have a talk with the Sheriff—''

"Then what are we waiting for?"

"I appreciate what you're saying, Mr. Gibbs, but I really can't ask you to inconvenience yourself."

"Meaning you wouldn't feel comfortable having me around unless I kept my mouth shut." Gibbs nodded. "Okay, I promise."

He turned in his chair to signal the waitress for the check but the long arm of coincidence—or, more precisely, her scrawny one—was already extended to deposit the bill on the table. "Thanks, Millie," he said.

Leaving his tip, paying at the cashier's stand, and conducting Amy through the lobby, Gibbs slowed his movements once they stepped out onto the sidewalk. "Mind doing a little walking?" he asked. "Nobody on your list is more than three blocks from here. That's one of the joys of living in a small town. Right offhand, I can't think of any other."

Their first stop was the office and showroom of Remsbach Farm Implements Co.; at least that's what the lettering on the display window proclaimed, and Amy had no reason to dispute it because she could see the tractor model looming up on the platform behind the windowpane.

Otto Remsbach's office was on the left-hand side of the hall just a few steps past the doorway. Gibbs held the door of the outer office open for Amy's entrance, then followed her, moving up beside the desk where a honey-blond secretary whom Amy judged to be about her own age sat behind a typewriter. She glanced up as they entered, her tentative smile broadening as she recognized Gibbs.

"Hi, Doris," he said. His head bobbed in accompaniment to the customary introductions. "Doris Huntley—Amelia Haines. It is Amelia, right?"

Amy nodded. "Pleased to meet you, Miss Huntley."

Gibbs' resonant voice broke in before the secretary could respond. "Miss Haines just got into town last night. She's doing a story about the Bates place so naturally she'd like to have a talk with Mr. Remsbach."

Doris Huntley's brown eyes focused momentarily on Amy in what seemed to be a quick reappraisal. But her reply was directed to Gibbs. "I'm sorry, he's over at the warehouse in Marcyville. Probably won't be back until sometime late this afternoon." Now she turned to Amy again. "Is there somewhere he can reach you then?"

"I'm staying at the hotel," Amy told her.

"Ask him to give her a call when he's free," Gibbs said. "Tell him from me that I think it's a good idea. That tourist trap he's opening could use a little good publicity for a change."

Doris Huntley nodded. "Soon as he gets back."

"Thanks. Be seeing you."

She nodded again, then leaned forward. By the time Amy and her companion reached the door the typewriter was already clattering away.

"She's very attractive," Amy murmured.

"Otto likes them that way," Hank Gibbs told her. "Can't say that I blame him."

Amy allowed her voice to rise to its normal level when they reached the street outside. "From what I saw, Fairvale hasn't yet moved into the world of computers."

"Not so. They have 'em at the bank, over at the super, and maybe four, five offices in and around town. I guess Otto's just holding out until he sees how things go on this Bates proposition. So far the Grand Opening's been postponed twice—once on account of some hangup bringing in furnishings, and of course that business out there last week meant another delay."

"I forgot to ask you about that," Amy said. "What's your theory?"

"My theory is that nobody knows the first damn thing about it," Gibbs said. "And they never will unless someone can come up with a motive. Who would want to kill an eleven-year-old girl like that? She wasn't sexually molested, had no problems with family or at school. It's a puzzler."

"Those reporters who came here after the murder," Amy said. "Did you talk to them about it?"

Gibbs nodded as they crossed the street. "They all hunted me up, first thing. Fella from Springfield, one from St. Louis, and a stringer covering this area for K.C. All I could do was tell them what I'd heard and turn them over to Engstrom, the coroner's office, and the Highway Patrol people. Guess they came up empty-handed because in forty-eight hours everyone was gone without bothering to kiss me good-bye. And there's been nothing in any of the papers since the first items were run."

He turned to hold the door open at the entranceway of a small, two-story structure imaginatively fashioned of concrete blocks shaped into a square with rectangular apertures for windows on the upper floor. Amy was under no misapprehension that the building had been designed by Le Corbusier.

"Rawson's office," Gibbs told her. And so it was, there on the left again, about the same distance down the hallway as Otto Remsbach's had been. The raised plastic lettering on the dark door spelled out CLIFFORD RAWSON, M.D.

Inside, the reception room offered the usual dingy discomforts accorded to patient patients by health-care professionals throughout the land. It occurred to Amy that at this very moment there must be several hundred thousand worried sufferers sitting on uncomfortable chairs and on edge in doctors' waiting rooms exactly like this one.

But at the moment there was no one else besides the two of them in the outer office and their stay was not lengthy. Gibbs went over to the glass-topped counter and rapped on the pane. The receptionist seated at the desk beyond appeared to be thirty-something, her hair jet-

black, eyes almost violet, and—wouldn't you know it?—
she was operating the keyboard of a small computer. Or
had been, until Hank Gibbs claimed attention.

Now the two of them were talking, but while she
smiled, nodded, and responded, Amy was quite conscious of her frequent side glances. The scrutiny concluded when she rose and disappeared into a corridor
area beyond the cubicle housing her desk and files.

Gibbs walked over to where Amy stood waiting.
"Doctor's in. I told her why you wanted to see him."

"Why do you suppose she was eyeballing me like
that?" Amy asked.

"Marge?" Gibbs chuckled. "Don't mind her. She
used to be my insignificant other."

Amy frowned. "What are you, some kind of comedian?"

"Not me," Gibbs said. "A comedian is somebody
who talks dirty for money."

The routine—if that's what it was intended to be—
ended abruptly now as the door to the inner office
opened and the receptionist nodded them forward.

Dr. Rawson's own private office was at the end of
the hall, past the two examination rooms and the storage
unit. There was a big desk, two small chairs facing it, a
bookcase against the wall opposite the window. The
wall behind the desk bore half a dozen framed diplomas
and certificates, all of which added up to attest Clifford
Matthew Rawson's rights as a physician, surgeon, and
one of the last of a dying breed of balding, horn-rimmed-
wearing general practitioners.

Once introduced he listened attentively as Amy
stated her purpose for the visit—very much, she imagined, as he would listen to a new patient's description of
symptoms. But when she finished, Dr. Rawson offered
neither diagnosis nor cure.

"I'm afraid there's not very much I can tell you," he
said. "It's true I was Lila and Sam's family physician,
but that's as far as it goes. Now that they're both gone, I

don't think I'd be violating confidentiality to tell you that Lila Loomis only came in once a year for a routine physical; as I recall it, she never had any serious problems. Sam had a slight heart murmur, but that's all. I put him on a low cholesterol diet and checked him out every six months." Dr. Rawson ran the fingers of his right hand across the side of his head to smooth nonexistent hair. He smiled apologetically. "I don't suppose that means very much one way or the other."

"What I was wondering about," Amy said, "is whether either of them might have happened to mention anything to you about the Bates case."

Dr. Rawson's smile vanished. "They never talked about it," he said. "And neither did I."

"I see." Amy nodded. "Thank you for answering my questions."

Dr. Rawson stared at her through the upper section of his bifocals. "Mind if I ask you one?"

"Not at all."

"Has anyone else here in town given you information about the case?"

"Not at all." Amy wondered how many more times she might have to use the same phrase today. *Not at all,* she hoped. But if this was any example of what she could expect to encounter—

"Let me say something to you, young lady. People around here just don't like to remember what happened. Frankly, I can't say that I blame them. What's done is done, and as far as they're concerned there's no more point in digging up those memories than there would be in digging up Norman Bates' body."

"You do have a poetic way of putting things," Hank Gibbs murmured.

Dr. Rawson's reaction was a self-conscious smile directed at Amy. "I'm sorry. I hope I didn't offend you."

"Not at all," Amy told him. *Here we go again,* she told herself.

And go she did, after the obligatory farewell

amenities. Hank Gibbs conducted her out and led her down the street. Traffic was brisker, Amy noted, and there were more cars angle-parked in front of the stores; the supermarket across the street had its own lot already more than half-filled now.

"My apologies," Gibbs said. "I should have told you the old boy is a little touchy."

Amy congratulated herself for restraining from replying, "Not at all." Instead she said, "I'm the one who ought to apologize, making you drag me around from pillar to post this way."

"No problem." Gibbs smiled. "Gives me something to pass the time. During the day I frequently suffer from insomnia."

"Maybe you ought to see a doctor," Amy said.

"About my insomnia?"

"No, about your sense of humor."

"Touché." Gibbs glanced at her. "Next stop?"

"Loomis Hardware."

"No such place. After Sam died and Bob Peterson took over he changed the name to guess what." Gibbs gestured toward the shop window directly ahead on their right.

Even a novice in sign language wouldn't fail to recognize the name which covered the entire upper surface of the hardware store's window. Bob Peterson had indeed taken over.

And a pity it was too, Amy decided, once they entered and Gibbs had introduced her to the proprietor. Peterson was middle-aged, a short man who was losing the battle of the bulge; his hair was pepper-and-salt, eyes and complexion grey. His smile of greeting vanished upon Gibbs' introduction, replaced by a stony stare.

"You the reporter staying over at the hotel?" he asked.

Amy nodded. "In that case I assume you may also know why I'm here."

"That's for damn sure." If anything the steel in his

stare was hardening. "Might as well tell you right off the bat that far as I'm concerned I got nothin' to say."

Hank Gibbs frowned. "Now look, Bob—"

Peterson ignored him, his stare still fixed. "Don't get me wrong, it's nothin' personal. Just that I made up my mind a long time ago I was never gonna talk about that business, never have and never will."

Amy waited him out, forming a reply that she never made. The sound of a phone ringing from a room behind the counter at the far end of the store put an end to further conversation.

"Sorry. Got to catch the phone." But Peterson didn't look sorry; it was warm relief that melted the steely stare as he turned and started off.

Amy followed suit, but in the opposite direction, Hank Gibbs moving up beside her, lengthening his stride to open the door as she approached it.

Sunlight nooned directly overhead as they emerged.

"My fault," he murmured. "Should have told you. He's got a thing about what happened to Sam Loomis and Lila in the store here. Wouldn't talk to those reporters either, but I hoped maybe he'd loosen up a little when he saw you." His smile implied a compliment, but Amy did not acknowledge it.

Instead she said, "I hate to say so, but most people here don't seem to go out of their way to be very friendly."

"You haven't seen anything yet." Gibbs shrugged. "As the captain of the *Titanic* used to say, 'It's just the tip of the iceberg.'"

The courthouse and its annex loomed directly ahead. Making their way past the artillery on the lawn, Hank Gibbs spoke again. "This time I'm going to warn you in advance."

"About Sheriff Engstrom?"

"You could include him, I suppose." Gibbs grinned. "But the one I really had in mind is that secretary of his—Irene Grovesmith."

"She hates reporters too?"

Gibbs shook his head. "Irene is impartial. She hates everybody."

"Any special reason?"

"Just old age, I guess. Engstrom should have gotten rid of her years ago. Irene ought to be grateful he kept her on, but she gives him a rough time. She gets her nourishment from biting the hand that feeds her."

Amy gave him a look, but it was nothing compared to the one she received from Irene Grovesmith upon entering the Sheriff's office in the annex.

"'Morning," Gibbs said. "Sheriff Engstrom around?"

"He's not in."

Gibbs nodded. "Must be over at State Hospital checking out what happened last night."

"Never mind where he is." The little old lady with the vinegary voice and matching expression would never be mistaken for Grandma Moses. Although it was he whom she addressed, Amy was still getting the look. And now a message came with it.

"I can tell you one thing right off," Irene Grovesmith said. "Even if he was here, the Sheriff wouldn't have anything to say to this young lady. When the time comes, he'll be handing out an official statement."

"Knock it off, Irene," Gibbs said. "Miss Haines isn't here to talk about what happened at the hospital, and you know it."

"What I said still goes." Now the voice poured vinegar directly for Amy's consumption. "And I advise you to do the same, Miss Haines. Just pack up and go. Nobody here wants to talk to you—"

The telephone rang on the desk beside her. *Instant replay*, Amy told herself, thinking of how the incident at the hardware store had ended.

This one was only beginning. Irene Grovesmith picked up the phone but said nothing. Whoever was at the other end of the line had already begun to speak and all she could do was nod repeatedly. As she did so her eyes brightened and her features defrosted. "Yes sir," she said. "Right away."

Replacing the receiver she turned and looked up with a triumphant stare. "If you're snooping around to try and find out who killed that little girl, you can forget it."

"What are you talking about?" Gibbs said.

"That was the Sheriff calling just now. They got the killer!"

·5·

THE sun had shifted slightly to the west when Amy and her companion made their exit through the annex door. Gibbs stepped into the shaded area at the left of the entrance and halted, nodding. "Cooler here," he said.

"Is that why you came out?" Amy asked. "They have air-conditioning inside. It didn't seem warm to me."

"It's going to be a lot hotter when Engstrom hauls that prisoner in."

"Then why did you tell his secretary we had to leave? Don't you want to see who they caught?"

"Sure do. That's why we're out here. At least we'll be able to get a look at him when he arrives. I somehow doubt that Engstrom would invite us into the holding cell for coffee and Twinkies."

"It isn't funny," Amy said.

Hank Gibbs nodded. "I know that. Probably better than you do. Don't forget, this is my town and these are my people. But if I let myself think too much about what all this is doing to them—" The way his voice trailed off added eloquence to his words.

"Have you got any idea whom they might be bringing in?"

"We'll see in a couple of minutes."

But they didn't. Normal traffic streamed along the street bordering the square but there was no sign of a car bearing the official insignia entering the reserved parking space at their left.

Gibbs consulted his watch. "What's holding them up?"

"The secretary didn't say where they'd be coming from," Amy said.

"That's right. But I should've guessed where they'd be going." Gibbs turned and opened the annex door. "Follow me."

Amy tagged along as he reentered, doing her best to keep pace as he strode down the corridor. "Engstrom's sharp. I just remembered he could take the back entrance to the main courthouse and sneak through to this side by way of the basement."

Once again Irene Grovesmith peered up at them as they came through the office doorway. "I thought you'd left," she said.

"Don't you wish." Gibbs' eyes semicircled the room and came to rest on the door to Engstrom's private office. "Where is he?"

"I've already told you it's none of your business. And there's no sense wasting your time hanging around here, Hank Gibbs. The Sheriff won't be talking to you until he's good and ready."

Gibbs winked at Amy out of the corner of his eye. "So much for southern hospitality," he murmured.

Irene Grovesmith glanced up quickly. "What's that you said?"

Before Gibbs could answer, the door to Engstrom's inner office opened abruptly and a uniformed deputy emerged, closing it behind him as he nodded at Gibbs.

"'Afternoon, Hank." He came forward, smiling. "Now I know what they mean when they say news travels fast."

"Happens we were here when the call came in. Just stepped out front in case you needed a welcoming committee." Gibbs glanced at Amy. "Miss Haines, I'd like you to meet Dick Reno."

As introductions were concluded the Sheriff's deputy was standing almost side by side with Hank Gibbs and Amy found herself inevitably—or was it automatically?—comparing the two men. Dick Reno was almost a head taller than the newspaper editor and at least a half dozen years younger, maybe more. He had dark, curly hair and would have been strikingly handsome were it not for the bridge of his nose, which was curiously flattened. Probably broke it playing football, Amy told herself, unless someone had broken it for him under other circumstances. Not an easy thing to do, if he'd been as trim and fit as he looked now. In any case, the slight irregularity of his features didn't mar his engaging smile, and just why the hell was she wasting her time over that one way or the other? *Business before pleasure.*

"Is there anything you might be able to tell us about what's happened?" The question was strictly business, but there was no harm in allowing a little hint of possible pleasure to creep into her glance and voice.

As a matter of fact, it seemed to help, and even more than she could have hoped. "It's up to the Sheriff," Dick Reno said. "But seeing as how you two already know we brought somebody in, I guess that part of it isn't exactly a secret. Fact is, we don't really know all that much more about him ourselves; not yet, anyway."

"I'll settle for a name," Gibbs said.

"Don't have one." Reno's smile was almost apologetic. "He refuses to identify himself and he's not carrying any IDs."

"Where did you find the suspect?" Hank Gibbs asked.

"He's not a suspect," Reno said. "That is, he hasn't been charged with anything yet. We just took him into custody for questioning."

"That's not the way I heard it." Gibbs gestured. "Irene here told us you got the killer."

Irene Grovesmith's eyes were like miniature ice cubes. Her mouth opened and the vinegar flowed. "Why, Hank Gibbs! I never said any such thing!" That made two indignant sniffs in a row, Amy noted, then wondered if there would be a third forthcoming now as the secretary directed her attention to Dick Reno. "As for you," she told him, "I think you've said more than enough already."

Apparently a third sniff was unnecessary because Reno nodded quickly, and when he addressed Amy the apologetic smile had returned. "Irene's right, Miss Haines. I don't think there's anything more I can tell you until you have a chance to talk to the Sheriff."

"Chance?" Gibbs' eyebrows rose. "You mean we've got to win the lottery or something?"

"Take it easy, Hank," Reno said. "He's just started questioning this guy now."

"Does he know we're here?"

Dick Reno shook his head. "I don't think so."

"Then it'll be a surprise." Gibbs moved past the deputy in the direction of the Sheriff's private office. As he did so, the voices of Reno and Irene Grovesmith rose and blended.

"Hey, wait a minute—"

"You can't do that!"

He glanced back for a moment, grinning. "Don't worry, I'm knocking." Actions followed words.

But not for long. The door opened partially; just enough for Sheriff Engstrom's head to emerge from the aperture.

"What's the big idea?" The question was obviously

rhetorical, and Engstrom made no pretense of waiting for a reply. Instead his stare focused on Reno. "Get these people out of here!"

"Come on, Sheriff." Hank Gibbs contrived a smile. "It's just a matter of common courtesy. Young lady here's been waiting to meet you—"

"Is that so?" Engstrom's stare shifted in Amy's direction. "Then why didn't she take the trouble to come over and introduce herself to me in the coffee shop last night?"

"I'm sorry," Amy said. "Actually, I wasn't quite sure who you were at that time."

"Looked to me as though you were listening up pretty good," Engstrom told her.

"Or else you were speaking pretty loudly," Amy said. Something happened to Engstrom's stare as she spoke; his eyes flickered momentarily and the corners of his mouth twitched.

"Now look here, young lady—"

"I am looking," Amy said, "but you've got the rest of it wrong. I'm going to be twenty-seven years old in another couple of months, which isn't all that young. And when I'm working, which I happen to be right now, I'm not that much of a lady. Come to think of it, I'm not a lady at all, not in your sense of the word. Because from what I've been able to observe around here so far it's just a word to you. As far as you're concerned, the idea is still to keep the young ones barefoot and pregnant and stick the old ones behind a stove—" Amy paused for an instant, glancing at Irene Grovesmith. "Or a desk," she concluded.

"Well I never!" The secretary sniffed in emphatic punctuation.

Somehow Amy resisted the obvious reply.

It was Engstrom who spoke for her. "That's enough, Irene," he said, then eased himself forward without opening the door any farther, glancing at Amy as he did so. "Be glad to set up something with you later. Right now I can give you five minutes."

"Thank you, Sheriff." Amy accompanied her nod with a smile. For a moment she debated whether or not to reach for the notebook inside the bag, then decided against it. Enough that she'd won; no sense pressing her luck. "Might I ask the name of the person you've taken into custody?"

"Sorry, I don't have that information." Sheriff Engstrom's pause was almost imperceptible. "Not yet."

"May I ask your reasons for questioning him?"

"My deputy didn't tell you?" Again the slightest of pauses; Amy imagined she could almost hear the wheels clicking inside his head. What she did hear next was, "Reno's been staked out over at the Bates property. This afternoon he picked up this prowler trying to break into the house."

"Then there is a charge," Amy said. "Breaking and entering."

"Well, not exactly." Amy revised her mental image. There were no wheels inside Engstrom's head; only a scale used for weighing his words. "When Reno picked him up he was trying the doorknob."

"Which makes him a suspect?"

"Let's just say it's a matter of suspicious circumstances. Here's this man showing up out of nowhere, no car, no ID. Doesn't even have a driver's license."

"Is that a crime, Sheriff?"

"No, but whoever killed Terry Dowson wasn't driving either. There was no sign of a car having been parked anywhere near the scene of the crime. But I guess you heard me mention that last night."

Whichever it might be, wheels whirring or scales weighing, didn't matter to Amy at this precise moment. What mattered was that she was watching Hank Gibbs. As she and Engstrom were talking he had begun to edge his way toward the door that stood ajar behind the Sheriff's back.

He had moved so slowly and cautiously that neither Dick Reno nor Irene Grovesmith seemed to notice; their attention was focused on the thrust and parry of the conversation. Thus they weren't aware that Hank Gibbs had hooked the heel of his right foot around the base of the door's far edge, pressing it toward him to gradually expand the opening.

Now the gap in the doorway was six inches wider. Staring past the Sheriff's head, she caught a clear glimpse of the inner office, and of the man seated there before the desk.

"Sounds like you're implying that these circumstances are all somehow connected to the person you just brought in." Amy shifted her gaze to Engstrom quickly as she spoke. "Are you saying you think he could have killed that girl?"

The Sheriff's eyes narrowed. "I'm not saying anything. But I'm going to find out."

"Let me save you the trouble," Amy told him. "He's not guilty."

The narrow eyes widened. "How do you know?"

Amy met his stare. "Because on the night of the murder he was in Chicago, in my home."

"Your home?"

"That's right. I had friends over for the evening who can testify they saw him when he showed up unexpectedly at the apartment. I told him I couldn't talk to him then, but made an appointment for an interview on Monday morning. Unfortunately, by Monday I'd read about what happened here and I was already on my way down. I'm afraid I forgot to notify him and cancel off."

"Interview?" Engstrom scowled. "What kind of an interview?"

"For the book I'm doing. He'd read a squib about it in the paper."

"Who is he?"

"His name is Eric Dunstable," Amy said. "He's a demonologist."

·6·

OTTO Remsbach was a good driver. He kept both pudgy hands on the wheel, both piggy eyes on the road.

Not very charitable, Amy told herself. But from what she had seen of Mr. Remsbach thus far there was little about him to inspire charity. For a moment she regretted having accepted his dinner invitation on the phone, but his call after she returned to the hotel had caught her by surprise. After all, she did have to eat dinner somewhere, and Remsbach was on her list, one of her lists anyway; although from what she had already observed he might also earn himself a place on another.

Having conceded her lack of charity Amy tried her best to be objective about obesity. But even if she could dismiss the common cultural prejudice and replace her image of Otto Remsbach with that of a man a hundred pounds lighter, it still wouldn't help. No matter how thin Remsbach became, everything about him would still be oversized. His vintage Caddy was too big, the diamond in his ring was not only too big but a bit too yellow. He had an outsized voice, and he used it constantly from the time he picked Amy up at the hotel until their arrival at the Montrose Country Club.

If the purpose of their meeting was an interview, he got the session off to a bad start. It was his big, booming voice that asked all the questions and Amy found herself floundering for answers in their wake.

"Is it Miss or Mrs.? What's with this 'Ms.' business

anyway? How come a classy lady like you didn't pick herself a husband and settle down? What do you do for a living? Yes, I know you're a writer, but what do you do for a living? That book you wrote—what was the name again? Does it have anything to do with Halloween? How come I never saw you on any of those talk shows? If you don't mind my asking, how much money do they pay for writing one of those things?"

Oh, Otto Remsbach was a pistol, and no mistake. That was the important part, Amy kept reminding herself. *No mistake.* She did her best to avoid making one while avoiding answering him too explicitly. Maybe he'd talk himself out by the time they arrived. And then it would be her turn. At least it was a carrot of hope at the end of the stick formed by the questions with which he kept prodding her.

Just outside Montrose they turned off onto the winding road that led up the hillside to their destination. Once the drive spiraled to the plateau above they drove through wide gates past lines of light that blazed and beckoned, then parked.

At first glance the Montrose Country Club looked very much like thousands of others—a recreational center for wealthy businessmen who have not yet been indicted.

Once inside Amy was pleasantly surprised to discover a large lounge area, complete with fireplace and bookshelves. At one time this must have been the living room of a large and imposing private residence. Carpeting, drapes, and paneling were recognizable holdovers, but the bar and the dining room beyond had obviously been added when the home was converted for its present use.

The bar was standard; booths lining the window wall, mirrored wall elongating behind the serving counter. The side walls were hand-muraled with desert scenes featuring sagebrush, cactus, burning sand, blazing sunlight, all artfully assembled to stimulate the viewer's thirst. The bartender wore a red vest, the barstools had red plastic coverings, the patrons had red, flushed faces. Time did not stand still here, but at least it was a bit wobbly; the cocktail hour stretched from five to eight. Actually there were only a half-dozen customers at the bar but what they lacked in numbers they made up for in volume; these greying, elderly men in their carefully tailored casual jackets and tattersall vests were used to talking just as loud as they goddamned pleased, both in the office and in public places. How they may have been forced to modulate their tone at home might be another matter. The point was they weren't at home, they were *here*, just having a drink or six to relax before dinner. Good ol' boys almost always cut their real deals over drinks and dinner; Mother ought to be used to it by now. At least she knows that's where the money comes from, and it wasn't like she had to just sit on her hands at home with nothing to do; she could always watch cable.

The dining room held a large number of customers but few surprises. There were no booths here, only square or round tables, each bearing a lighted, glass-sheathed candle and a bud vase containing a single rose. Since the room was a comparatively recent addition it didn't boast a chandelier, but the indirect lighting was pleasantly nonfluorescent. Amy noted a preponderance of middle-aged and elderly patrons but almost half were wives and mothers. The conversational level was lower, and about one out of three of the male diners wore neither vest nor necktie, but none were in shirtsleeves. Out here at the source of what advertising copywriters would describe as down-home country goodness, country club dining was still a form of ritual, separating the men from the good ol' boys.

Apparently some things had never really changed. The maître d' who greeted and seated them was white, but the waiters and busboys were black; still the same old setup, boss man and hired hands. The waiter, whose name was Quentin, was very good; he took Amy's order for a vodka martini and twinned it with a double Daniel's on the rocks without Remsbach having to request it.

Obviously her dinner partner's preferences were well known here. Amy consulted the menu before deciding on her brook trout almondine, baked potato and dinner salad, coffee later. But Otto Remsbach didn't bother to order; at proper intervals they served him his shrimp cocktail and a second drink, then his porterhouse medium rare and a Daniel's redoubled.

All of which Amy noted out of the corner of her mind. Most of her attention was concentrated upon Remsbach's continuous conversation which, like the liquor, flowed freely. It was interrupted only twice early on; the first time being when a couple identified only as Mr. and Mrs. Aversham nodded a greeting as they passed en route to a table. "Mayor of Montrose and his better half," Remsbach told her, nodding in the direction of their departing figures. "No point introducing you— they wouldn't have anything you want. Besides, he hates my guts and she's gonna spend all night trying to figure out what I'm doing here with a foxy lady like you." This observation came after the shrimp cocktail and the second drink but Amy noted that his accompanying laughter was already a trifle above the ordinary decibel level here. Good ol' boys will be boisterous.

The other interruption followed almost immediately and she welcomed it. This one did involve an introduction to the thin, sharp-featured, middle-aged man whose most attractive attribute seemed to be a comely wife twenty years his junior. Number two, Amy guessed, then amended her estimate after a downward glance. Custom-made alligator shoes worn in these surroundings were indications of taste that might easily run to a higher number of nuptials.

"Hey there, Charlie!" Remsbach cocked his head up at the couple, ignoring the woman completely, even though it was she who nodded in response to the greeting. Probably not his wife after all, Amy decided, but outside of the AA meeting in the bar this seemed to be a fairly stuffy place; it would take a considerable amount of nerve to bring a bimbo into a roomful of self-described decent, respectable wives and mothers. Come to think of it, Remsbach had his quota of nerve too, bringing a bimbo like herself into the same surroundings. So much for snap judgments; nevertheless she was eager to be introduced to this particular stranger. Now Remsbach gratified her wish.

"Senator, I'd like you to meet a friend of mine. Miss Haines, this here's Charlie Pitkin. Better watch what you say about me when you're around him, on account he happens to be my attorney."

"You're the writer, I believe?" As Amy nodded the thin man offered her a thin smile. "In that case, I think I already know what brought you here. Otto can probably answer most of your questions, but if there's anything else you think I might be able to tell you, I'll be around for most of the week. You can reach me through my office."

"That's very kind of you," Amy said.

Charlie Pitkin shook his head. "Actually it's just a sneaky way of trying to get my name into your book." He gestured to Remsbach. "Give me a call on that other matter."

"First thing tomorrow."

Amy's gaze joined Remsbach's as they watched Pitkin and his unidentified companion move to the waiter who had been standing patiently a dozen feet away during their halt at the table. Now he turned and they followed, moving past a pillar to disappear at a table directly behind it.

"Is he really a senator?" Amy asked.

"Sure is. Been in the State Legislature three terms now." Remsbach's laughter had a rasp to it. "Never hurts to have yourself a lawyer who knows his way around politics. Got to hand it to him—he's one smart little jew-boy. Sure been a big help to me."

At the moment Amy would have liked nothing better than to say farewell to Fairvale. And she would, she promised herself, once her mission was accomplished. Getting information for the book was the problem that had brought her here; the sensible thing was to accept people like Remsbach as part of the problem. Amy recalled some of the people she'd interviewed for the first book, the hookers, dope dealers, gangbangers. By comparison Otto Remsbach, on a scale of one to ten, was scarcely more than a four. She could deal with him. As the thought came, sheer coincidence echoed it in Remsbach's words.

"—deal," he was saying. "He set it all up so's I could get hold of the Bates property out there. That's where politics comes in. Thing I figured was just putting up the house and part of the motel and running tourists through it at maybe two, three bucks a head. Pitkin's the one who came up with improvements."

And it was Quentin, their waiter, who came up now with a cart bearing the two plates, the tall wooden pepper mill and the big wooden bowl. "Toss your salad, Mr. Remsbach?"

"Yeah. Just as long as you don't try serving it to me." Again the rasping laugh.

Amy took the opportunity to break in quickly. "Would you mind telling me what gave you the idea of rebuilding in the first place?"

"Cartoons," Remsbach said. "Got to thinking one day. For thirty years now I've been seeing cartoons and hearing jokes about Norman Bates and his mother. Seems like people out here remember him just like they do that woman back East, Lizzie Borden or whatever her name was. So I said to myself, if I can get my hands on the property that the state's been holding onto all these years, maybe it'd be worth a try. Call it something like the Bates Murder Mansion, run a few ads around the area, see what happens."

Quentin served Amy in silence, pantomimed profferment of the pepper mill, accepted its rejection, and wheeled the cart away—all without interrupting Remsbach's monologue for a moment.

But Amy wasn't standing on courtesy. "You mentioned something about your attorney making suggestions."

Remsbach nodded. "He's the one who got the idea about selling souvenirs—room keys, ashtrays, stuff like that you could sell from the motel. He even talked about towels and shower curtains, but I told him wait and see how the other stuff goes first. But I went for his pitch about getting some postcards printed up and later on he wants to get out some kind of booklet with pictures of Norman and the old lady, maybe have somebody like Hank Gibbs write up a little piece for it."

"Getting back to the building project," Amy said. "Did you have much trouble finding furnishings for the house?"

"That part was easy." Ice cubes rattled as Remsbach put down his empty glass. "Pitkin reminded me that they were gonna do a movie seven, eight years back, some outfit named Coronet Pictures. It never got made, on account of what happened, and they sold off the studio in some kind of conglomerate deal. But Pitkin remembered they'd already started shooting the picture before the trouble started, so they must of had props and furniture. He contacted somebody out there and sure thing, the whole *kapoosta* was in storage, along with the sets or whatever you call 'em. He made a deal and they shipped the whole lot here direct. The dummies were the hard part."

"They didn't come from the studio, did they?" Amy said.

"No." Remsbach glanced up as Quentin reappeared with the cart that, this time around, bore their entrees.

Good customer scowled at faithful servitor. "Hey, you forgot my drink!"

"No sir." Quentin lifted the tumbler from its hiding place between the domes of the casseroles covering the two plates. His fingers curled around the glass, mahogany against crystal, as he set it down before Remsbach.

A quick gulp later, conversation was resumed where it had left off. "Charlie Pitkin gets credit for the dummies too. Had them made out there in L.A., someplace that does them for movies." He leaned to one side as Quentin set the porterhouse platter down before him, then reached for his glass again. "Damn things cost a fortune, but like Charlie says, it makes all the difference in the world." Gulp. "All the difference in the world."

Down went the glass; up came the steak knife. As Amy might have suspected, Otto Remsbach's eating habits were governed more by enthusiasm than elegance. She averted her gaze while filleting the trout as best she could; evidently Montrose Country Club's silver service did not include fish knives. But the trout was excellent.

When she glanced up her dinner companion gestured to Quentin as he passed by their table on his way to the kitchen. Apparently Remsbach had already finished off almost half of his steak and needed another Daniel's for additional gravy.

"I got to hand it to them, whoever made those things sure did a job." Remsbach nodded, then chewed and swallowed for punctuation. "Get 'em in the right light and you'd swear they were real people. Mother—old lady Bates, I mean—is some scary-looking sight."

"So I've heard," Amy said. "It's one of the things I wanted to see."

Remsbach scowled. "What I want to know is, who the hell stole her?"

"That's part of the mystery, isn't it?" Amy said. "I was hoping you might have some ideas."

Otto Remsbach chewed over the thought along with

his steak. "I got ideas, all right. Might of been Reverend Archer. I don't think he'd be up to it himself but he could get somebody to do the job for him. He's got his whole goddamn congregation turned against me. Damn fools can't see what this proposition is gonna do to bring business into town."

He paused long enough to launch another frontal attack on his drink, and when he thumped the glass down again his scowl faded. "Le'me tell you something, they're all gonna hafta change their tune once we get started. Charlie says just as soon as he can finagle the permits we'll put in a parking lot and a couple refreshment stands. He's got a crazy idea about serving some special kind of hamburgers covered with ketchup— wants to call them Murderburgers. With a side order of shower-kraut." Remsbach drowned his rasping laugh in drink. "Sounds pretty weird if you ask me, but it just might work."

Amy nodded. One thing was certain; Remsbach's drinks were working.

And his timing was perfect as he caught Quenin's eye when the waiter turned from a nearby table. Then he turned to Amy. "'Scuse me. You like another drink?"

"Only my coffee," Amy said, raising her voice just enough so Quentin heard before he moved on.

Remsbach pushed his plate away. "Pitkin's got some other notions too, but they'll stay on the back burner until later. Y'know we hadda postpone the opening twice already, first on account of some stuff coming in late, and then when that business happened out there last week. Terrible thing." He hunched forward, head and voice lowered. "You been talking to people in town today. Any of them come up with ideas about what happened?"

Amy shook her head.

"What about Hank Gibbs? He generally puts in his two cents' worth about everything that goes on."

"I didn't get any confidential information, if that's what you mean," Amy said.

Otto Remsbach's voice became a rumbling whisper. "Wouldn't have too much to do with him if I were you. He's a real weirdo. I couldn't get him to put that damn paper of his behind this Murder Mansion proposition either." The scowl returned. "For all I know, maybe he stole the dummy."

"Not likely."

"Well, somebody did, that's for damn sure. And nobody's doing anything about finding it. I been after Engstrom and Banning too—he's in charge of the State Highway Patrol around here—but I can't get any action."

He did, however, get his drink and Quentin served Amy her coffee as Remsbach continued. "You're a reporter, right? You must of come up with some ideas about what happened out there last week."

Amy shook her head. "I haven't even seen the place."

"That's easy." Otto Remsbach raised the tumbler to his lips, then lowered it to the table. As his pudgy fingers relinquished their grasp they marched forward to encamp on Amy's wrist. "What say you and me take a run out there right now and look around?"

Amy knew the answer to that question and she hoped it wouldn't be necessary to utter it. Instead she tried to free her wrist from its five captors.

But the fat fingers tightened their grasp and the voice slurred on. "Y'know, one room in that motel is all rigged up—shower, bed, the works—"

Suddenly the slurring ceased and the fingers fled as Remsbach looked up. Amy followed his gaze.

Sheriff Engstrom was standing beside their table.

Remsbach's mouth gaped, then managed a lopsided smile. "Well, whaddya know? We were jus' talking about you—"

The Sheriff ignored him. When he spoke his words were directed at Amy.

"Come with me, Miss Haines," he said. "You're under arrest."

· 7 ·

THERE was one thing Amy had to concede; Engstrom got her out of the dining room quickly and quietly, without attracting undue attention or provoking any objection from Otto Remsbach.

So far the Sheriff had lucked out, Amy told herself, but once they got to the parking area he was going to be due for a big surprise.

Instead it was her turn to be surprised when they emerged and he led her to the shiny late-model Olds that half blocked the circular driveway directly before them. Engstrom opened the passenger door.

"Hop in," he said. "You're not under arrest."

"Then why—?"

Engstrom slammed the door as she slid across the seat, speaking through the open window. "That was just for Otto's benefit. Anytime you mention a word like 'arrest' it tends to shut people up in a hurry. I just figured you didn't want to drive back to town with a drunk."

"But how did you know about him?"

Engstrom circled the front of the car and climbed in behind the wheel before responding. "Friday night at the Club," he said. "Happens around the same time every week. I generally make it a point to look in just about now, just to see that they take good care of him." Closing the door, he started the motor.

"What will they do?"

The Olds looped around the driveway and down the long flambeaux-guarded entryway, then turned left on the road beyond. "Nothing much. Take him upstairs to one of the guest rooms and let him sleep it off for a couple of hours. Don't worry, he'll be on his way to town before midnight, safe and sound." Engstrom gave Amy a sidelong glance without seeming to divert his attention from the road ahead. "Hope he didn't give you a bad time."

Amy smiled. "Let's just say I was glad to see you."

"Old Otto's not really as bad as he sounds," Engstrom said. "More bark than bite."

Another sneak peek out of the corner of his right eye. "Did he happen to introduce you to anybody else out there?"

"Somebody named Charlie Pitkin. I couldn't quite get it straight whether he was a business partner or just his attorney."

Engstrom nodded. "It's hard to get anything straight when it comes to Pitkin. He's an operator."

"He had a lady with him," Amy said. "We weren't introduced."

"Pretty girl?"

"Very. Tall, blonde, green eyes—"

"That was Charlie's daughter. He's been a widower about three years now."

Once again Amy felt the snap go out of her judgment. But Engstrom seemed in a talkative mood and she might just as well take advantage of it. "Are you married?" she asked.

"Right."

"Any children?"

"No." There was a slight smile lurking beneath Engstrom's mustache. "Don't get home all that often."

The smile disappeared. "Figure it out for yourself," he said. "Department's got two cars. That calls for three deputies working on eight-hour shifts. There's another three doing warder duty at the jail, and Irene handling the office, thank God. She may have a leaky mouth but she runs the whole shooting match."

"There doesn't seem to be too much crime around here," Amy said.

"Any crime is too much, as far as I'm concerned. The way I see it, with a small setup like ours, prevention is easier than detection so I spend most of my time just moseying around, sort of a troubleshooter. Like tonight, when I heard you were up at the Club with Fatso." His dry cough was followed by quick correction. "Mr. Remsbach, I mean."

"Don't worry, I know the nickname." Amy smiled. "And I really do thank you for your concern."

Sheriff Engstrom's grunt was noncommittal. "That's my job. Besides, it wasn't just concern."

"Curiosity?"

"That's my job too."

"And mine," Amy said. "But I'm afraid we've both been disappointed. I didn't find out anything from him tonight except what I already knew."

Engstrom rolled down the window beside him. "Too much draft on you?"

Amy shook her head. "Fine with me. It cooled off a little tonight, I noticed."

"Now that we're finished with the weather," Engstrom said. "Exactly what is a demonologist?"

"Would you mind running that past me once again?"

"What's a demonologist?"

He'd caught her by surprise—intentionally, of course—but now she was ready with her answer. "Someone who specializes in demonology, a branch of learning dealing with beliefs and superstitions about demons and evil spirits."

Engstrom grunted again. "That much I know. We have a dictionary kicking around the office. I looked it up."

"So did I."

"Definition I read says it's also a systematic religious doctrine. Do you believe in such stuff?"

"No—do you?"

Engstrom shrugged. "I'm just a cop," he said. "I was hoping maybe you could fill me in a little more. Didn't Dunstable tell you anything about it?"

"No." Amy glanced at him quickly. "You were the one who questioned him. What happened after I left this afternoon?"

"First thing I did was check, long distance, for those names you gave me; people who saw Dunstable when he came to your apartment. They confirmed what you told me."

"Then what?"

"I turned him loose."

"You wouldn't happen to know where he went?" Amy said.

"Pretty damn nosy, aren't you?" This time the dry cough sounded more like a dry chuckle. "Well, so am I. Jimmy Onager, one of my deputies, was coming off his shift when Dunstable left. I gave him a little overtime out of uniform. He tailed Dunstable straight to the bus station. Turns out his luggage, wallet, and ID were all stashed in a locker there."

Amy frowned. "You searched him when you picked him up. Where did he hide the key?"

"Onager says it was lying right back of the edge above the top locker."

"In plain sight?"

"Only to basketball players." Engstrom's mustache masked another smile. "Must have figured he might be collared so he stowed everything away. Then he hitched a ride out to the Bates place. He wouldn't tell us anything except that it was with some truck driver who was just passing through. Says he doesn't want to make trouble for him."

Amy nodded. "He's not a troublemaker."

If there was such a thing as a dry sigh, Engstrom uttered it now. "Maybe not intentionally. And neither are you. But if you stay here and make waves there's bound to be trouble. My advice is that you get out of town before anything happens."

"I'm here because I'm writing a book. I still have work to do."

"So do I." Engstrom frowned. "Thing that bugs me is, why would a demonologist come here? What kind of work does *he* have a mind to do?"

"Where is he now?"

"Your boyfriend? Last I heard he checked into the Fairvale Hotel for the night."

Amy shook her head. "Haven't I made it clear to you? He's *not* my boyfriend!"

"Too bad." Engstrom's voice and stare were level. "He's got room 204, next to yours."

·8·

WHEN Amy heard the tapping on her door she wasn't frightened.

At least she could thank Engstrom for that. But it was still disturbing to know what waited on the other side of the door at this time of night. Or was she disturbed because she didn't know? Outside of that one brief exchange a week ago and a thousand miles away, the presence in the adjoining room remained a complete stranger. Now the muffled tones of his unfamiliar voice sounded above the persistent rapping.

"Miss Haines—"

"Yes?"

"This is Eric Dunstable."

"I know."

"Please, let me in. I've got to talk to you."

Amy hesitated. Letting him in meant letting him into her life. And what would she be letting herself in for? There was enough to contend with here already; the last thing she needed right now was to be involved with the plans and purposes of a rival seeker of information.

But how could she be sure he was a rival, and just what were those plans and purposes? There was only one way to find out, and she'd better take advantage of the opportunity to ask some key questions.

She called to him.

"Just a moment. I've got to get the key."

The key dropped out of her purse and, moments later, Eric Dunstable dropped in.

As Amy opened the door and caught sight of her visitor she wondered again if she had made the right decision. She wondered too about Sheriff Engstrom's insinuation. How could he possibly imagine that she could be conducting a liaison with this man?

Eric Dunstable was thin, bearded, bespectacled, and bowlegged; at first glance he looked like a tall Toulouse-Lautrec.

Not that she held any conscious bias against painters, handicapped or otherwise. But there was more to this package than just the wrappings. Behind the thick-lensed glasses the left eye twitched spasmodically with a life of its own. The rhythmic tic was disturbing, a soundless punctuation to the words that issued in a hoarse half whisper, accompanied by gesticulations of bony hands and almost pencil-thin fingers.

All right, Amy told herself, *so he isn't exactly a Rambo.* Just who and what he was were questions for which she needed immediate answers. Instead, she asked, "How did you know I was coming here?"

"I knew." His eyes twitched at her across the threshold. "Aren't you going to ask me in?"

"Of course, Mr. Dunstable." Amy covered embarrassment with a nervous giggle, then checked herself as he entered. This was not the time or place for schoolgirlish giggling, but the nervousness was real. Not because she had a man in her hotel room—if indeed this wimpish weirdo was a man—but because of that simple phrase he had half whispered in response to her question. She gestured to him to take a seat in the armchair at the far corner near the window, and as he did so she spoke.

"You said you knew I'd be coming here. What made you so certain?"

Dunstable shrugged. "There's nothing mysterious about it, Miss Haines. I read the same papers and listen to the same newscasts as you do. And when I learned about what had happened here last week it became obvious why you left town so suddenly and what your destination would be."

"Then I hope you'll forgive my breaking our appointment," Amy said. "I really should have let you know, but I left in such a hurry—"

"I quite understand." Dunstable nodded and twitched at her. "What's really important is that you arrived when you did. If you hadn't seen the Sheriff this afternoon I'm afraid I might still be behind bars."

Amy pulled the chair out from behind the little writing desk and seated herself. "You came here by bus?"

Dunstable nodded. "I don't drive," he said. "And I have a strong aversion to plane travel. 'The demons of the air,' I suppose."

It was Amy's turn to nod, but she wasn't quite sure what she was nodding at. "Demons of the air"—was that meant to be some sort of a joke or was it a serious allusion? She vaguely remembered the phrase as a quotation but couldn't recall its source. What she did remember was another question relative to the same subject, and this was her chance to ask it now.

"Just what is a demonologist?"

Eric Dunstable actually smiled. "A demonologist is not necessarily an old man with a long white beard, dressed in flowing robes and wearing something that looks like a dunce cap. He's not a sorcerer or black magician, carries no magic wand, and has no magic powers. For that matter, a demonologist isn't even necessarily a *he*. There are women who study the subject too—and I suppose that's as good a definition as any. A demonologist is a student."

"Please, Mr. Dunstable, don't hide behind the dictionary definition." Amy leaned forward. "I'm interested in how you got into all this, and just exactly what it is that you do."

"I can tell you how I got into all this, as you put it. I'm a failed seminarian. Not because of my grades, but because of my faith—or lack of it."

"I don't understand."

"Neither did I. That was the insolvable problem. To me, the theological concept of good and evil seems valid and self-evident. But while modern religion pays lip service to the abstraction it rejects the reality behind it."

"In other words, you are saying you believe demons are real?"

"It's not a question of belief. I *know*."

"Have you ever seen one?"

"No." Again the whisper, again the tic. "A demon is a discarnate entity—it's incorporeal. The shapes it may assume when conjured up are, of course, hallucinatory. Perhaps a psychologist versed in ethnology and anthropology could explain why a Tibetan demon would appear radically different than a Nigerian or a Romanian one."

It crossed Amy's mind that she should be taking notes, but the thought vanished almost as quickly as it came. Better to channel it through a more direct route—in one ear and out the other. Nevertheless she wanted to hear more. "You say that demons are disembodied and appear only as hallucinations. How can you prove they exist if you can't see them?"

"One sees them indirectly through the people whom they possess."

Much to her surprise, Amy didn't find it all that easy to smile in response. Sitting late at night in a strange room in a strange town with a strange man who might have come straight out of a horror comic wasn't really all that disturbing. It was obviously Dunstable who was, in a polite euphemism, disturbed, and that didn't alarm her. What did was her own reaction to what they were talking about. It was all superstition, of course; this much she knew and accepted on the intellectual level.

But below that level, far below, below common sense and even consciousness, something stirred.

"Just how do people become 'possessed'?" she said.

Dunstable shrugged. "Think of evil as a communicable disease. A virus attacks the body when one's defenses are down. Evil seeks out entry points in the mind and spirit."

Amy frowned. "Are you talking about hypnosis?"

"This has nothing to do with suggestion. Possession takes advantage of situations involving loss of conscious control—during anesthesia, nightmares, at the extremes of manic-depressive states, or in some situations involving drug abuse, including alcohol." His tic winked at her in the lamplight. "Of course the easiest point of entry is during heightened emotional states—extreme rage, hysteria, sexual or religious frenzy."

Amy found herself smiling. "I know some people who might take offense at your last two examples."

"I know a lot of people who might just tell me I'm flat-out crazy," he said. "But in my profession I've learned to accept this as an occupational hazard."

Amy shook her head. "You told me demonologists are students. Now you say what you're doing is a profession. Are you talking about things like ghost-hunting or witch-finding?"

Eric Dunstable's nictitation served as confirmation. "Hunting and finding, yes. But it's after that the real work begins."

"Which is—?"

"Exorcism." The hoarse voice placed odd and added emphasis on the second syllable.

So that's it, Amy told herself. She glanced up quickly. "But I thought exorcism can only be performed by ordained members of the clergy."

"Exactly the sentiments of the faculty at the seminary." The bearded man sighed. "They expelled me when they learned I'd been experimenting on my own." He shrugged. "I've been on my own ever since. Fortunately, my parents left me a modest inheritance some years ago, so I'm more or less free to live as I choose. And while I was denied elevation to holy orders, I don't need to take orders from anyone, holy or otherwise."

Amy waited for the tic, then broke in. "Is that what you intended to do when they caught you trying to enter the Bates place?"

"That house has an aura of evil—I could feel it." Behind the thick lenses his eyes caught hers in a solemn stare. "Death lurks there."

Again Amy felt something stirring deep below the level of consciousness, something that reacted irrationally to all this nonsense about death and demons. Death, of course, was, is, and will be a reality, but demons—

"This isn't why you wanted to see me in Chicago," she said. "Neither of us knew about the house then. I'm here because I want to write a book about Norman Bates."

"And I came to exorcise the demon that possessed him."

Why didn't I quit when I was ahead? Amy asked herself. But it was too late now. "It's generally believed Norman assumed the personality of his mother. That

doesn't exactly fit your definition of demonic possession. And it wouldn't matter if it did. You can't exorcise
a dead man, and Norman Bates is dead."

"The demon still exists." In this context, Dunstable's wink was almost confidential. "When Norman died
it took possession of Adam Claiborne. It left him last
week to seek out another instrument for its purpose."

"What purpose?"

"The ultimate purpose of evil is to destroy, to kill.
Often its essence as an entity is nourished by returning to
its former haunts. That's why it came to the Bates house
the other night and took over whoever it was that killed the
little girl. Then it returned to Claiborne, when he attacked
Dr. Steiner. After Claiborne collapsed I think it went on to
a stronger, healthier body. If it left Claiborne then, someone else in this town must be possessed."

"How can you tell?"

A pause, a blink, a shrug. "I can't. But I understand
they're holding a memorial service for that little girl tomorrow. Everyone will be there." The hoarse voice
sounded its own echo. "That's when I'll know."

·9·

AMY was free to sleep in, and because her
sleep proved to be mercifully free of nightmares, it was
midmorning when she awoke.

Strangely enough, the lengthy rest didn't seem to
have refreshed her. Perhaps it was the fault of the

weather; as she opened the window it became obvious that the day would be hot, muggy, overcast. It was too warm and too gloomy, and so was she.

The source of the warmth was obvious, but the reasons for gloom eluded her. Even under cloudy skies, in the morning light her impressions of Eric Dunstable clearly revealed him for what he was. She only wished he hadn't shown up here to complicate her own situation. But neither his unwelcome presence nor his equally unwelcome prescience could account for her feeling of depression.

Most likely what bothered her was the idea of attending today's memorial service for Terry Dowson. Yes, that was it.

Amy always tried to avoid funerals, and had no strong desire to attend her own. Even though on this present occasion the corpse and casket would be absent, she had an uneasy feeling about the whole affair.

Maybe breakfast would help. But when she slid the watch onto her wrist after showering Amy realized that the best description of the meal would be brunch. There was no question of wearing her best for an appearance in the downstairs coffee shop. Memorial services didn't begin until three o'clock, so she'd have plenty of time to change into more formal attire before driving out.

The coffee shop was deserted; Amy had slipped through the crack between breakfast and lunch. For a moment she wondered if it would have been a polite gesture to invite Eric Dunstable to join her. But if she had, he'd probably bring his theories about possession with him, and she wanted no part of demons in her present mood or present meal. Checking the sandwiches on the menu, Amy quickly decided against the deviled ham.

What she did order was satisfactory, and after her second cup of coffee she was able to consider Dunstable with less distaste. Could anything that he had told her last night be of possible use to her when she sat down to write the book?

For a moment the notion seemed tempting; including such fantasizing would add a touch of spice to the dull fare of data she'd accumulated. But such sensationalism would defeat her purpose. The book must deal with murder and its impact on a small town, and do so realistically. So thank you and good-bye, Mr. Dunstable.

Thank you and good-bye to the waitress-cashier, then back upstairs. Once again in her room, Amy checked the wedge of sky beyond the window and noted little improvement. Adjusting the thermostat made the air-conditioning unit hum in a lower key but didn't seem to lower the temperature. It was going to be sticky at the memorial services, in more ways than one.

Amy pulled out her notebook and sat down at the tiny desk in the chair which Eric Dunstable had occupied last night. Which was appropriate enough, inasmuch as she was jotting down what she remembered of his conversation.

But why? Amy paused for a moment, frowning. Hadn't she just told herself that this material would be wrong for her purposes? What prompted her to waste time making notes about invisible entities commuting back and forth between various bodies in order to do the Devil's work?

Or had Dunstable mentioned the Devil? She couldn't recall, but what she did remember kept her occupied throughout the noon hour. Amy still hadn't changed her mind, but just in case she ever did, the notes were here.

Now it was time for a careful application of makeup and a careful decision about dress. Obviously the occasion called for wearing something dark and discreet, which left her with no choice at all. The only garment fitting that description was the heavy suit she'd hastily folded up in the overnight bag before making her hurried trip to O'Hare Airport the other day. What would have been cool and comfortable for Chicago was hot and irksome here; the suit was unsuitable, but so be it.

She put on the skirt before putting on makeup, then donned her blouse and jacket just before departure. The outfit looked better than it felt, but she knew she would welcome the air-conditioning in her car because it worked as well as hummed.

There were only three people in the lobby, none of whom Amy recognized as she crossed to the exit. The sky outside withheld sight of the sun but filtered its fire as she made her way into the parking area. Approaching the rental car she was surprised to find it a bit smaller than she had remembered. For some reason or other its height seemed to have shrunk overnight, or had it merely wilted in the midday heat?

No such thing. Some bastard had slashed the tires. Amy seethed, steamed, then boiled over.

There was no doubt about what happened; the deep gashes scoring the treads were outrageously obvious. And Amy was obviously outraged as she marched up to the counter of the reception desk to report what she'd discovered.

Young Chambers stared at her, but neither his eyes nor his features registered any hint of emotional reaction. He told her he was sorry, he couldn't imagine what had happened, they'd never had anything like this here before, and several other lies. At least Amy thought they were lies, but she really didn't give a damn. All she wanted now—and insisted on—was for the clerk to call the nearest service station and get somebody over here immediately.

Immediately turned out to be twenty minutes later. The pickup that pulled into the parking slot beside her car came from SMITTY'S SERVICE STATION and its driver was none other than Smitty himself. He wore the obligatory bill-cap, khaki trousers, and a khaki shirt rolled up to the elbows. As he stooped to inspect the damage, Amy admired the tattoos on his forearms. She was still staring as Hank Gibbs drove up behind the truck and climbed out of his car, leaving the engine running.

"Hi, Smitty," he said. And to Amy, "What's going on here?"

She told him quickly, and halfway through the telling he frowned. By the time she finished her account the furrows on his forehead seemed permanently fixed.

"I don't like it," he said. "You're going to give this town a bum rap when you leave here."

"Looks as if somebody here doesn't want me to leave," Amy said. "I've got to get out to the memorial service."

"That's where I'm headed for," Gibbs said. "Come on, I'll give you a lift."

"But what about my car?"

Gibbs walked over to the man from the service station. "Think you can help the lady, Smitty?"

The bill-cap bobbed in nodding response. "No problem. Whitewalls, I'm positive. Radials I can get from Kleemann."

Gibbs glanced at Amy and she shook her head. "Never mind the radials," he said. "Just see if you can get the job done this afternoon. The lady's staying here at the hotel. Any idea what this is going to cost?"

Smitty ran a tattooed nude across his sweaty hairline. "Got to see how this size runs when I get back to the shop. Then there's the labor—"

Hank Gibbs smiled. "Just remember, you owe me."

"Okay, okay, I'll hold it down."

"You want me to sign anything?" Amy asked.

Smitty shook his head. "I can't make out an order until I check the price list. No point you waiting until I get back here. I'll get your name and address from the register when I leave the bill at the desk."

"Thank you," Amy said.

She repeated the words to Gibbs as they drove away. He nodded but she noted his forehead was still furrowed.

"Anything wrong?" she said.

"You park your car in plain view on an open lot facing Main Street, then somebody comes along and slashes all four of your tires. Sounds wrong to me." The car curved onto a county trunk road at the far end of town. "What did Engstrom have to say?"

"I haven't reported it."

"Why not? Don't you have any ideas about what could have happened?"

"Ideas, yes. I think somebody may have asked the desk clerk at the hotel about what I was driving."

"You're talking about young Chambers."

Amy nodded. "I have a strong impression he doesn't like me, but that doesn't prove anything. And if I make a fuss it's only going to stir up more hard feelings."

Gibbs shrugged. "Maybe you're right. I'm just sorry you had to run into all this trouble."

"It's not your fault. Nobody asked me to come." Amy's jawline tightened as she spoke. "But now that I'm here nobody's going to scare me away."

Which was the truth, Amy told herself. This was no time to back off. If anything, what had happened to the car strengthened her determination. Added to it now was a new element—suspicion. Given the circumstances she could understand why someone might tell her to get out of town, but slashing those tires was more than a suggestion; it was a threat. A threat from someone out there who was capable of slashing more than tires—

Amy found herself forcing a smile to hide the thought behind it. But hidden or not, the thought remained. And once again the feeling of depression surfaced as Gibbs headed the car into the parking area on the far side of the church at the crossroads. The sight of its white spire looming against the lowering sky evoked memories of Amy's high school art classes years ago. The church was pure Grant Wood; the clouds were something out of Hieronymus Bosch.

Abandoning the cool comfort of the car, they

emerged into the swelter and stifle surrounding the lone structure that soared against the background of open fields and sullen sky.

The time was ten minutes to three, and they were by no means the first to arrive; perhaps thirty other vehicles had already parked and several more turned in as they climbed the church steps to the open entrance.

The former occupants of the cars outside clustered in the area that joined the main body of the church with the smaller sections on either side. Amy had no idea what might lay behind the closed door of the right-hand wing, but the left opened on the chapel. At the moment only a few people were seated there; the majority lingered in the lobby. Most of the women were matronly, pleased to be out of housedresses and into their Sunday best; high heels elevated both body and spirit. Many of the males offered a sharp contrast as they stood sweating into suits worn only at weddings, baptisms, and funerals. Awkward and ill at ease here, they had the look of men who'd be handy around the house, and kept power tools in the garage, along with their fishing gear and hunting rifles.

Generally the sexes were separated into small groups conversing in the muted murmur inspired by their surroundings. Whose idea was it that one must whisper when in the presence of the Lord?

Amy ignored the irreverence as irrelevant, but she could not shake off the feeling of depression. If anything it was heightened here. Church or no church, the air of sanctity had not been cooled by air-conditioning, and body heat did nothing to alleviate the humidity. Even the mumbling seemed to add to the lobby's oppressive atmosphere. Too many people grouped in too small a space; the result was cluster-phobia.

All of which made it uncomfortable for Amy when Gibbs started to introduce her around. At the same time she realized it might be her only opportunity to identify some of the people whose names were bound to crop up in the book. During the next five minutes she met and exchanged polite greetings with the glum local fire chief, the grim-visaged principal of Fairvale Elementary School, and the beaming president of The First National Bank. His sunny smile was probably prompted by the fact that Fairvale didn't have a Second National Bank.

But happiness, like fresh air, seemed in short supply here. It certainly wasn't reflected in the faces she recognized—Dr. Rawson, Bob Peterson, Attorney Charlie Pitkin, or Irene Grovesmith. Gibbs pointed out Terry Dowson's parents but did not introduce her to them. She would have recognized them anyway, for both were dressed in mourning, their features gaunt with grief. What startled Amy was the bulge beneath the waist of the black dress—Terry's mother was pregnant. *In the midst of death is life.*

Gibbs also introduced her to Robert Albert, the mortician in charge of the proceedings. In the midst of death Albert seemed neither overjoyed nor grief-stricken; he greeted her politely enough, but his eyes kept searching for new arrivals, like a theatre manager counting the house.

Now organ music sounded from within the chapel and the clutter began to converge toward its entrance in response. Excusing himself, the mortician went over to Terry Dowson's parents and escorted them into the chapel. Gibbs started to move forward but Amy touched his arm. "Let's wait a minute," she murmured. "I'd prefer the last row, but if I sat there before the place starts to fill up it would be too conspicuous."

"Gotcha." Gibbs smiled. "In case you don't like the show you want to sneak out without anybody noticing."

Amy shook her head. "I'm interested in the audience, not the performance. Which reminds me—I don't see any children here. Where's Mick Sontag?"

"She went into shock after the murder," Gibbs said. "Doc Rawson told her father to take her on a vacation.

They're probably in Disneyland right now, and I wish I was there with them."

"I understand." Amy shrugged. "But duty calls."

"Better sit down, folks. We're gonna start, next couple minutes." It was not duty who called, but one of the mortician's ushers; he had the suave, courtly manner of · a high school basketball coach.

As they moved into the chapel Gibbs' murmur blended with the music. "Kids are in school today. There was some talk about making this a half holiday for Terry's classmates, but busing them over would be a hassle." Amy moved into the second seat of the last row; only then did she notice Irene Grovesmith was just two seats away at her left. Gibbs had already taken the aisle seat at her right, and it was too late to move farther upfront. Instead she glanced forward toward the lectern on the podium, seeking the source of sound. But there was no organ, no organist; somewhere in another room stereo piped its sacred strains into the chapel's secular speaker system.

Now she turned her attention to the audience seated ahead. There were only a few people Amy might possibly recognize face-to-face, let alone from behind, but she tried to search them out. It was a vain effort; Sheriff Engstrom wasn't here and she couldn't find Doris Huntley or the desk clerk and waitresses from the hotel. Some people had to work. What did surprise her was the absence of most of the people she'd seen last night, the country club set. And where was Otto Remsbach?

She leaned over and voiced the question to Gibbs. His response sounded against the hymnal background.

"He won't show here, because of the feud over the Bates place. He and Archer hate each other's guts."

"Not so."

The voice was scarcely more than a shrill whisper, yet clearly audible. Amy glanced up into the wizened fae of a tall, white-haired, bearded man with the eyes of an Old Testament prophet.

He had entered from the lobby and come up behind them unobserved; now, as he bent forward to address Gibbs, there was no need for further identification or introduction.

"I don't hate Otto Remsbach," said Reverend Archer. "My feeling is directed only toward his project, his plans to capitalize on the suffering and torment of others. Don't you realize if he hadn't built on the Bates property that little girl wouldn't have had any reason to go out there? She'd still be alive today!"

Even though the whisper was soft, its shrillness carried. Nearby, heads were beginning to turn, and Gibbs nodded hastily. "I know your position on this, Reverend," he murmured.

"Then why don't you take a stand on it? Remsbach has his Opening scheduled there for day after tomorrow. Once that happens there's no telling what it may lead to. It's high time you ran an editorial."

"I'll think about it."

"Do so. One way or another, this man must be stopped before we find ourselves with more blood on our hands." Now and only now, his gaze pierced Amy's. "We have enough to live down already, thanks to the media," he said. "The last thing we need is strangers coming into town to blacken its name and—"

The music halted abruptly, and so did Archer's voice. But he himself did not halt; straightening, he moved briskly down the aisle in the direction of the lectern on the podium.

Amy and Gibbs exchanged glances, and his slight shrug said it all. To the left, Irene Grovesmith had turned to listen as Archer spoke; now, even in this muggy heat, Amy was chilled by her icy stare.

There was hostility here, no doubt about it, but thus far nothing to indicate demonic possession. Unless, of course, Eric Dunstable could make good his claim and recognize it.

Dunstable. She scanned the heads and shoulders in

the rows ahead, quickly but in vain. Why wasn't he
here? Had something happened to him; had something
been *made* to happen to him? A foolish idea, of course.
Just because some of these people looked hostile that
didn't necessarily mean they were dangerous.

Reverend Archer's attack was merely verbal, and
this only because he had no other targets. She and Gibbs
were the only press people here today, because as far as
major media was concerned the story was dead. Like
Terry. There were no leads so no reason for them to follow up on a murder where no one would ever find the
killer. Unless Dunstable was right.

Reverend Archer mounted the podium, gripped the
far sides of the lectern and the attention of his audience.

"Let us pray," he said.

Heads bowed obediently as Archer's voice boomed.

*"O Lord, we are gathered here today to invoke thy
blessing upon the soul of Theresa Dowson—"*

As Archer's voice rose, so did Amy's gaze. Disobe-
diently she glanced toward the podium, trying to discover what there was about it which disturbed her. Then
she realized there were no floral offerings, no wreaths or
bouquet on the platform behind the speaker. It was only
after a moment of reflection that she could understand
the reason; after all, this was a memorial service, not a
funeral. Probably plenty of flowers still on Terry's grave
right now, wilting in the late afternoon heat.

*"—memory of that poor child struck down shall not
be forgotten, but we console ourselves with the knowledge that our lamb is safe in the bosom of God. It is we
who remain in mortal peril as long as the evildoer is
abroad."*

Did he stare at Amy when he spoke those last words
or was it just her imagination? She wasn't sure, but now
the bowed heads before her were gradually rising as the
pretext of prayer yielded to the demands of stiffening
neck muscles.

"But the sacrifice of the lamb was not in vain. It

teaches us that we must repent of our wickedness and forsake its ways."

Was he talking about her? But her ways weren't all that wicked. And it was up to Dunstable to find the real evildoer. If there really was a demon here, this was his chance for a demonstration. Better Dunstable with his tic than this fanatic with the relentless stare.

"Hear us, O Lord, as we resolve ourselves to walk in the paths of righteousness in loving memory of that sweet innocent lamb. In the words of the psalmist, 'lead us not into temptation'—"

Amy was only half listening, but now his words intruded on her thoughts. Could he be reading her mind? Was he referring to the temptation of using Dunstable's crazy theories in her book?

And it was a temptation, of course. She'd done well with the first one, even without any special attention from the good folks at Stacy Publishing Company. Reviews and sales had been better than anyone expected, good enough to gain her double the advance on this effort. A thoroughly researched account of the Bates case and its mystique would probably do even better.

But even better wasn't good enough. Admit it, what she wanted was a smash. Full-page ads, top talk shows, the nationwide tour with a limo waiting at every airport, the works. She was tired of telling people she was a writer and hearing them say, "Yes, I know, but what do you do for a living?" She was tired of being introduced as "Miss Hayes." Why settle for that when she had a sales gimmick like demonic possession right here in her hot little hands? It might destroy the credibility of the book, but it could create a name for her. *Amelia Haines, media personality.* And as far as that goes, there were millions of people out there who did believe in demons, ghosts, supernatural powers.

So why not take advantage of the opportunity? And quickly, before somebody else beat her to the draw. All she really had to do here was take a look at the Bates property; stick around for the Grand Opening, day after tomorrow, then get out.

"—*let her memory abide in our hearts even as we erase the memory of the other, his memory, from our minds. For his was the way of the transgressor and it is doubly a transgression for those who seek to resurrect his memory for gain. Let the dead bury the dead—*"

He was a fine one to talk, Amy told herself. In his own way Reverend Archer was capitalizing on the death of that child just as much as Otto Remsbach. Or herself, if she yielded to temptation.

"—*It is for us, the living, to cherish loving thoughts of the lamb who has departed from our flock and returned to the green and eternal pastures of heaven—*"

Amy wasn't all that interested in the sheepherding business, but the townsfolk down front seemed moved and there was audible sobbing from the first row where Terry's parents and relatives were seated. She glanced to the left toward Irene Grovesmith; her ice-cube eyes had melted into tears.

As she did so the voice ceased sounding from the podium; gazing forward, she noted that Reverend Archer's head was again lowered in silent prayer, though only for a moment.

Then the invisible organ sounded again, this time in an accompaniment for an invisible choir. A thought suddenly occurred to Amy as the voices sounded. Wouldn't it be funny if God didn't like singing?

She glanced to her right. Whether or not God was a music lover remained debatable, but obviously Hank Gibbs was not. Sometime during the last few minutes he'd left his seat and headed for the exit.

Why hadn't he let her know his intentions? Just a nudge would have done the trick. Unless there was something wrong—

The thought prompted Amy to rise and propelled her to the doorway. In the lobby, electronically evangelical voices echoed. There was no sign of Gibbs' presence.

Perhaps he'd gone outside to escape the sound and capture a breath of fresh air. If so, he'd acted sensibly; even though the lobby was deserted the stagnant, odoriferous heat persisted here.

Filtering through the speaker system from the chapel Amy caught a few words of the hymn sung by the choir, something to do with "The blood of the lamb." An unfortunate phrase, in view of Reverend Archer's sermon.

She turned toward the lobby door, eager to make her exit before hearing any further sanguinary references.

As she did so the door opened to admit a figure momentarily silhouetted against the outer sunlight. Amy saw that the man was not Gibbs, but long before he reached her side she recognized the rumpled suit, the hair and beard; today he was wearing shades that concealed ocular spasm but didn't improve his general appearance. If anything the dark glasses added a slightly sinister touch that, in his case, seemed superfluous.

Amy greeted him softly as he approached. "Mr. Dunstable, I've been looking for you. Why weren't you at the memorial service?"

"I misjudged the length of time it would take me to get here from town," he said.

"You walked here? In this heat?"

Eric Dunstable nodded. "I had no choice. None of the cars headed in this direction would stop and give me a lift." If his sigh was accompanied by a rueful smile his beard concealed it. "Not very hospitable around here, are they?"

But very cautious. Amy's response was silent. No point trying to explain to Dunstable that Fairvale citizens took a dim view of strangers who might have emerged from the pages of *Gross-Out Comics*. Particularly when the stranger in question claimed to be a demonologist.

"I'm sorry," Amy said. And she was. After his long

hike here in the heat Dunstable aroused her sympathies rather than her suspicions.

Nevertheless, she glanced around before speaking again. Sound piping forth from the chapel indicated ceremonies there hadn't concluded. But aside from herself and Dunstable the lobby held only shadows.

"You didn't happen to see Hank Gibbs drive off when you got here?" Amy murmured.

"The newspaper editor?" Dunstable shook his head.

"He might have gone up the road in the other direction." As she spoke Amy realized her voice had dropped almost to a whisper. What was there about this lobby that still retained the power to subdue speech as well as spirit?

Whatever it was Eric Dunstable felt it too. Weary and bedraggled, he seemed suddenly revitalized, alert and aware amid the shadows. He was watching, waiting, listening, though not necessarily to the ethereal voices of the choir.

Staring at him, Amy reconsidered. The way his head was poised didn't indicate a response to sound; absurd as it might seem it reminded her of something entirely different. *A bloodhound catching the scent—*

Now he spoke, and the shadows listened. The shadows listened, and she heard the whispered words. "I was right. There is evil here."

"Yes. I sense it too." Amy turned at the sound of Reverend Archer's voice. He was standing directly behind them. And now his only forefinger jabbed out toward Dunstable as he spoke again.

"*You are the evil one!*"

·10·

IT was deputy Dick Reno who broke it up before their voices escalated into a shouting match. He came through the front door just as the audience started to emerge into the lobby from the chapel. The organ music continued to sound, and this helped; at least it served to muffle Archer's angry outbursts and Dunstable's hoarse rejoinders.

But it required Dick Reno's physical intervention to separate the two men before their altercation was generally noticed, and it took the combined efforts of Dr. Rawson and grey-haired Mrs. Archer to pull the angry clergyman aside.

For a moment Amy's full attention was diverted as wife and physician led Reverend Archer across the lobby and into a narrow hallway beyond. When she turned to locate Eric Dunstable he was no longer at her side and Dick Reno shook his head. "Minute I let go of his arm he took off like a bat outta hell. Mind telling me what that hassle was all about?"

Amy cast a sidelong glance at the crowd moving toward the exit, then shook her head. "I'd rather not talk about it now."

"Just as well." Reno nodded. "It'll be easier for you when you're in the car."

Amy frowned. "Don't tell me I'm under arrest again!"

Reno shook his head. "Hank Gibbs was pulling out just as I drove in. Asked me if I'd mind driving you back to town. Said he didn't know services would run so late. He has to put the paper to bed for tomorrow, and asked me to give you his apologies."

"I understand." Amy paused. "Do you?"

"Do I what?"

"Mind driving me?"

"My pleasure." Reno led her down the steps, then followed the driveway to the far side of the church. "I parked in back," he said. "Figured people might get the wrong idea if they saw you climbing into a patrol car."

"Thanks." Amy smiled. "I appreciate that." Which was true; the last thing in the world she needed right now was to have the good citizens of Fairvale mistake her for a criminal. She had already been convicted of being female and was suspected of being a writer as well as an out-of-towner to boot.

Once the patrol car swung out into the narrow single-lane road behind the church she felt more secure. Safe from prying stares and insulated from muggy heat. Apparently Reno had already mapped out a route that would take them into town along the back roads, and she was grateful for his consideration.

As he peered forward through the windshield the flattened outline of his nose marred his profile. When he glanced toward her the imperfection vanished.

"Comfortable?" he said. "I can turn up the air-conditioning if you like."

"This is fine." Amy smiled. "I was just thinking— maybe some of your locals resent me but the rest of you go out of your way with hospitality. I haven't had to drive myself once since I got here."

"Don't knock it," Reno said. "Might as well save wear and tear on the tires."

Amy frowned, and he caught it. "What's the matter, did I say the wrong thing?"

Amy shook her head. "No, you just reminded me of something." Having gone that far she decided to go all the way and told him about what had happened to her car in the hotel parking lot.

He listened without comment until she finished. "Want to file a complaint?"

"Be honest with me," Amy said. "What good would it do?"

Reno shrugged. "Not much, I guess. People around here—well, you saw them at the services. Some of them can get pretty uptight over anything to do with what happened out there at the Bates place last week. Hell, some of them are still uptight about what happened there thirty years ago."

"I know," Amy said.

"That's one of the things they're uptight over—what you know, or what they think you know. I'm talking about the real diehards now, folks like Reverend Archer, Irene Grovesmith, and those older people. The rest of us would just as soon forget the whole thing."

"Us?" Amy met his gaze. "Meaning you feel that way about it too?"

"I guess I can speak for most people my age who were born and brought up around here," Reno told her. "I was only five when it all started, and I can still remember the way those Sunday drivers jammed the streets. The whole town was crawling with reporters, curiosity-seekers, people coming in from as far away as New York and California. Tell the truth, it was pretty exciting, seeing all those strangers and looking at all of those out-of-state licenses."

Amy nodded. "I can imagine it would be, for a five-year-old."

"Trouble was, I turned six. That's when they began busing me to school over in Montrose. Kids were enrolled there from all over the area and every last one of them knew about the Bates case. Anyone who came from Fairvale got dumped on, and I don't know which was the worse—the older kids trying to beat up on us or the younger ones trying to tell those stupid Norman jokes."

"I know what you mean," Amy said. "I've heard them too."

"But not for twelve years running," Reno said. "Seems like they never let up, and the more jokes they told, the less folks were laughing back in Fairvale. I can't explain it, except that the shadow of those murders hung over the town like a cloud that never cleared away. I guess that's one of the reasons I was glad to go off to the university—until I got there, that is. Because when they found out where I came from the jokes started all over again."

"What was your major?" Amy asked.

"It doesn't matter now," Dick Reno said. "I had some idea about ending up in law school. But I said the hell with it and dropped out at the end of my freshman year. Came back here, passed the tests, and hired on as a deputy."

"Any regrets?"

"Yes and no." Reno hung a sharp left and suddenly they were moving along a street between two rows of tract housing. "For a few years after I got back it looked like things were improving; the younger generation wasn't all that steamed up about what had happened way back when. I guess most of us knew Norman Bates was still alive over at State Hospital, but you might say he was really just a name to us. And nobody bothered going over there with candy or flowers." If Reno was attempting to lighten up, his tone of voice didn't match his words. "Then Bates escaped and Dr. Claiborne flipped out—well, you know the rest. After that it started all over again. And last week—"

"Do you have any ideas about what happened?" Amy asked.

For a moment Reno didn't reply; his attention was focused on parking. Glancing up, Amy was startled to realize that they had pulled into the area adjoining the hotel. Then he spoke. "Notice your car's back," he said. "Looks like they put on a new set of tires for you."

Amy followed his gaze and nodded her confirmation. "So I see. But you still haven't answered my question. I'd like to know if you have any ideas about what happened last week."

Dick Reno leaned across her, his hand reaching out to open the door on the passenger side. "Tell you later," he said. "At dinner."

Amy hesitated. Was he coming on to her? Right now the answer didn't matter. More important were answers to questions about the murder case. That's what she had come here to get, and if somebody wanted to throw in a free meal, why not? It certainly couldn't be any worse of an ordeal than last night's dinner with that sophisticate and raconteur, Fatso Otto.

"Thanks for the invitation." Again she hesitated, but only for a moment. "You weren't thinking of eating here at the hotel, were you?"

"Don't worry, I can feed you better than that." Now it was Reno's turn to pause. "Just one thing. I'll be going back on duty after we finish. Would it embarrass you if I wear my uniform?"

"Not if we're having dinner somewhere out of town." Amy smiled. "It may even help me feel protected."

"Good thinking." Reno pulled the door shut after she stepped out of the car.

"Suppose I pick you up right here at six-thirty."

"That sounds fine to me." Amy waved as he put the car into gear. "See you."

But there were other things to see before that time. First, the bill for tires and service awaiting her at the counter of the reception desk. She received it and her car keys from a matronly-looking lady clerk whose features resembled those of the waitress Amy had encountered last night in the coffee shop. A sister, perhaps?

Amy dismissed the possibilities of nepotism as she

considered the realities of the bill. The total for tires and
labor came to two hundred and sixty-five dollars, which
seemed reasonable enough; apparently Smitty had
heeded Hank Gibbs' warning and inflated the tires rather
than the price.

Once again she made a mental note to check on the
rental car agreement and the status of her insurance coverage, and once again she neglected doing so after reaching her room. Instead she spent the next half hour
adding to her notes. Nothing earthshaking had happened
at the memorial services today and neither Reverend
Archer's sermon nor his dust-up with Dunstable would
probably get more than a passing mention in the book.
Still, one never knows, and it was best to put things
down before details faded from her memory.

By the time she finished Amy's watch told her it
was five-thirty. The clouded sky beyond her window
had a sickly yellowish cast, which indicated the weather
was still hot and sticky. And so was she.

In the shower she debated what to wear for the evening. It would help if she knew the sort of place she'd be
dining at, but aside from that there were other factors to
consider. Somehow she must combine comfort with
looking her best. All she really had beside the suit was
the blue dress, which she could wear with the black bag
and the heels. Too formal? After all, Reno warned her
he'd be in uniform. And if he had to go back on duty at
nine he'd be staying in uniform, worse luck.

Toweling dry, Amy made a face at herself in the
bathroom mirror. What put that thought in her mind;
who was really coming on to whom now?

Might as well admit it, Reno did attract her and after
all it had been a while since she and Gary split, just before the book came out. Come to think of it he and Dick
Reno both had one thing in common; men with dark,
curly hair seemed to get to her every time. Of course
Gary had been shorter and his nose wasn't broken. He
was a lover, not a fighter, and at first this was no prob-

lem. It took her several months to learn that he was also slightly wimpish and very much of a mother's boy. The old barracuda ran his life and had some weird ideas about how he should live it. Amy should have suspected Gary's mother from the first; after all, what kind of a woman would name her son after a dead movie star or a town in Indiana?

Still, there'd been good times and smooth sailing until the barracuda roiled the waters and Gary went overboard. There'd been no one since and during the past six months the only man in her life had been Norman Bates.

She needed a change, and quickly, but tonight was definitely not the night. And even if the opportunity arose, she wasn't all that certain it would be a wise thing to get involved with a small-town deputy sheriff. Not in this particular town anyway. All the same, there was no harm in paying particular attention to her makeup after she'd pulled the dress over her head and fluffed out her hair. She sprayed her cologne in strategic spots at six twenty-six, picked up her bag and dropped her room key into it outside her door at six twenty-seven, and emerged from the lobby exit at precisely six-thirty.

Twilight time, but no breeze had risen to dispel heat or humidity. Most shops along the street closed at six; customers and owners alike had gone home for dinner, and there were few drivers passing to note Amy's escort and his vehicle as he arrived.

As she climbed into the passenger seat the streetlights came on and they took off, rounding the far corner. Once again Dick Reno seemed to have mapped out a route that would render them inconspicuous. This time they headed for the freeway; here too the traffic seemed light.

But that term didn't describe Reno's mood. He'd greeted her cordially enough and there was no doubt about his reaction to her appearance. But even in their small talk about the weather his voice was pitched low and his shadowed features seemed immobile. A dark mood.

Amy tried to fill gaps of silence with comments on her surprise at the reasonable price Smitty had charged for replacing her tires. Responding to Reno's lack of response she did her best to deliberately avoid discussing matters of greater concern. But before she could stop, she found herself saying, "Maybe I should have asked Smitty to keep the car in the garage overnight. I hope that whoever did a job on my tires won't decide to try again."

Dick Reno shook his head. "Wouldn't worry about that. Seemes to me what happened last night wasn't vandalism. Looks to me it was supposed to be some kind of warning."

"Like get out of town and stay out?" Amy nodded. "But I didn't get out. So what happens next?"

"There's a regular drive-by along Main Street every half hour or so. Engstrom's given orders to keep a special lookout to see if your car's okay. I don't think there'll be any problem."

"You're my problem," Amy said. "You sound as if you're down. Did something happen after you dropped me off this afternoon?"

"I'm all right. Haven't eaten anything since breakfast, so what I probably need right now is to put a little food in my stomach."

"And a drink."

"Not now. Don't forget, I'll be going back on duty, but don't let that stop you—the drinks here are special."

The size and variety of the various rum concoctions at Wing Chu's were surprising, as was the presence of a mandarin cuisine Chinese restaurant nestled on the hillside just beyond the freeway's second turn-off ramp.

She told Reno so, and for the first time since his greeting tonight a smile accompanied his reply. "Place is really run by a Swede. Even the name's a fake. Wing Chu—reverse it."

"Chu Wing?" Amy laughed. "I get it. But you say the food here is good?"

"Take a look at the menu." She did so, while sipping at the drink she'd ordered, a combination of fruit salad and alcohol ignorantly identified as a *Tahitian Zombie*. There were, Amy realized, no zombies in Tahiti—but there was enough rum in this drink to create one right here.

She manipulated her straws carefully, watching as Dick Reno made do with his ice water. The booth was comfortable; obviously he was not.

"Find anything you like?" he said.

"Suppose you order for us?"

And he did. The waiter was short, his complexion saffron, though his accent indicated origins closer to Mexico City than to Beijing. But the names of the dishes that Reno rattled off sounded authentically oriental.

Reno glanced at her as the waiter departed. "Hope you'll like what I ordered."

"I'm not worried," she said. "I trust you."

"Thanks."

"But why don't you trust me?"

"Never said I didn't."

"Level with me. Something *did* happen after you dropped me off at the hotel." Amy leaned forward. "It's connected with the murder case, isn't it?"

"No—but you are."

"What's that supposed to mean?"

"Engstrom asked me what I was doing for dinner tonight, and I told him. He made some suggestions."

"Such as?"

"Seeing what I could do to discourage you from running around and asking all these questions."

"I know he doesn't like me," Amy said.

Reno shook his head. "Wrong. He thinks you're a neat lady. It's your book he doesn't like. And neither do I."

"Hey, give me a break! How can you be judgmental about something that hasn't even been written yet?"

"Because of all the other stuff we've seen before. Hasn't been a year gone by without some newspaper or magazine article coming out with the same old story on Norman, and new ones of their own. Was Norman fooling around with his mother before she died? How many other girls could he have murdered and buried in the swamp? Don't forget, they came damn close to making a movie about him until Claiborne messed that up for them. And what he did only made things worse; they started doing pieces on Claiborne too. Now you're going to dump the whole mess into a big fat book."

"No such thing," Amy said, then halted as the waiter wheeled up the cart bearing their order. They sat silently as he served them; Amy recognized the chow mein, some of the Chinese vegetables, and most of the scents, but the rest required exploration.

Lifting her fork, she explored and, as she did so, explained. "I've researched most of that newspaper and magazine material you mentioned, and I agree a lot of it is sensationalism and sheer speculation. It all adds up to what you said—a real mess—but you're wrong about what I intend to do with it. I'm not going to dump all this garbage into my book; if it turns out to be big and fat that's because I intend to fill it with facts. The reason I'm here is to establish as many of those facts as I can and try to set the record straight."

"You really think that's going to do any good?"

"Tell your friend the Sheriff he and I are really in the same business," Amy said. "Both of us are searching for clues. And yes, I do think my book will do some good. This afternoon you were telling me about what it was like to grow up haunted by memories of those murders. The only way to deal with the jokes, gossip, and those wild legends is to get at the truth. If I can manage to set it down once and for all, Fairvale will be rid of its ghosts. And these sweet-and-sour shrimp are delicious."

"I hope you're right," Reno said. "About the book, I mean. I sure as hell don't like the idea of my son growing up here and having to cope with all that crud."

"Son?" Amy's fork dug into a slice of abalone, then halted. "You're married?"

"I was." Reno seemed slightly more relaxed now as he started to eat. "David's eleven now, same class in school as Terry. What happened last week shook him up pretty bad. I'd like to talk to him about it."

"Why don't you?"

"Divorce papers say I can see him twice a month, on Sundays. Way the schedule works out my next chance comes this weekend." Reno scowled. "One of these days I'm going back to court to get custody. That kid belongs with me, particularly at a time like this. I hate to think of him sitting there in the house night after night because of the curfew—"

"No wonder I haven't seen any children around."

Reno nodded. "Been ordered on since the day after Terry was killed."

"Sheriff Engstrom didn't tell me about that." Amy paused; the abalone was good too. "I guess he's not anxious for me to know everything that's going on."

"Neither was I, until you explained about the book." Reno's frown vanished and he started to eat again. "But Engstrom and I don't always see eye to eye. For one thing I don't buy his idea that a transient could've committed the murder. Banning's people with the Highway Patrol picked up a couple the day after it happened, but both of them had alibis that came out clean. Way I figure it, if a vagrant was involved then why didn't he rip off some of the stuff in the house?"

"Something was taken," Amy said. "That wax figure of Mrs. Bates." She hesitated. "But maybe it helps to prove your point. Why would a vagrant want to steal a thing like that?"

"Why would anyone *make* a thing like that in the first place?" Reno's scowl was back again. "You think your book will help? Forget it, lady; nothing's going to help as long as that damn Remsbach is around. When he opens that tourist trap of his day after tomorrow he'll really trash this town for keeps. He'll trash the lives of our kids too. Talking to David isn't going to do any good, any more than trying to talk to Remsbach."

"I'm sorry," Amy said. "I didn't mean to spoil your dinner."

"Not your fault." Reno did his best to transform his scowl into a smile. "Let's not talk about that business anymore. Here, how about trying a little fried rice?"

Amy tried the fried rice, tried not to talk about anything connected with the case, tried to elevate Dick Reno's spirits with small-talk. By the time the meal ended she had seen no recurrence of his frown, and when they parted back at the entrance to the hotel Amy was reassured his mood had shifted. One thing was certain; she'd hate to get on his bad side. Maybe that was the reason for the divorce—

"Thanks for coming with me," he said.

"Thanks for asking."

"Hope I didn't spoil your evening," he told her. "Maybe you'll give me another chance before you leave."

She nodded. "We'll be in touch."

"Good. Time for me to punch in. Got to get moving now."

As he drove off she turned away. Behind her the town seemed to have settled down for the night, streets and houses sleeping under a dark blanket.

But not Amy.

·11·

FAT Otto Remsbach grabbed the tab and tossed it on the floor. Ignoring Doris Huntley's stare of disapproval he had himself a nice long swig.

What the hell was wrong with Doris tonight? Maybe her mother had told her it wasn't nice for a gentleman to drink beer out of a can when he's in bed with a lady. But where did Doris get off, thinking she was a lady? And if her mother was so uptight about drinking out of a can why didn't the old bitch come along with Doris and pour his beer into a glass?

Remsbach erupted a belch, indicating both appreciation of his drink and of his wit. Doris was scowling, but to hell with that too. This wasn't Remsbach's first drink tonight and it wasn't going to be his last, either; if his little chicky-baby didn't like it she could go stuff herself. He'd had it with Doris—too many times, and you can say that again. Somebody ought to tell her that smoking in bed isn't ladylike either and maybe injurious to your health, particularly when the guy you're balling kicks you out on your big fat butt.

Right now he was getting a good look at it because she'd stubbed her cigarette in the bedstand ashtray and settled down on the pillow with her back turned. That's another way ladies hint their dissatisfaction with their bed-partners. Well, when it came right down to it he wasn't all that satisfied himself. Another thing; just thirty seconds after she turned she started making those noises. Real ladies don't snore.

Remsbach dropped his empty beer can on the floor beside the bed and opened a fresh one. He was starting on the second six-pack already, but he might as well drink up before the rest of the cans got warm. What he needed was some kind of portable refrigerator in here, some place to put the beer and keep it cold. Maybe he could build shelves in Doris; she was frigid enough.

Remsbach substituted his chuckle for a belch. Hot-damn, he was really on a role tonight—a regular Johnny Carson—and all off the top of his head too.

Now he took another gulp of beer because the top of his head didn't feel so good; too much strain on the brain today. A lot of the stuff he'd ordered came in this morning, parcel post and Federal Express. Postcards with a picture of the Bates house, Bates Motel stationery, and those damn fool souvenir buttons reading *Norman Loves Mommy.* The buttons were Pitkin's idea; a lot of this deal was his idea, including all those ads that had to be proofed for the papers in Montrose, Rock Center, and the six other weekly rags in the surrounding counties. Too early to risk what it cost running them statewide or pay big-city advertising rates, but if these one-shots in the nearby weeklies pulled in enough suckers for the Grand Opening day after tomorrow, Pitkin wanted to give the dailies a shot. Next step would be radio, then TV.

Right now he had his hands full just keeping track of orders and deliveries. Tomorrow somebody would come along to haul this crap out to the property and stash it in the motel office ready for displays and sales. At least Remsbach hoped somebody would be coming around; that was Charles Q. Pitkin's department. He was in charge of all hiring, from one-time truck deliverymen to the full-time staff out at the motel. "Full time" was maybe stretching it a little; they'd be starting out with one girl handling sales at the motel and two guys who would spell each other for the guided tours, motel and house both included. Open ten to six, closed Sundays. If they lucked out the next thing would be staying open nights—Charles already had some kinky notions about spooking things up for the evening trade. And they'd pave over and fence in a parking area with gates and a tollbooth.

If they lucked out. Otto Remsbach tackled beer number—who-the-hell cares. They'd better luck out, after the bundle it was costing him just to get started. But like Charles said, he had to do something, because agrobiz was sure as hell ruining farm implement sales; the little guys were going belly-up and the big guys bought their supplies and equipment at quantity discounts from outside sources.

So it was time to fish or cut bait. Nothing to worry about; Charlie only gambled on sure things and his dice were always loaded. What was it he'd said? "You'll know business is good at the motel when you've gotta make a reservation to use a pay toilet."

Charlie was a smart-ass but he sure's hell could come up with ideas that landed him on the profit side of the ledger. And this was just the beginning. The next step would be to build a *real* motel out there. Then they'd need statewide advertising, and after that they'd go national. *Visit the Bates Motel and the Houses of Horror!*

That was another one of Pitkin's brainstorms. Not just a wax museum but a whole string of separate exhibits. If they could have a motel office for Norman and a house for the old lady, then why not build something for characters like the Boston Strangler, the Manson family, and all those famous weirdos? Hell, with enough loot they could put up a whole street like London in the old days and do Jack the Ripper.

"Theme parks," that's what they call such places now. With the right kind of luck it could end up with something like Disneyland or Universal Tours. And the big money wasn't just from admissions. The real name of the game was concessions. Jesus, think how much you could take in just from the beer franchise alone!

The thought of beer triggered another belch, and its echo awakened his companion. Doris Huntley rolled over on her back and blinked up at him, bleary-eyed.

"Wha' you say?" she mumbled.

"Nothing, I was just thinking about beer."

"That's pretty much all you ever think about. So what else is new?"

"Not this beer, dummy." Remsbach gestured with the hand holding the can. "I'm talking beer sales out at the Bates place." His hand uncurled and dropped the empty container to the floor.

"Don't you have to have a license?"

"Sure, and one for fast-food stands too. That's where your boss comes in."

"Don't be too sure. I know Charlie's gotten liquor licenses for a couple of clients before, but it wasn't easy. Took a lot of doing and a lot of time."

"I can wait." Remsbach rewarded his promise of patience with another beer from the six-pack. "We're gonna need permits for the motel and the concessions first before we get into the big stuff."

"Know something, Otto? You ought to kick the beer habit." Doris favored him with a frown of virtue as she lit a cigarette. "Get loaded like this and you don't make any sense."

"Hell I don't!"

To prove it he explained what he had in mind. How much came from him and how much came from Charlie didn't matter—once this thing got off the ground it'd be bigger than both of them. Plastic souvenir knives, with *Yours truly, Jack the Ripper* stamped on the handles. A roomful of waxworks in nurse's uniforms, like those eight girls who got themselves snuffed in Chicago years ago. Maybe a bunch of murderer masks, at least the dead ones who couldn't sue for invasion of privacy.

"How about that?" Remsbach laughed. "Bastards

like that always squawking about somebody invading
their privacy, right after they invaded somebody else's
privates with a butcher knife."

"You're disgusting!"

"Am I? Well, there's one hell of a lotta people out
there who don't think so. They're gonna come see, and
your boss and I are gonna make megabucks."

Doris abandoned her cigarette and reached for her
undergarments. "What makes you so sure all this will
work out the way you think?"

"Because it damn well better work out, that's why."
Remsbach scowled. "Every goddamn thing I own is rid-
ing on this, plus what Charlie got from mortgaging stuff I
really don't own yet. Not that I'm telling you anything
you don't know; hell, you're the one who drew up most
of the papers on those deals. This idea just eats money,
chews it up and spits it out." Remsbach's scowl became
a full-fledged frown. "Christ, I wish I knew who stole
that goddamn Mother waxwork. Why the hell would
anybody do a thing like that?"

"I don't know," Doris said. Nor was it apparent that
she cared as she sat on the side of the bed and pulled her
dress over her head.

"Goddamn piece cost a fortune. Charlie got hold of
the outfit that made it out on the coast and he ordered us
another, only it won't be done in time for the opening."

"Too bad." Doris stood up, wriggled her skirt down
over her thighs and stepped into her shoes. "Maybe
they'll send it to you for Mother's Day."

"That's okay, we can get along without it now."
Remsbach's scowl was reshaped into the philosophic
smile of someone who believes in looking at the bright
side. "Whoever killed Terry Dowson really did us a
favor—all that extra publicity is gonna boost attendance."

Doris Huntley's hair was a mess, but if she had har-
bored any intention of combing it out, Remsbach's re-
mark about the Dowson kid changed her mind. Grabbing
her purse from the nightstand she turned and stormed

out of the bedroom, but not before giving Otto Remsbach instructions which, owing to the limitations of human anatomy, would be impossible for him to fulfill.

Otto Remsbach hurled his half-empty beer can after her; it struck the upper panel of the door, then splattered its way to the floor.

Hell with it. Hell with her too. Have 'nother beer. Good stuff. 'N good riddance. Because even before he could get the can open, the phone rang. And whaddya know?

It was Amy.

Friggin' betcha, Amy Haines herself, coming to you live, not on tape, none other than the same little snotty bitch who walked out on him last night.

Otto Remsbach did his best to eliminate the slur from both his voice and his thoughts as he spoke. Did a pretty good job of it too, but why not? Doing deals over the phone came easy to him; like Charlie used to say, he was born on the horn.

Beauty part was he didn't have to make any deal at all. The way it went down the only thing he had to do was say yes. "I know it's late and short notice, but I'd really like to see you for a few minutes if you can spare the time," she told him.

It sure as hell was no problem saying yes to that; the trick was to keep the surprise out of his voice.

"Half an hour?"

"Sounds good to me."

He hung up, or tried to; it took several attempts before he managed to cradle the phone, and it wasn't just the effects of drink that hampered him. Remsbach felt a surge of mingled anticipation and excitement, but overriding both was triumph.

Her walking out on him that way had been bothering the back of his mind all day. So he had a couple drinks with her out at the Club, no big deal. He remembered inviting her to come back to the house with him, but that was no big deal either. Thing was, she turned him down. Thing is, tonight she'd changed her mind.

Or had she? Maybe there was something she was after, something he could tell her, some favor he could do for her. Well, whatever the hell it was she wanted, the lady was going to get herself a lot more than she bargained for.

Half 'n hour. Jus' time for a drink before he got dressed. Or maybe not. Maybe better give himself a couple minutes to relax, put himself together.

He probed his right cheek with a fatty forefinger. Yeah, he could get by without shaving again. Save him 'nother couple minutes.

Turn off the lamp. Close your eyes. Relax. But don't go to sleep. Ten minutes, that's all you got now. Relax. Take deep breaths. Gotta remember make this bed when you get up, get rid of those beer cans an' all that other crap. And don't forget those goddamn cigarette butts with Doris' lipstick smeared all over them. Now *that* was good thinking. And good resting.

Here. In. The. Dark.

Remsbach came awake with a start. Must have passed out cold. How the hell long had he been lying here? Did Amy come and go while he was sleeping? He couldn't remember.

She must have come, but on what happened next he drew a blank. All he knew was that she hadn't gone. He could feel the curve of her bare hip against his own.

Almost reluctantly he broke contact to turn away and switch on the nightstand lamp. Then he turned back for a better glimpse of his bed-partner.

It wasn't Amy.

It wasn't Doris Huntley either.

The face that leered up from the pillow beside him was Mother's.

·12·

AMY entered the hotel lobby, grateful for its comparative coolness after the swelter of the street. The desk clerk looked up from his comic but she ignored his stare and crossed to the waiting elevator.

Usually elevators triggered off a touch of claustrophobia, but tonight Amy was grateful when the door slid shut and she ascended in solitary confinement. There had been too many people today, too many stares. The whole town had gotten a chance to look her over, talk her over.

So what? Amy shrugged as she left the elevator, fishing in her purse for the room key. Let them whisper behind her back, just so long as nobody stuck a knife in it.

Not exactly the kind of thing she wanted to think about while opening the door on darkness and fumbling for the switch beyond the threshold. The overhead light fanned across a room occupied only by herself; still, she gave a start when the phone began to ring.

Closing and bolting the door behind her she hurried to pick up the receiver, giving herself three guesses as she did so. Who would be calling her tonight—Hank Gibbs, Sheriff Engstrom, Eric Dunstable?

"Good evening, Miss Haines. I hope I'm not disturbing you at this hour."

"No, I just came back from dinner." Amy paused. "Who is this?"

"Nicholas Steiner."

"Dr. Steiner!" Amy paused again. "I'm sorry—I didn't recognize your voice."

"Neither do I." Steiner's chuckle was weak and he spoke slowly. "I'm still trying to untangle my vocal cords but I wanted to give you a call as soon as possible and tell you I'm sorry about breaking our appointment."

"You're apologizing to me because somebody tried to kill you?" Amy said. "I'm afraid you'll have to come up with a better excuse than that."

Steiner's chuckle of response seemed stronger. "Would you be willing to settle for another meeting?"

"Of course. Are you at the hospital?"

"They released me this afternoon, on condition I don't go back on my regular schedule until next week. I'm resting, taking it easy, and bored stiff."

"So I'm your last resort."

"I prefer to think of you as my first concern."

"That's very kind. Most of the people I've run into around here don't seem to feel that way," Amy said. "I get the idea the only thing they're concerned about is how soon I'll get out of town."

"When will that be?"

"I haven't decided yet." Amy hesitated. "Do you think it would be possible to see me tomorrow?"

"Possible and pleasurable. What time would be convenient?"

"Offhand I think afternoon would be best. If I could have an hour with you, say around three o'clock—"

"You've got it, Miss Haines. Make it three-thirty. Gives me a chance to nap first after lunch."

"Good. I'll see you then." Amy prepared to hang up, then voiced a final question. "How is Dr. Claiborne doing?"

"Not too well. They've got him over at Bancroft Memorial Hospital and I can't get a straight answer out of anyone on staff there. Maybe I'll know more by the time we meet tomorrow."

"Thanks, Doctor. I'm looking forward to seeing you, but please take it easy until then."

"Don't worry, I intend to do just that." Once more, the dry chuckle. "I may not even shave."

After hanging up Amy reached for the smaller of her notebooks, though not to record the time of tomorrow's appointment; she was in no danger of forgetting that. But now it was time to review future plans again, checkout for possibilities or impossibilities.

On the basis of what Steiner had just reported, Dr. Claiborne sounded like an impossibility. She'd have to count on getting a fix on him from what Steiner could tell her. Meantime, a scrub for Adam Claiborne, M.D. A scrub for Bob Peterson too, and another for Dr. Rawson; as for people like Reverend Archer, there was no sense in even listing their names.

Hank Gibbs? Might be worthwhile talking to him again, and Sheriff Engstrom too, if she could only find a chink in his armor. So far the little man seemed to be an Achilles without a heel.

Who else was left? Instinctively Amy recoiled from the notion of a personal interview with Terry Dowson's parents. There was no reason to exploit their grief, no point in sensationalizing the sorrow of the victim's friends and classmates. It wasn't going to be that kind of a book.

But just what kind of a book *would* it be? Amy tried to deal with that question as she scanned her notes. Face it, so far she hadn't really come up with all that much new material; maybe because it was nonexistent. Perhaps this attorney, Charlie Pitkin, knew where the bodies were buried, but she had a strong hunch he wouldn't be doing any grave-digging for her. You don't get to be a hotshot state senator by giving away secrets, and from what Otto Remsbach had told her, good old Charlie wasn't in the habit of giving away anything.

Amy quickly considered and disgarded Irene Grovesmith, Doris Huntley, Dr. Rawson's receptionist—

Marge or Margie, whatever she went by. Scrub Captain
Banning too; she hadn't seen him around, and even if
available the chances were he'd be another Engstrom
type.

Dick Reno was no Engstrom, that's for sure, but she
already knew what she could get out of him. And if she
hung in here for another couple of days she'd probably
accept it, out of sheer boredom. So scrub him too; the
last thing Amy needed right now was to get tangled up
with a small-town deputy and his problems. The book
was still going to be about the Bates case and had nothing to do with hang-ups over ex-wives or the custody of
eleven-year-old sons. *You're a nice guy, Dick Reno, but
right now I've got no time for hitting or getting hit on; go
cry in your own beer, not mine.*

Still, Amy knew that in a way she owed him after
what he'd told her over dinner about Otto Remsbach's
future plans. These would be very much a part of the
story and Remsbach himself had dropped hints about
them last night, but only hints. Amy was sure there was
more if she could only pry it out of him.

But when? That was the question. Even if she hadn't
made an appointment with Steiner that tied her up during part of the afternoon, it was a good bet Remsbach
would be tied up himself all day and all night in prepa-
ration for his Grand Opening the following morning.

Which left her with no alternative except to wait until after the Opening. And it was strange how her thinking had changed about that.

When she arrived, attending the event had been a
top priority, but now she no longer felt any commitment.
Amy wondered why; was it the result of the hostility she
felt directed toward her in town here, at the Country
Club, or the memorial services today? If so, appearing at
the Grand Opening would be another ordeal. And, actually, an unnecessary one. No matter how few or how
many customers showed up, this was one event that was
bound to attract plenty of press coverage, to say nothing

of radio and TV. As far as getting information about the event itself there'd be more than enough in print or on tape to provide her with all the gory details.

As for herself, Amy wasn't interested in gore. The details she needed concerned the actual reconstruction of the house and the motel. How authentic was it, had some actual artifacts from the original structures been salvaged for use here, did the settings convey the feel and the atmosphere of the place where Norman lived— and others died?

A complicated question, but one with a simple answer; she'd just have to go out there and see for herself. Not alone, of course, but not as part of a guided tour mob scene at the Opening, either. What she needed was an opportunity to examine whatever interested her, in depth and at leisure.

Once again Amy reviewed her options. Tomorrow was out. The day after tomorrow, the Grand Opening, was out too. Even if she changed her mind and stayed yet another day the place would still be open for business; she'd have no privacy. There had to be some other solution.

Was tomorrow really out? As far as she knew now, her only commitment was the afternoon appointment with Steiner. That Remsbach would be tied up all day was a natural assumption. But suppose she could talk him out of it? Suppose she could get him to drive her over there in the morning, or when she returned from the interview with Steiner?

Amy glanced at her watch; the time was nine twenty-two. Not too late for someone to give Remsbach a call—

Someone else, that is. It was too late for her; had been, ever since she'd walked out on him at the Country Club. What made her think that all she had to do was pick up the phone and say, "Hi, Fatso, remember me? That's right, Amy Haines, the gal who did the dump on you in front of all your buddies last night. I know you're going to be busy tomorrow, but why don't you just drop everything and drive me out to the Bates place when I'm ready to go?"

Amy shook her head. Fat chance she had of selling that idea to Fatso. But what other chance would she have, what other choice?

Frowning, she crossed to the window and gazed out over the flat rooftop. The clouds had thickened and it was only for a moment that she caught a glimpse of the crescent moon before it vanished. Her frown vanished with it.

Crescent. Female sexual symbol. What did it have to do with her situation? Why was she suddenly thinking about *Tricks or Treats?*

Because of Bonnie Walton, that's why. True, Amy had written the book, but Bonnie had lived it. She'd wasted no time mooning over female sex symbols; there was little or nothing she didn't know about the realities. And if she had found herself facing a problem like this she'd come up with a solution.

And so would Amy. All she had to do was to think like Bonnie. It had been easy enough to adopt Bonnie's mind-set while writing about her. Now the time had come to make use of it for a practical purpose.

Suppose Bonnie had insulted a trick by walking out on him in public—and that now she needed a special favor from him?

Only two steps were involved and their order was obvious. First the apology, then the request. But Amy already knew this; she didn't need to get inside Bonnie Walton's head just to find that out. And she also knew Remsbach wasn't going to accept her apology or honor her request. At least—

"Not over the phone, dummy!"

Amy gave a start. Was she inside Bonnie's head, or was Bonnie inside hers? For an instant there she could have sworn she'd actually heard Bonnie Walton speaking.

In any case, she knew what Bonnie was thinking. Gaining Otto Remsbach's forgiveness would require not just a personal apology but a personalized, in-person one, and a lot of stroking. Pitching a request for a special favor would almost certainly involve physical presence; perhaps even a bit of physical activity. Just a bit, because the mere idea was repugnant. The phone call was still necessary, but only as a means of gaining access to her mistreated trick.

That's the way Bonnie would have figured it and Bonnie was a smart girl. Amy remembered one of the things she'd said. "All the world can be divided into three kinds of people—whores, pimps, and customers."

Amy picked up the phone.

She knew what she was.

·13·

WHEN she hung up Amy didn't know whether to smile or to frown.

There'd been no difficulty arranging a meeting after her preliminary apology, so she didn't anticipate any trouble when she repeated it after her arrival. That was something to smile about.

The problem, and the frown it inspired, rose from the realization that Otto Remsbach was skunk-drunk.

Not that she was afraid; if Bonnie Walton could deal with drunks, so could she. On the other hand, she really hadn't promised Otto Remsbach that she'd be coming out alone.

She glanced at the door on the far wall. Maybe she wouldn't have to go alone. If Eric Dunstable was in his room it shouldn't be too hard to persuade him to accompany her. What would Bonnie say? Probably tell him Fatso Otto was possessed by evil spirits. Mainly alcoholic ones, but there'd be no need to be that specific.

Amy went into the hall and tapped softly on the upper panel of his door. Tapping gradually became rapping but there was no response.

On the off-chance that he still might be in there sleeping, Amy decided that the best way to rouse him was by phone. She dialed direct and waited, hearing the ring echoing both from the receiver and beyond the wall, but there was no answer.

Where could he be?

A useless question, under the circumstances. A more useful one concerned who else she might get to go with her. Hank Gibbs, perhaps?

Reno had said Gibbs would be at work getting out the paper for tomorrow, but asking him was worth a try. And as in the case of Remsbach, Bonnie Walton would probably advise her to make her request in person rather than just a phone call.

Amy decided to stop by the newspaper office on her way. One trip to the bathroom, one last-minute inspection of hair and makeup, then time to get moving.

The desk clerk gave no indication that she had improved her appearance; he didn't even bother to look up from his comic as she crossed the lobby to the exit.

It seemed warmer outside now than it had been half an hour ago. The clouds overhead had thickened into a lid clamping down to confine the heat, and the air had the deceptive stillness of water just before it starts to boil.

There would be rain before the night was over, no

doubt about it. Instinctively Amy quickened her pace as she made her way to the car.

Main Street was a morgue aside from a few bars where, presumably, wakes were being held. Not just for Terry Dowson but for what had once been a way of life for youngsters in small-town America. Main Street was mourning the passing of its movie house, the bowling alley, the soda parlor. Kids didn't patronize such places anymore, and neither did their parents.

Rural residents had changed over the years. Today farmers were pudgy, middle-aged men wearing baseball caps and horn-rims; big heads on TV screens complaining about not getting enough rain or getting too much rain. In either case the price of foodstuffs would rise in the fall and they wanted more government subsidies.

These weren't the kind of people who needed to go to the movies, and neither did their kids. Television was their window on the world; given the cirsumstances it was difficult to understand how Hank Gibbs could compete with the prime-time nightly news.

But the lights were on in the building fronted by the *Fairvale Weekly Herald* office. When Amy parked and stepped out of the car she could hear the muffled combination of hum and clatter that serves as a lullaby whenever a paper is put to bed.

Once she entered the office the sound was scarcely soothing, and the accompanying vibrations were more nerve-wracking than the noise.

Amy had opened and closed the door quietly; it was difficult to believe anyone could have heard her come in with all this racket. But he did.

He waddled through the print-shop doorway and peered up at her through the lower hemispheres of his bifocals. That's when the shouting match began.

"Yes, miss. Something I can do for you?"

"I'm looking for Mr. Gibbs."

"Hank? He ain't here."

"You happen to know where I might reach him?"

The man in the leather apron shook his head. "He left about an hour ago. Didn't say where he was going."

Amy smiled. "Thank you, Mr.—"

"Homer." He raised his eyes and his voice simultaneously. "Be back anytime now. You want to leave word?"

"Just tell him Amy Haines stopped by. I'll phone him tomorrow."

"Okay."

They exchanged good nights but Amy's heart wasn't in it. As far as she was concerned this wasn't really a good night—not if she had to go up to Otto Remsbach's house alone. But at least there was a moment of welcome relief when she escaped from the newspaper office; the noise was bad enough but the vibrations had set her teeth on edge.

It was quieter here on the street. Hot and humid too. She hoped the rain would come quickly now, breaking up the clouds and easing the pressure. Perhaps Gibbs would also be coming soon, but she had no time left to wait for his arrival.

Reluctantly Amy climbed back into the car, switching on ignition and lights, then the air-conditioning. Where could Gibbs have gone this evening? Maybe he'd just stepped out for a bite to eat after getting the press-run started. She probably should have asked Homer if there were any fast-food places open nearby. And while she was at it, she could have asked whether Homer was his first name or his last. Not that it mattered one way or the other, any more than it mattered where Hank Gibbs might be at the moment.

Besides, what was she worrying about? Fatso Otto wasn't going to attack her, and she didn't have to worry about being stopped or mugged here on the street. This was Fairvale, remember? Good old Fairvale, U.S.A., where you don't have to worry about crime and violence.

So who killed Terry Dowson?

And why did Eric Dunstable pick this place to come

looking for demons? Because it was so quiet? Because it was so dark?

Ominously quiet and ominously dark, here on the side street slanting up the hillside to the house that stood alone within the semicircle of trees. Tall trees, motionless in the sweltering still of the clouded night.

Amy made a right turn which took her into the driveway, then braked quickly. There was something wrong about the imposing two-story house looming ahead, the red-brick house with the white wooden pillars flanking the entryway. If not wrong, at least odd or peculiar.

There were eight windows visible from the angle at which she was approaching—four upper and four lower—but not one of them was lighted from within. Gazing ahead, Amy noted the ornate iron grillwork supporting the two outside lamps on either side of the double-paneled front door. At least these should be lit in expectation of a guest's arrival, but both were dark.

Dark night, dark trees, dark house. Amy switched foot pressure from the brake to the gas pedal, gliding along the driveway past the entrance. Common sense told her there was probably nothing wrong here; Fatso Otto was just so bombed he'd forgotten to turn on the lights. In which case there wasn't much sense trying to talk to him.

But more important than mere common sense was the fact that she was frightened. It was the real reason she had no intention of going into this darkened house alone. What she was going to do was get the hell out of here, right now.

Or almost now. Because as she reached the other side of the driveway she noted its bifurcation; at her right was a stretch of pavement bordering the far side of the house and leading to a garage at the rear. Again she paused, long enough to observe its door was raised and Remsbach's big Caddy had been parked within.

But what about that other car, that beat-up old red Pontiac standing just outside the garage, facing inward? It certainly couldn't be Otto Remsbach's second car, not a junker like that. And if it belonged to another guest why wasn't it parked in the outer driveway? Unless, of course, the purpose was to conceal its presence from anyone passing by on the street.

In which case somebody had been careless and left the car radio on. The music was clearly audible, probably loud enough to be heard from the street. Of course it was possible that the driver had just entered the car, turned on the radio, and was preparing to leave. Highly possible; what Amy had failed to note at first glance was that the Pontiac's headlights were on, and it was their beams which had so clearly revealed the presence of Remsbach's car in the opened garage.

Amy waited for a moment, ready to reverse if the Pontiac started to back out of the side driveway. The car didn't move, but the lights stayed on and the music continued to sound. Had the driver left it like that and gone into the house?

Amy peered down the driveway, focusing on the shadowy blur vaguely visible beyond the Pontiac's rear window. The car was occupied; someone was sitting behind the wheel. And something was wrong.

Amy switched off her lights, turned the key in the ignition, then dropped it into her purse as she left the car and walked up the driveway along the far side of the house. The air was stiflingly still; the calm before the storm. It had to come soon.

As she moved up to the left side of the Pontiac the blare grew louder from behind the glass and the seated shape became more distinct.

Only the figure wasn't seated; it was slumped forward over the wheel. Was the driver drunk, ill, passed out from the heat?

Amy tapped the window glass, her nails counterpointing the car radio's raucous rhythm. There was no response, so she added a vocal accompaniment. "Hey— anything wrong? Open up—"

Still no answer. Something was definitely wrong,

and Amy reached down to grip the handle below the closed window. The door swung wide, releasing a blast of sound and a blur of moving shadow.

She must have been partially leaning against the door because when it opened she fell sideways, to land face upward on the pavement. In the shadow cast by the car her features were indistinct and Amy frowned for a moment before recognition came. Yesterday's meeting had been brief but she remembered the name.

It was Doris Huntley.

Doris Huntley, lying there with eyes wide open, head cradled by a swirl of blond hair. She wore a dark dress, its exact color indeterminate in the shadows, and a pendant necklace.

As Amy looked down the lightning came, flashing from above and behind and only for an instant, but that was long enough. Enough to reveal that Doris Huntley wore no necklace. The beads were blood, trickling from the crimson slash encircling her throat.

Amy's gasp was lost in the roar as thunder came. Then something touched her shoulder. Turning, she stared into the face of Sheriff Engstrom.

·14·

HIS name was Al.

There was no way of telling when or what he had for dinner but apparently it was still creating a problem because now, seated behind Engstrom's desk, he was chewing on a toothpick.

That in itself didn't bother Amy; this red-haired, freckle-faced, skinny specimen of what passed for humanity might be a sheriff's deputy but she wasn't intimidated by his uniform. It was the way he eyed her, as though he were looking at some exotic animal newly escaped from the zoo. But then they'd all stared at her like that; Engstrom, the deputy who had driven her here to the courthouse annex, and—most upsetting of all—Irene Grovesmith. What was she doing at the office here in the first place, at this hour?

Silly question. She was here because Engstrom had called and told her to be here. Somebody had to hold the fort while he stayed beside Doris Huntley's corpse, waiting for the paramedics to arrive. Maybe that's what life is really all about; just one long wait until the paramedics come.

Morbid thought. Amy frowned it away, but she didn't like what replaced it—the sudden, seering image of Doris Huntley's face in the lightning flash. Her face and her throat. Drops of blood dripping down her neck; drops of rain dripping down outside the office window. The storm had broken then and it would continue. Here at the courthouse annex and back there on the pavement where the rain ran red.

Thunder rumbled. So did Al's stomach. "Storm's pretty bad," he said, talking around his toothpick. "Good thing you didn't get caught in it."

But I did get caught. That's why I'm here. Amy almost spoke the words aloud but it wasn't necessary; the deputy grinned apologetically, toothpick teetering.

"My mistake, lady. I didn't mean it that way."

"That's okay."

She would have said more but her attention was distracted by the sound of voices and footsteps echoing from the outer office where Irene Grovesmith sat. Amy swiveled in her seat to glance through the open doorway. At the sight of Dr. Rawson and Sheriff Engstrom entering the room behind her, she started to rise from her chair.

As she did so, deputy Al involuntarily reached toward the weapon in his holster.

Amy caught the movement out of the corner of her eye and turned quickly. "That's not necessary," she murmured.

Al's hand retreated to the desktop. "Sorry," he said. "Sheriff's orders."

"Don't worry. I won't harm him."

And even if she'd had the intention she lacked the opportunity. Irene Grovesmith had risen and moved to close the door of the inner office, shutting off sight and sound from behind it.

Lightning flashed outside the window. Rain spattered, thunder boomed. A pity Al wasn't wearing a baseball cap and horn-rims; Amy could have asked him if this was good or bad for the crops. But Al wouldn't know. He was just a sheriff's deputy and besides he wasn't fat enough.

Amy wondered if she was flaking out. Why a thought like that at a time like this? Was it a sign of hysteria, or just common sense to opt for frivolity over morbidity?

Al wouldn't know the answer to that one either. As he toyed with his toothpick Amy found herself straining at the sound of muffled voices from beyond the door. Deep bass alternating with shrill soprano indicated Dr. Rawson and Irene Grovesmith were engaged in conversation; sharp staccato punctuated by short pauses suggested that Engstrom was talking on the phone. But even if she'd been spared the constant crashing of thunder Amy couldn't make out what was being said. Sound and fury, signifying nothing.

Nothing except sweaty palms, a tendency to grip her purse too tightly; telltale tension along the inner lengths of her legs as she leaned forward in the chair, unable to relax. If Al didn't get rid of that damn toothpick pretty soon, she'd do it for him. The odds were three to one she could yank it out of his mouth before he could yank that gun out of his holster. Be a mighty sad thing if she couldn't beat a hick deputy sheriff to the draw.

Funny? Maybe not, but it was the best she could do. And the best wasn't good enough, because whenever she blinked she found Doris Huntley's face staring at her from the darkness behind her closed eyes. Each time it was only for a moment, just long enough to reassure her the image hadn't faded. And *reassure* wasn't the proper term; why couldn't she think straight? What was Engstrom doing on the phone, how much longer would he keep stalling her like this?

More questions that Al wouldn't be able to answer. Amy stared up into the light, trying to keep her eyes open without blinking. The deputy removed the toothpick, tossing it into the wastebasket, and in gratitude she asked him a question he could answer.

"What did you have for dinner?"

"Pizza."

Might as well take refuge in her role as a reporter and ask him what kind. Fortunately it wasn't necessary, because the door behind her opened at last and Engstrom hurried in. Al rose to his feet hastily, but not in time to deflect the Sheriff's scowl.

"Move," Engstrom said. "Now!"

Standing, the deputy towered over his superior by a good six inches, but without his toothpick he seemed defenseless. By the time Engstrom replaced him behind the desk Al was gone, closing the door behind him.

"Didn't mean to keep you waiting so long," he said. "Couldn't get through to the chief of staff over at the hospital. Sounds like something's up there. I told Doc Rawson to keep calling."

For a moment Amy wondered why Engstrom's uniform was dry, then remembered that both he and Dr. Rawson had worn hats and ponchos when they entered the outer office. As he spoke Engstrom's voice was dry too.

"All right," he said. "Where is Eric Dunstable?"

"I don't know."

"When was the last time you saw him?"

"Late this afternoon, at the memorial service. He had an argument with Reverend Archer—"

"We know that." Engstrom leaned forward. "The other night you said you'd met Dunstable in Chicago."

"Yes." Amy nodded. "I gave you the names of the people who were with me when he came to my apartment that evening. Didn't you try to reach them?"

"Sure thing. Your alibi checks out and so does his." The Sheriff paused. "Of course they had no way of proving this was really the first time you and Dunstable met."

"Why should I lie to you about that?"

Engstrom shrugged. "I wouldn't know. Why should you have adjoining rooms?"

Amy tried to keep her voice under control. "I told you there's nothing between us."

"Except murder." Engstrom paused again. "You two in on this thing together?"

"Of course not. What reason could we have?"

"You're writing a book."

"True. But Eric Dunstable has nothing to do with it."

"Look, Miss Haines. Fairvale's only a flyspeck on the map but we get television here, same as in Kansas City or St. Louis. That's where the real money comes from, doesn't it? First you write a book, then you sell it to some producer for a movie or a miniseries on TV." Engstrom nodded. "Don't tell me you haven't thought about that possibility."

Amy countered his nod, shaking her head quickly. "Possibility, yes. But it's not very likely to happen. There are hundreds of books written about mysterious killers that never sell to television or films. There generally has to be some unusual angle—"

"Like demonic possession?" Engstrom hunched forward. "Dunstable's theories might be just the extra touch you've been looking for."

"That's ridiculous!"

"Maybe." The Sheriff's mustache twitched with the suggestion of a smile. "I'm not accusing you two of collusion, mind you, just asking. There's a lot of things we need to find out about and we will, one way or the other." As he spoke, the hint of a smile vanished. "For starters, what were you doing up at Remsbach's place?"

"You've already answered that yourself. I'm writing a book. My only reason for visiting him was to get information." Amy paused. "But I suppose you already know. The desk clerk at the hotel must have been eavesdropping on my calls again. He phones and tells you I'm going to visit Mr. Remsbach at his home and you come charging after me, is that it?"

Engstrom shrugged. "More or less. Stopped by at Peachey's on the way."

"Peachey's?"

"It's a bar. Had to break up a little disturbance." The Sheriff gave her a pointed look. "Couple of out-of-towners."

"If you'd come directly maybe this thing wouldn't have happened," Amy said. "At least you saw me arrive—"

"Correction. We saw you opening the car door. That's when we switched off our lights so we could slide in without you noticing."

"I hope you noticed I didn't have a weapon."

The Sheriff nodded.

Amy hesitated for a moment, waiting for him to speak. But he said nothing, and it was she who broke the silence. "Do you know what the weapon was?"

"Pretty sure of it. Six-inch butcher knife, notched handle grip, bit of a curve in the blade." His voice was flat, his stare sharp. "Sound familiar?"

"Why should it?"

"Because you could have had it with you when you came."

"To kill Doris Huntley?" Amy's voice rose above distant thunder. "I didn't even know she was there."

Engstrom was sitting up straight now. "Of course not. Must have come as a surprise for both of you—you see her getting in her car, she sees you getting out of yours. You walk over to her, maybe she opens the door to talk. Meanwhile you get the knife out of that big purse of yours and—"

"Why?"

"To get rid of the only witness who could testify seeing you there. After you killed her you went inside. Maybe five, ten minutes later, you came out and checked again to make sure she was dead. That's when we showed up."

"Don't play guessing games. I didn't kill that woman! I never went inside, I didn't carry any weapon."

"Well, somebody did."

The sound of thunder was scarcely more than an echo now, and Amy spoke before it subsided. "You found the knife?"

"That's right."

"Where? Was it in the house?"

"It was in Otto Remsbach's chest. Whoever left it there stabbed him thirteen times."

·15·

THERE was no more thunder. The rain had stopped, the storm was over, and the air had cleared.

But that was outside; here in the Sheriff's office, tension remained. Tension in the deep-set lines bordering Irene Grovesmith's lips as she monitored the tape. Tension in Engstrom's voice as he asked the questions that once again took Amy through the events of the evening. Tension in her replies, tension that came in sudden succession like the aftershocks following an earthquake.

For some reason, hearing about Remsbach's murder was even more disturbing than the actual sight of Doris Huntley's body. But both victims were equally dead.

Double Event.

Where did that come from? It took Amy a moment before she remembered the source. The term had originated over a hundred years ago when two victims were killed on the same night by Jack the Ripper.

Had his weapon been a butcher knife? Nobody knew. And today, more than a century later, his identity remained unknown.

There had been another Double Event tonight, but at least they'd found the weapon. Would they ever find the killer?

Engstrom had just concluded his interrogation when another thought occurred to her, and it was then that she voiced the question.

"May I ask you something, Sheriff?"

Engstrom's nod both dismissed Irene Grovesmith with her recorder and also signaled Amy to continue. "Go ahead. It's your turn."

"What makes you so sure both murders were committed by the same person? Couldn't there have been two instead of one?"

"How do you figure?"

"Suppose Doris Huntley killed Remsbach with that knife. And when she left, somebody was waiting for her outside."

"Somebody." Engstrom shook his head. "You'll have to do better than that."

"There should be prints on the knife."

"I doubt it." The Sheriff stretched the skin below his left cheekbone between thumb and forefinger. "I've got a feeling this isn't Amateur Night."

"But that doesn't rule out the possibility that two people were involved in the murders."

"You and Dunstable, perhaps?"

"I've already told you I haven't seen him this evening. And you know I came to Remsbach's house alone."

"He could have walked. Or driven out in another car."

"I don't think he even knows how to drive," Amy said. "And he doesn't have a car here. But someone else could have come and gone before I arrived. There could be tire marks—"

"Not after this storm. Rain'd wash 'em out." Engstrom pushed his chair back. "Which reminds me. I had your car driven over here. It's in the lot."

"Where are my keys?"

"I'll tell Reno to give them to you." Engstrom rose.

"Thanks."

Amy had about forty-five seconds between the Sheriff's departure and the moment when the office door opened again to admit Dick Reno. She used the interval to open her purse and inspect herself in the compact mirror, prompted by curiosity rather than vanity. After tonight's experience it came as a surprise that there seemed to be so little change. True, her eyes did look tired but some fresh liner would take care of that.

Amy smiled at her image in the mirror. Maybe curiosity was just another synonym for vanity after all. As the door opened behind her, she closed the compact, dropped it back into her bag and zippered it before Dick Reno reached her side.

He must have left his poncho in the outer office, for his uniform showed no indication of storm damage. It was only when she glanced down that she noted his boots were caked with mud at the heels and streaked along the ankles.

Then something jangled and she looked up; he was holding out her car keys. "How do you feel?"

"Much better, now that I've got my car back." Amy

zipped her purse open again to deposit the keys. "I take it this means your boss trusts me not to sneak out of town tonight."

"Are you really okay?" Reno said. "They told me what happened. It must have been an awful shock."

"I'm all right now." Amy glanced down again at the deputy's boots. "But where were you when all this happened?"

"Sheriff told me to go find Eric Dunstable."

"Where did you look for him—in a swamp?"

"No, but that's an idea. There *is* a swamp, not too far away."

"Away from what?"

"The Bates place." Dick Reno nodded. "Engstrom thought Dunstable might have headed out there."

"I take it you didn't run into him."

Reno nodded again. "I didn't run into anything, except rain and mud. Way I figure it, you had more chance of seeing him than I did."

Amy rose. "You and Engstrom do a lot of figuring, don't you? I guess theorizing comes easier than finding out the facts. But just for the record, let me tell you just what I told him. I didn't see Eric Dunstable tonight, I have no idea where he went, and the two of us didn't join forces to commit murder."

"I never said that." Reno spoke quickly. "And I wouldn't be handing you back your car keys if the Sheriff really thought you were a suspect."

"Then why was he pressuring me?"

"When something like this happens, there isn't much choice. He needs all the information he can get, and fast. But for what it's worth you're pretty much in the clear. Sheriff knows we had dinner together. The clerk up at the hotel filled him in about how you talked to Steiner and Remsbach and tried to call Dunstable. We know when you left the hotel and if your story about seeing Homer at the newspaper office checks out, there's no way you could've had enough time left to kill either

one." Reno smiled. "Let alone put Mother in Otto Remsbach's bed."

"What?"

"They found that wax figure lying next to his body.
You didn't know?"

Amy didn't answer. She strode to the door, yanked
it open. The outer office echoed a babble of voices and
the buzzing of unanswered phones. The deputy named
Al, Irene Grovesmith, and Sheriff Engstrom were taking
calls at three separate desks, but the instruments on
three other desks continued their clamor.

Amy moved up beside Engstrom without slackening
her stride. As she halted he concluded his conversation,
forefinger poised to plunge down and establish connection with another call. "Damned phones been ringing off
the hook," he muttered. "Rock Center, Montrose, *Kansas
City Star*, you name it. Beats me how in hell the word
always gets around so fast."

"Me too." Amy's words rose through the confusion
loud and clear. "Particularly when you take such pains
to withhold information."

Engstrom's finger faltered. "Come again?"

There was no hint of faltering in Amy's voice. "Why
didn't you say anything to me about finding the wax
dummy of Mrs. Bates in Remsbach's bed?"

"Who told you that?" The Sheriff scowled. "I gave
everybody strict orders—"

"To withhold evidence?"

"I have my reasons. You've got no right to question
them."

"And you've got no right to give me the runaround."
Amy's voice dropped to its normal level. "Don't worry,
I'm not doing a story for the newspaper." She paused,
glancing around. "Speaking of which, where's Hank
Gibbs? You'd think he'd be interested in getting hold of
this kind of news."

"That's right." Engstrom frowned. "Unless he *is* the
news."

·16·

ENGSTROM'S phones may have kept ringing all night, but when Amy drove back to the hotel there were no messages of any calls awaiting her there. The male desk clerk had finished his shift—and, presumably, his comic book—but Amy had no doubt that his female replacement would continue monitoring her line.

Nonetheless, the first thing she did after kicking off her shoes when she reached the room was to try Eric Dunstable's number. Again there was no response.

Where could he possibly have disappeared to, and why? The questions rose and once more she pushed them aside, or tried to. Hard to push when you're so tired, when so much has happened and there's so much to think about.

Only she wasn't going to think about anything more tonight. Tomorrow would be time enough, after she got some rest. It was already close to midnight, and while she had to remove her makeup, the shower could be put off until morning.

Shower put off and nightgown put on, Amy was ready for sleep. But sleep was not ready for her.

At least she was grateful for one thing; closing her eyes no longer evoked a vision of Doris Huntley's face. The problem now was not what she'd seen but what she hadn't seen.

Otto Remsbach, horizontal. The butcher knife in his chest, vertical. Thirteen stab wounds. Bloody bed. Bled like a stuffed pig. And Mother—was she bloody too?

Amy had never seen Mother and she didn't want to, but the only way she could avoid it now was to keep her eyes open. Keep her eyes open and keep her mind off what had happened up there at Remsbach's house tonight. Maybe Sheriff Engstrom was right after all; it was none of her business.

Business. Now there was something she could think about. Her business was to write the book and—to be brutally honest, totally honest—what had happened tonight meant that business was going to be very good.

There'd be no more talk about leaving town tomorrow, or the next day, not after what had just occurred. Of course it was horrifying but it would be hypocritical of her not to admit that it was also exciting. Much of the horror lay in what she imagined; her excitement was rooted in reality.

All of those daydreams about a career were going to come true, and there was no point having any guilt feelings about it. Once again Amy reminded herself she hadn't been responsible for what happened, couldn't have anticipated or prevented it, and certainly couldn't change matters now.

Perhaps Dr. Steiner might help put things into their proper perspective tomorrow. Now it was more important than ever that she interview him; his was the voice of reason. By the same token it would be imperative to have a talk with Eric Dunstable. His was the voice of unreason, but reason alone couldn't account for the bizarre turn of events tonight.

Could Dunstable himself have been involved? And what about Hank Gibbs? Did the Sheriff really suspect him, and for causes as yet unrevealed? Or was it just due to the fact that his whereabouts were unknown? Absence makes the heart grow fonder—or, in this instance, beat faster. Hank Gibbs, a somewhat cynical knight in somewhat battered armor, a serial killer? Eric Dunstable seemed creepy but harmless; were his creepy ideas harmless too? And when you got right down to it, the

Bates property wasn't the only place where Dick Reno could have gotten mud on his boots. In any case, wouldn't the rain have washed it off? The rain could wash away bloodstains just as easily.

And there she was, coming full circle again to what was the Sheriff's business, not hers. If Dick Reno had blood on his boots, it was his problem. That didn't make her Lady Macbeth; there was no blood on her hands.

No blood on her hands, and a nice clean makeup job when she went on those talk shows. And she would go, the book would go, all the dreams would come true. The good dreams, anyway. Bad dreams were what she didn't want; dreams about Doris Huntley and her necklace, Otto Remsbach and his heart surgery. Nothing to joke about, but sometimes a laugh smothers the scream.

No, this was business, serious business. And she would do a serious, straightforward job when she started the book. In light—or dark—of recent events, it might be well to have another meeting with the publishers up-front. This was going to be a much bigger project than either she or they had anticipated; big enough and time-consuming enough to justify renegotiation.

Blood money? Again Amy reminded herself that she wasn't accountable for the events that had taken place here both before and after her arrival. Nor did she intend to capitalize on them. In which case why was she thinking about her book in the language of a bookkeeper? What were words like "accountable" and "capitalize" doing in the vocabulary of someone who considered herself a serious writer? These weren't the right terms.

Terms. She really owed it to herself to renegotiate the terms of her contract. But what she really owed to herself most of all was honesty. If that meant admitting she was as mercenary as anyone else, so be it. Nobody ever said that Shakespeare gave his work away for free.

Which brought her right back to Lady Macbeth again, and to hell with it. Good night and God bless you, one and all.

It wasn't quite that simple, but in the end Amy did manage to drift off into sleep that was mercifully deep and dreamless.

Bright sunlight heralded the morning, and so did the phone at her bedside. Sudden light blurred her vision; sudden sound had a similar effect on what she heard after raising the receiver. Somebody from A.P. was calling from downstairs and would like to do an interview, how soon would it be convenient for him to come up or would she prefer to meet in the lobby? Amy's instinct was to tell him to drop dead, her watch told her it was eight o'clock, and she told her caller he could expect her down at eight-thirty.

As she stepped into the shower the phone rang again. Towel-wrapped, she responded. This time it was someone from a St. Louis paper but the conversation was the same.

Before she could do more than open a bureau drawer there was another call. The Montrose radio newscaster wanted to do a tape.

It wasn't until then that she realized her mistake. Interviews might be good publicity, but in the long run it meant she'd be giving away material that should be saved for her own use in the book.

After she hung up she phoned the desk and told the clerk to hold all calls. He promised to take messages instead.

All of which got Amy into a bra and panties and she was just completing the makeup job on her freshly scrubbed face when the desk clerk broke his promise.

"No, he didn't," Hank Gibbs told her. "I had to blackmail him to get this call through. But I just wanted to warn you the enemy has landed in full force, so prepare for a hit."

"Where were you last night?" Amy said.

"Tell you when I see you."

"But those people in the lobby—"

"Will come racing up to your room if you don't

show up when you promised." Gibbs paused. "Or do you want to get out of this?"

"You're a mind-reader! But how—?"

"Help is on the way."

"Wait—"

He hung up. And by the time Amy finished wriggling and started zipping he was rapping at the door.

Shoeless, she admitted him. "My hair's a mess," she murmured. "I can't go down there looking like this."

"You aren't going down there at all." Gibbs nodded. "Far as I'm concerned your hair looks great the way it is, but if you want to fiddle around with it, bring a comb and a mirror. My car's over on Second Street."

"Think we could get there alive?"

"Positive. Unless somebody's captured the service elevator."

But that hadn't happened, and they landed safely in the hall just off the kitchen, then left by way of the delivery door at the rear of the hotel. The alley that bordered it was empty and so was the side street beyond. Turning right at the corner, Hank Gibbs led her to his car.

Her compact mirror confirmed he'd told her the truth; a good thing she remembered to bring a shower cap, because her hair hadn't gotten wet and all it needed was a quick comb-through. By the time she finished, the car was picking up speed.

"Where are we going?"

Gibbs grinned. "You ever hear a definition of the word 'impossible'?"

"Tell me."

"'Impossible' means finding a Chinese restaurant that's open for breakfast."

"If you're saying what I think you are, we had dinner there last night."

Gibbs glanced at her quickly. "We?"

"Dick Reno and I."

"Then you're in for a surprise. They serve the best

country-style ham and eggs breakfast this side of Spring-field."

Now they were leaving the town behind them. Gibbs glanced at her as she settled back in the seat.

"Feeling better?"

"Much. Thanks for rescuing me. I wasn't really awake when I agreed to all those interviews. I could have spent half the day giving free handouts."

"Don't feel guilty. The same thing happens to me, and that's why I wanted to get away. Minute a big story breaks in a small town, every stringer in the state shows up, then it's radio and the television crews. They've got to deal with the local lawmen but that means waiting for a handout or a personally delivered 'no comment.' So the first thing they do is track down the editor of the local paper and try to get a story out of him."

Amy nodded. "Was it as bad as this when Norman Bates escaped and the Loomises were killed?"

"Bad enough. Thing is, after it blew over, nobody expected something like that would ever happen again. But now—"

He broke off in midsentence as they approached their destination and there was no further conversation during parking or entering the restaurant.

At the moment there were only a few other customers. On the way to their table Amy noted Gibbs hadn't exaggerated; the ham and eggs looked good and she enjoyed an enticing preview of hot rolls, freshly squeezed orange juice, real marmalade in glass jars rather than synthetic glop in tiny plastic containers.

By the time they were seated and placed their orders from a menu entirely devoid of oriental cuisine, Amy was well pleased with Gibbs' surprise.

"Was dinner good here last night?" he said.

"Very."

"I'm not just talking about the food. Did you get anything worthwhile out of Reno, anything you could use?"

"I didn't accept his invitation in order to use him."

"So the lady says." Gibbs grinned. "But the lady also happens to be a writer, and writers use everyone and everything. It takes one to know one."

Amy found herself smiling. "All right, you win."

"Did you?"

She shook her head. "Not really. That is, I didn't learn anything new. But he made it very clear how people around here feel about being saddled with guilt by association. They don't like what Norman Bates did, they don't like the idea of living in his shadow."

"Can you blame them?" Gibbs paused as their juice and coffee arrived. Amy discovered the cream was genuine too; this was a day for surprises.

She put some real sugar into her real coffee and glanced up. "I stopped by your office last night," she said. "Where were you?"

"Didn't Engstrom say?"

"No. He was looking for you too."

"I forgot. When I got back and heard the news I went over there, but by that time you'd already left." Gibbs smiled. "Guess I owe the Sheriff an apology. He couldn't have told you before I told him." The smile disappeared. "Matter of fact, I'm not so sure I ought to tell you now. Don't want to spoil your breakfast."

"Whatever it is, I'm going to find out anyway sooner or later," Amy said.

"True. But it's not the kind of surprise I had in mind when I brought you here."

"Are you going to tell me or aren't you?"

"All right. Last night I was over at Baldwin Memorial Hospital."

"I remember the name." Amy nodded. "That's where Dr. Claiborne is."

"Was." Gibbs' voice was flat. "He died last night."

"What happened?"

"Another heart attack—a big one."

"Does Steiner know?"

"I assume so, by now. The first call came to me at the office; that's why I went out there. They wouldn't give me much by way of details, but I know there'll be an autopsy within a day or two. Not that anyone is going to pay any attention, considering what's been going on over here."

Amy took a sip of coffee but she couldn't taste it. Her senses were playing her false, senses and emotions. In this instance surprise should register as shock, but it didn't. And compassion was oddly interlaced with irritation; why couldn't she have had a chance to interview Claiborne before he died?

She stared at Gibbs across the table. "So that's where you were."

"If you don't believe me, ask your friend Engstrom."

Amy shook her head. "He's not my friend."

"Nor mine." Gibbs was frowning. "Told me to get off his back and not mess up his investigation. When he got hold of me at his office he couldn't wait to call Baldwin Memorial and check out my alibi."

"He suspected you?"

"Why not? He suspected you too. That's the name of the game."

"Who do you suspect?"

Gibbs frowned. "Have to think about that. Might help if you told me what happened to you after you left Dick Reno last night."

Amy obliged, but not until after the rest of their breakfast order arrived and they started to eat. Her taste buds were beginning to function again and for this she was grateful.

As for Gibbs, he seemed grateful with her information. When she concluded, he began. "What do you think really happened?"

"I'd know more if I could come up with some possible motives."

"Try insanity."

"That's one of the things I intend to go into with Dr.

Steiner," Amy said. "I'd like to get a professional opinion about the personality profile of someone capable of breaking into the Bates property, stealing that dummy, and killing a harmless little girl."

"Have you come up with any candidates on your own?"

Amy hesitated. "Norman would do it. Or someone who thinks like Norman."

"Claiborne fits that description. But he's dead now, and at the time Terry Dowson was murdered he was confined." Gibbs speared a slice of ham with his fork and didn't continue speaking until he'd stopped chewing. "Wild guess," he said.

"Who?"

"Eric Dunstable. I get the distinct impression that his elevator doesn't stop at every floor."

Amy shook her head. "Not unless he has an identical twin. You're forgetting he was with me in Chicago on the night Terry was killed."

"If you told the truth." He grinned quickly to counter her frown. "Only kidding. I know Engstrom checked up on your alibi, same as he did mine." Gibbs nodded. "Okay, Dunstable's off the hook as far as Terry Dowson is concerned. But where was he last night?"

"I don't know," Amy said. "I couldn't reach him in his room then or this morning. It's possible he might have run off without checking out."

"That's really Engstrom's problem. You can bet he'll be looking for him or some other fanatic."

"Fanatic?"

"I suggest you try to feel out Steiner on the subject when you see him. There've been some rumors floating around that a local resident is getting outpatient treatment from him."

"At State Hospital?"

Gibbs shrugged. "Not that many shrinks available in this neck of the woods. Though God knows we could use a few."

"Any idea who this local resident might be?"

"I talked to Steiner a while back and he refused to give names. But he didn't deny he'd been seeing someone. If I was the Sheriff I'd start looking for a weirdo."

"Or someone who wants people to *think* it was a weirdo."

"Why?"

"To cover-up their real motive, of course." Amy took a final sip of her coffee. "That might go along with your hunch about a fanatic being responsible. Someone with far-out ideas but rational enough to make those murders look like the work of a psychotic." Amy put her cup down. "But that doesn't mean fanaticism is the only possible motive. We can't rule out things like envy, revenge, jealousy—" She hesitated, frowning. "Did Doris Huntley have a boyfriend?"

Now it was Gibbs who frowned. "Not for publication."

"But you know who it is?"

Gibbs rose. "Let's go. Maybe we could get a chance to talk to him before Engstrom does."

·17·

THE office door was locked, but Gibbs reached down and rattled the doorknob.

"I know he's in there. His car's parked out back."

Amy hesitated. "Under the circumstances, maybe we shouldn't disturb him—"

But they already had. The door opened abruptly and a disturbed Charlie Pitkin peered up at them, standing in shadow and blinking at the light from the hallway. As recognition came he relaxed.

"Hank?"

Gibbs nodded toward Amy. "You remember Miss Haines, don't you?"

"Of course." Pitkin stepped back. "Come in." Once they entered he closed the door behind them and the shadows deepened. "My apologies," he said. "I'm keeping the blinds drawn. Officially we're closed for the day; I told my girl not to come in and I'm not taking any calls."

As if to prove his assertion the phone on the desk in the outer office began to flash and ring. Ignoring it, he led them through the reception area and into the even darker depths of his private quarters beyond. Here a lamp cast a fan-shaped wedge of light over the desk. Atop it another phone flashed, then ceased to signal.

Pitkin took his place behind the desk and gestured them forward. "Please sit down." He glanced at Amy. "Sorry about lights. I'd rather not let the media people know where I am right now." The phone flickered again but he ignored it.

Amy and Gibbs settled into chairs facing the attorney. He stared at them expectantly for a moment and it was Gibbs who broke the silence.

"Seen Engstrom yet?"

"He just left."

"Have there been any new developments?"

"Why don't you ask him yourself?" Pitkin shook his head in sharp-nosed profile, then turned toward Amy as the phone's light signal faded. "Please excuse me, Miss Haines. I don't mean to be rude. It's just that this has all been quite a shock—"

"I understand."

"But Hank doesn't." Again the attorney directed his attention to Gibbs. "You know better than to think Engstrom would clue me in on what's going on. As far as he's concerned, I'm still a possible suspect."

Gibbs nodded. "But not enough of a one to be placed under arrest."

"I did give him an alibi, in case you're interested." Once more the desk phone came alive with light and once more Pitkin ignored it. "I assume that's what you really came to find out."

Amy stirred uncomfortably. "It was thoughtless of us to bother you at a time like this. We'd better go—"

"Please." Pitkin gestured quickly. "I gave you an invitation the other night at the Club."

"But that was before all this happened. If you'd rather not talk about it—"

"What I told Engstrom is now a matter of public record. No reason why you shouldn't know. My daughter and I were out at the lake last night. We have a cottage there. First we heard about what went on was around seven this morning when we caught a news bulletin. Needless to say, it hit me pretty hard at first. Otto's been my friend as well as my client for so many years. He had so much ambition, so many plans. All gone now, and Doris too—"

The attorney's voice broke off simultaneously with the flicker of the phone, then resumed. "Emily knew how upset I was. She didn't want me to come in, but the Sheriff meant to see me and I thought it would be easier on her if I spoke to him alone."

Gibbs leaned forward. "But won't Engstrom be seeing her too, just to confirm your alibi?"

"I suppose so. But he won't lean on Emily the way he leaned on me. At least that's what I'm hoping, but with the kind of pressure he's under right now, anything is possible."

"There's just one other thing I'd like to know," Amy said. "Do you have any idea who might be responsible for what happened last night?"

"None. And as I told you, the Sheriff didn't volunteer to fill me in."

"I can do that much," Gibbs said. "During the time before Miss Haines met me at the hotel I heard at least six versions of various rumors already floating around. What most of them boil down to is the usual mysterious stranger who was seen by somebody—no one quite knows who— coming into town or leaving town during the storm. There's no explanation why he was wandering around on foot without an umbrella, but everyone is absolutely convinced that he is definitely an escaped lunatic, a gay with terminal AIDS—or a child molester who killed Terry Dowson and has now graduated to bigger things."

Pitkin spoke slowly. "That's nothing to joke about."

"I'm serious. And so are they, which is what really bothers me. If this case isn't solved quickly, we're due for a witch-hunt."

"I'm afraid you're right, but there doesn't seem much that we can do about it." Pitkin glanced at Amy. "I only hope that when you write your book it won't be necessary to compare Fairvale with Salem, Massachusetts in 1692."

"That's not my intention," Amy said. She turned, nodding at Gibbs. "I think we should go now." As she rose, the phone's flashings flared across her face. "It was kind of you to see us, Mr. Pitkin. You've been very patient."

The attorney gestured, rising. "No need for that. Let's just hope we meet again soon under more pleasant circumstances." He nodded at Gibbs. "Let me show you out."

"I expect to be in and out of the office all day, after Homer finishes up on the route," Gibbs said. "If you want me, get in touch."

"Thanks."

Amy didn't speak until they reached the car. "What do you think?" she said.

"I'm not sure. Want some coffee?"

"Somebody's bound to spot me."

"There's a hot plate and some instant at the office," Hank Gibbs said.

"I'll settle for that." As Gibbs started the car she spoke again. "Will you do me a favor?"

"Name it."

"I noticed there's a drugstore across the street from the courthouse. Would you get me a package of cigarettes?"

"Sure. What brand?"

"Anything mentholated."

"That's funny. I didn't know you smoked."

Amy shrugged. "I haven't, not since I finished my book. But now that I'm starting another—"

"Sounds to me as if you're getting uptight," Gibbs murmured.

"What about you?"

"A little." He shrugged. "Guess it comes from writing too many obituaries."

They parked in the alley, motor running, while Gibbs ran his errand at the pharmacy. A gap between the building and the structure on its left gave Amy a view of the courthouse and annex across the street. In the parking lot a TV remote crew was doing a shoot with a couple of deputies. Because of the distance and the clustering crowd Amy could not identify them. No matter; the important thing was that she had escaped the risk of sound-bites. It would be bad enough when the time came to get in front of the cameras and plug her book. But right now it made no sense going on television just to plug somebody else's murder.

Now where had *that* come from? She was beginning to sound like Hank Gibbs. But she was thankful for his presence and grateful for his return with a package of Salem Ultralights 100s.

Salem, as in Salem, Massachusetts, 1692. *Salem, as in witch-hunts.* No wonder she was uptight. And where was Eric Dunstable?

Reaching into her purse she pulled out the lighter. Flame rose with a flick; the fluid hadn't evaporated. And neither had her need to smoke, in spite of the resolution made so many months ago. The fact that she'd continued to carry the lighter with her almost hinted at precognition. *And where was Eric Dunstable?*

Gibbs was frowning at her. "Trouble?"

"No." Amy dropped the cigarettes into her purse. "Just resisting temptation." Which was a lie, of course; she'd decided not to risk breaking a fingernail opening the package while the car was in motion. Besides, the first cigarette would taste better with a cup of coffee, no cream, regular sugar please.

But the cubicle at the rear of the print shop was not a restaurant, and while the coffee was instant as promised, it took a good ten minutes for the water to boil on the hot plate. They sat talking as they waited.

"Sorry this place is such a mess." Gibbs' gesture encircled the small room's clutter. "Seems as if we're spending most of our time sneaking in and out of back rooms by the back way."

"I'm not complaining," Amy said. "But now that we're here let's get back to the question. What do you think?"

"About Charlie Pitkin? Frankly, I don't know. He could be hiding something."

"Like law books, perhaps?" Amy nodded. "I noticed he didn't have any in his office."

"Tell you a little secret. A good lawyer doesn't need them."

"Not even for trials?"

"Especially not for trials." Gibbs leaned back his hands steepling. "Take homicide, for instance. Chances are an average suspect is male, aged somewhere between eighteen and thirty-five. When arrested he's in dirty jeans, a tank top, bare feet, has a scraggly beard, maybe a couple of porno tattoos on his arms above needle marks.

"Then he gets himself an attorney. And when the trial begins he'll be wearing a white shirt, a plain tie with a small knot, conservative three-pieced suit, black oxfords,

and a close shave. I don't even have to mention blow-dry."
The sides of the steeple fell away to form a funnel.

"A good trial lawyer today is just a combination
hairstylist, fashion advisor, and drama coach." Gibbs
paused, smiling. "Besides, Pitkin does have a law library
in his other office, up at the state capitol."

Amy listened, trying to conceal her impatience,
thinking *Everyone had a weakness and his is self-appre-
ciation. My weakness is the patience I have for listening.*

As if sensing her thought, Hank Gibbs halted
abruptly. "Sorry, I got carried away." He glanced at the
pot on the burner of the hot plate, confirming that its
contents had not yet begun to bubble. "Anything else
strike you about Pitkin or the office?"

"Pictures." Now it was Amy's turn to glance at the
water, but a watched pot never boils. "Two photographs
on his desk, both in silver frames. And maybe you didn't
notice because it was so dark, but there's a big one hanging in the corner on the wall opposite the window."

"The little girl?"

"His little girl. I saw his daughter the other night
and her features haven't changed all that much. The
photos on the desk are more recent."

"He's very fond of her."

"Obviously." Amy paused. "I didn't notice any pictures of his late wife. What was she like?"

"I wouldn't know. She died when Emily was still in
grammar school. Cancer. It was Charlie who did most of
the parenting."

"How old is Emily?"

"I'd say twenty-three or -four. She graduated from
college three years ago."

"Let me guess the rest. No boyfriends, no live-ins.
She came straight back home to take care of Daddy."

Gibbs leaned forward. "Slow down, I think you're
driving too fast. And on the wrong road."

"I'm not suggesting any actual physical relationship.

But there does seem to be a strong bonding between them."

"Drive a little further. I'm not sure where you're heading."

"To an obvious conclusion. A daughter who really loves her daddy might be willing to provide him with an alibi."

Gibbs shook his head. "Let's try a detour for a moment. What makes you assume that Charlie Pitkin would risk his professional and political career by committing murders that would point to him as the principal suspect? It's not just that he was Remsbach's friend and attorney; the two of them had some kind of joint setup in this Bates Motel deal. Now, with his partner dead, Pitkin may end up with everything. But he wouldn't pull such a dumb trick and hope to get away with it. Charlie's too sharp for that."

"Is he?" Amy's sidelong glance shifted to the pot; the water was beginning to simmer. "Remsbach kept telling me about all the clever promotion ideas Pitkin had come up with for the tourist trade. But the man we saw—"

"—had just been cross-examined by the Sheriff as a principal homicide suspect," Gibbs interjected. "He'd probably gone through a sleepless night and faced the prospect of hiding out in his office all day. If he's innocent, you can imagine what a shock it was, losing the two of them at once—his partner and his girlfriend."

Amy frowned. "Did his daughter know about his relationship with Doris Huntley?"

"I'm not sure. What difference would it make?"

"So far there's no evidence to show that these murders couldn't have been committed by a woman."

"Spoken like a true feminist." Gibbs looked up. "I think our water's boiling."

Amy rose. "Let me do the honors."

"Here's my mug. You can use Homer's, over there on the shelf—it's clean. Sugar's in that little bowl behind the coffee jar. Got the ashtray over the top to keep the flies out.

You need a spoon, there's a couple in the drawer. And I don't think Pitkin's daughter is the guilty party."

"But you don't know." Amy played instant housewife with the instant coffee.

"I can find out." Gibbs took a sip, grimaced, then set the mug down. "Watch out, it's hot." He stood up and started toward the doorway leading to the print shop and the front office beyond. "Only be a minute," he said. "Might as well get this thing settled while the coffee cools."

Following his previous directions, Amy located the sugar and a spoon. As she stirred the contents of her cup she could hear the echo of Hank Gibbs' voice from the room beyond, but the sounds were too faint for precise word identification.

Explanation, and his cooling coffee, had to wait until Gibbs returned.

"Just talked to Leona Hubbard. She and her husband are Pitkin's neighbors out at the lake. Told me she called Emily last night to ask about some church social this coming weekend. Neither Emily nor her father answered the phone."

Amy stopped stirring her coffee and met Gibbs' gaze. "And—?"

"Mrs. Hubbard tried again about half an hour later, but by then the phone was out of order; I guess the storm was really heavy there. She wanted her husband to take a hike over to the house and see if anyone was home, but he said forget it. Old Lloyd's arthritis acts up on him in bad weather and he wasn't about to go any farther than the kitchen window. Even with the rain coming down he was able to point out that the yard light was on over at Pitkin's place and both cars were in the carport."

"So?"

"Mrs. Hubbard saw Emily around eight this morning, right after her father left to come into town. She knew what had happened, of course, because the phone was working again and Engstrom had just called.

"Emily told Mrs. Hubbard that she and her father had been home together since six-thirty last night."

"Are you buying that?"

"Apparently Sheriff Engstrom is. According to Leona Hubbard he called to ask her the same questions over an hour ago." Gibbs picked up his coffee cup and took a tenative swallow. "Cooler." Now, a gulp. "Unless somebody's lying, it doesn't look as though Doris Huntley was killed by a jealous daughter."

"I still think jealousy could be the motive," Amy murmured. "But perhaps we ought to forget Doris and concentrate on Remsbach. You happen to know if he's been involved with any other women?"

Gibbs slammed his coffee mug down onto the table. "Holy Christ—why didn't I think of that?"

"Who is she?"

"Sandy Oliver."

"That's a new name to me."

"An old one to her. Took it back after the divorce." Gibbs nodded. "She was married to Dick Reno."

·18·

THIS time Amy went into the print shop with Gibbs, perching on a stool beside the counter as he made his call. After dialing there was a lengthy period of silence, but Gibbs continued to grip the receiver.

"Same old story." He sounded annoyed. "Nobody

wants to answer the phone. It's a wonder they ever make any appointments."

"They?" Amy said. "I thought you were calling Sandy Oliver."

"I am," Gibbs told her. "She's got a job doing nails over at the beauty parlor." His annoyance dissolved into a grin. "You can imagine what it must be like over there this morning. Maybe they can't even hear the phone with all that cackling going on."

But somebody did, because Gibbs turned away from Amy and directed his next remarks into the mouthpiece. "Hi, Ada. Hank Gibbs here. Can I have a fast word with Sandy? Only take a minute—"

He broke off, his grin giving way to an annoyed expression once again. "Okay. It wasn't all that important." Gibbs paused. "No, they haven't found the murderer yet." Another pause. "I haven't got the faintest idea. Unless you did it."

After a final farewell he replaced the receiver and turned. "Sandy's not there today. Called in sick."

"What does it mean?"

"She's the only one who can answer that." Gibbs glanced at his watch. "There's still time to drive out to her place if you like."

"Hadn't you better call first?"

"I don't think so. Way I figure it, staying home from the beauty shop, particularly on a day like this, she doesn't want to talk."

"If she won't talk with people she knows she certainly isn't anxious to see a newspaper editor and a total stranger."

"Which is why I don't intend to give her any warning."

"You sound as though you really think she could be a suspect."

Gibbs' gesture was equivocal. "So far we can't accuse her of the actual murders. But if there's anything to the jealousy angle you brought up, she might still be involved."

Amy frowned. "There's always a chance she really could be ill. And even if she isn't, she probably won't talk to me."

"Want to bet? Anyone working at that beauty parlor knows more about what's going on in town than I do. You've probably been a chief topic of conversation right up until what happened last night. Don't worry, she'll see you, if only out of curiosity."

Gibbs lost no time leading her back to the rear exit, and it was Amy who remembered to disconnect the hot plate before they left. As they walked out to the car she shook her head. "If you ask me, you're the one with the curiosity."

"Maybe so. But there sure as hell wouldn't be much use trying to run a newspaper without it."

"I understand." Amy's voice rose above the sound of the motor as Gibbs turned the key in the ignition. "You're the fisherman, and I'm the bait."

"Makes a good combination. Let's see what we can catch."

As they drove Amy glanced through the windshield and noted the thinning ranks of houses on both sides of the street ahead. "Have we far to go?" she said.

"She lives about ten miles outside of city limits. Closer to the Bates place than she is to town."

"And Dick Reno—?"

"He's got the old Murray property, about three miles farther on. Just this side of the swamp." Gibbs gave her a sidelong glance. "You know about the swamp, don't you? Norman's disposal."

Amy's nod both acknowledged and dismissed the thought. Once again she diverted her attention to the view beyond the windshield. They were traveling through an area of rolling hillsides topped by pines rising against the vivid blue of a cloudless sky.

"I love the scenery around here," she said.

Gibbs shrugged. "I guess it's all right if you like beauty."

Amy smiled, then sobered. "Mind if I ask you something?" she said.

"Go ahead."

"Are you really that cynical? Or is it some kind of an act?"

"Both." As he spoke he avoided her gaze, peering at the roadway ahead. "I guess it's what our friend Steiner would call a defense mechanism. Leoncavallo would have cast me as Pagliacci."

"If it's all a front, what's behind it?"

"Envy, I guess." He kept his eyes on the road as he spoke. "Envy of people like you."

"Why me?" Amy paused. "I wrote a book, is that it?"

"Partly. The big thing is that you wrote something you wanted to write, something you believed in. Now you're going to write another, probably lots of others. And when I'm an old man with a long gray beard and a short fuzzy memory I'll still be writing up Sunday school picnics and high school basketball games for the local paper."

"Any law says you have to stay here?"

Gibbs nodded. "Law of economics says there aren't too many people around looking to buy a small-town weekly with poor circulation. Law of nature tells me my own circulation isn't all that great—I don't have the energy to start all over again. And even if I could beat out all those kids with degrees in journalism and land a job with some metropolitan daily what difference would it make? I'd still be writing nonnews about nonpersons." Gibbs shook his head. "These being the laws, it looks like I'll serve a life sentence."

He spun the wheel and the car veered left onto a narrow dirt road tunneling beneath towering trees. "Sorry to bend your ear, but you asked for it. One of these days I'll get around to writing my unauthorized autobiography."

Self-pity, Amy told herself. *Whoever would have guessed it?* Or was it something which required guess-work? A montage of images flashed through her mind—Dad, her sister Fran, Bonnie Walton, ex-lover Gary, Dick Reno. And last but not least, that not-so-celebrated au-thoress and researcher, Miss Amelia Haines. Admit it, self-pity is one trait most of us share in common. But we seldom share it openly with others. Why had Hank Gibbs momentarily removed the mask? Was that his way of coming on to her?

Vanity. That's another common trait commonly con-cealed, if Gibbs itched for her he'd have made his move by now, and they would have been parked back there behind the trees instead of emerging into the sunlight.

Its rays were reflecting from the windowpanes of the two-story structure at the end of the road directly ahead. The barn behind it indicated that the white frame house had once functioned as a farmhouse, but the open field area beyond showed no present signs of cultivation.

As they parked in the rutted side yard, chickens clucked a greeting from somewhere inside the barn. Emerging from the car Amy confronted a tan-and-white collie bounding from behind the house with mixed sig-nals—a menacing growl and a wagging tail. She chose to believe the tail, but still felt more secure when Gibbs came around the front of the car and stooped to pat the dog before moving toward the back door.

She followed him as the growl, tail, and dog itself vanished as quickly as they'd come. Now her attention was directed to the woman who opened the door in re-sponse to Gibbs' knock.

Sandy Oliver was neither as tall or as heavy and her nose had never been broken, but her complexion and facial features bore a marked resemblance to Dick Reno's; she could easily have passed as his sister rather than his ex-wife. Short-cropped curls and the ambiguity of boots and jeans accentuated a sense of unisexuality, betrayed only by the bulge of heavy breasts beneath the khaki shirt.

Gibbs smiled at her. "'Afternoon, Sandy," he said.

His smile was not returned. "What the hell do you want?"

"Like you to meet a friend of mine." He indicated Amy with a nod.

"Cut the crap." Her eyes were still fixed on Gibbs. "You gonna answer my question or not?"

"Maybe it would be better if we talked inside. I wouldn't want the chickens to hear."

Sandy Oliver's reaction indicated she would never make a meaningful contribution to a sitcom laugh track. For a long moment she stood motionless, then stepped back abruptly. "Okay, but make it short."

Gibbs gestured and Amy was the first to cross the threshold and enter the kitchen beyond. She did her best to ignore the scowl on Sandy's face but there was no escape from the acrid reek of her breath. No escape, and no mistaking: the lady had been recently smoking a joint.

Or several. When Gibbs moved up beside Amy in the kitchen their reluctant hostess glared at them with pinpointed pupils.

"Start talking," she said.

Gibbs nodded. "First of all, I'd like to introduce—"

"Never mind, I already know who she is. That's all they've been talking about the last couple of days. Every customer in the shop keeps telling me what she's been up to and where she went, like it was the second coming of Christ." Now the eyes were pinpointing Amy directly. "Ever since you hit town and stuck your snotty nose into what's none of your business, we're in trouble. On top of it, now you got the nerve to show up here. Well, honey, just let me tell you where you can stick that snotty nose of yours—"

"Cool it!" Gibbs gestured quickly. "The only reason Miss Haines is here is because I invited her to ride along."

"And I'm inviting her to get the hell out of my house." Sandy Oliver's gesture was neither as quick nor as firm as Gibbs', but her voice was strong and strident. Now she focused her glazed glare on Amy's companion. "That goes for you too, Hank Gibbs. I wouldn't use that goddamn newspaper of yours to line the litter box for David's dog!"

Somewhat to Amy's surprise, and not altogether to her approval, Gibbs grinned. "I'm not trying to drum up circulation," he said. His grin softened to a smile. "Look, Sandy, I know you're not feeling well and we didn't come here to upset you. All I need is two minutes, just long enough to ask you a couple of simple questions."

"Like where I was last night?" There was a rasp in Sandy Oliver's laugh that betrayed more anger than amusement. "I'll tell you where. I was over at Otto Remsbach's place, sticking a knife in him and cutting Doris Huntley's throat."

There was no trace of a smile or grin on Gibbs' face now. "Sandy, for God's sake—"

"That's what you want to hear, isn't it?" Ignoring his shocked stare she moved across the kitchen to the cupboard area beneath the sink. "Damn good thing I left that butcher knife stuck in Otto's gut. Maybe if I had it here now I'd use it on both of you."

Still speaking she stooped. "Lucky for me I got this." Rising, she faced them with the leveled revolver.

"Sandy, no—"

"Now it's my turn. Where were you last night?"

"Baldwin Memorial Hospital. You can check—"

"Shut up. I'm asking her."

The muzzle of the revolver moved ever so slightly, ever so emphatically. But before Amy could answer, Sandy shook her head.

"Never mind, I already know." Her voice shook too, but not her hand. "Wasn't more 'n nine o'clock before I get this call from Ruth Potter. Said she just got home from that lousy Chinese restaurant out on the county trunk and she saw Dick having dinner with that female reporter from Chicago. How do you think I felt, with David sitting right there finishing up his homework and having to listen? His own father, messing around with another woman in public—"

Amy broke in quickly. "I thought you and Dick were divorced."

"That's none of your goddamn business! You got no right to shame me and my son in front of everybody, do you hear me? Answer me, you little bitch, do you hear me?"

"Loud and clear."

It was Dick Reno's voice, and he moved quickly into Amy's field of vision. Reno had entered so quietly that none of them were aware of his presence until now. By the time Sandy glanced up he was already wresting the weapon from her hand. "This is what I came looking for," he said. "Where've you been hiding it?"

"None of your business where!" The rasp in Sandy's voice was edging upward to a screech. "Gimme that! Damn you, I gotta keep something around to protect myself!"

She clawed at him but Reno shoved her back. "So do I," he said.

"What the hell for? You already carry a gun at work."

"Not anymore." Reno shook his head. "I've just been fired."

·19·

SOMEWHERE along the way, either from the late Otto Remsbach or her customers at the beauty salon, Sandy had acquired a wealth of raunchy invective. Her vocabulary seemed far from exhausted when Amy and Hank Gibbs made their abrupt departure.

A moment later Dick Reno joined them, still carrying the gun as he slammed the door behind him to stem Sandy's scatological flow. His car was not visible; it had been parked on the far side of the house. Apparently the tan-and-white collie was checking it out, but the chickens acknowledged Reno's presence as he walked Amy and Gibbs to their vehicle.

Gibbs eyed him warily. "Want to tell us what happened?"

"No, I don't." His scowl merged with a crooked grin. "But I might as well. You'll find out anyway, I'd better give it to you straight before you put a write-up in next week's paper."

Reno glanced at Amy. "After I dropped you off last night I got on the squawk box to Irene at the office. Usually I draw city patrol first, then one of the county trunk routes, but this time Engstrom left orders assigning me in reverse.

"Point is, he'd detailed me to cover this area. Things looked pretty quiet the way they do on a weeknight when the kids aren't out playing cowboy. Thinking about kids reminded me of what we'd been discussing at dinner, how Sandy had custody of David, and that started to steam me up."

Reno's lopsided grin had disappeared but the scowl remained. Now he took a deep breath. "Next part's off the record. Okay with you, Hank?"

"Shoot."

"That's what I damn well felt like doing, the more I thought about Sandy and how she'd screwed-up—not just her life, but David's and mine." He hesitated. "Like I say, no traffic around. Everything was under control out there on the trunk; everything but me. I went from steam to boil. Next thing you know I headed for the house here."

Hank Gibbs' eyes narrowed. "What did you have in mind?"

"Murder." Again Dick Reno hesitated, then shook his head. "But that's where it stayed—in my mind. What

I felt like doing and what I actually did are two different things. By the time I drove up here last night I'd simmered down a bit, enough to talk to Sandy without blowing my stack."

"What time did you arrive?" Gibbs said.

"Around ten, maybe a little earlier." Reno shrugged. "What I should have done was check things out with the office. Last time I called in was about nine forty-five, just before heading here."

"You didn't say where you were going?"

"I told Irene I was making a second run, just to double-check on a couple of truckers who'd parked their rigs outside the Pig-Out Inn. Wouldn't want to see them back on the highway carrying two loads instead of one."

Hank Gibbs nodded. "So Irene didn't log where you were actually going?"

Dick Reno sighed. "If she knew about me pulling a stunt like that on duty she wouldn't be able to wait to blow the whistle. I know I goofed, but it seemed like a good idea at the time."

Hank Gibbs nodded again. "Right."

"Wrong." Reno's gaze flickered to Amy. "Look, there's no point my boring you with all this stuff."

"I'm not bored," Amy said. Then, quickly, "In case you're wondering, it's off-the-record with me too." She smiled. "I don't even have a whistle."

Hank Gibbs cleared his throat, then glanced expectantly at Reno. "You were saying?"

"We talked about David. At least that's what I tried to talk about, but the minute I brought up the idea of custody it was the same old story, forget it, no way. I told her I damn well wasn't going to forget it, and there was a way, even if it meant going to court and telling what I knew was going on between her and Otto Remsbach." Somewhere in the background the chickens clucked their disapproval before he continued.

"Surprised I heard about that?" His grin was rueful

and fleeting. "So was she. I could see, even though she didn't let on, just told me to get the hell out."

"Did you?" Gibbs asked.

"Had to, before I lost my temper. Got all the way back to the county trunk by the time I cooled down enough to remember I was overdue calling in. By then they knew what had happened up at Remsbach's place and when Irene asked me where I'd been I figured the best thing to do was tell the truth."

Amy glanced up at him. "Did they believe you?"

"Sometime after midnight Engstrom contacted Sandy. I don't know whether she'd heard the news from somebody over the phone, but she sure as hell put me on the spot. Said she hadn't seen me last night at all, let alone the time those murders were supposed to have taken place."

"I'm surprised Engstrom isn't holding you," Gibbs said.

"He probably would, if he had anything positive to go on. As it is he fired me."

"For suspicion of murder?"

Reno shook his head. "Two charges. The first is failure to report in on schedule. The second is revealing classified information."

Amy frowned. "What does that mean?"

"It means I told you they found that wax dummy of Norman Bates' mother in Otto Remsbach's bed."

"Hell you say!" Hank Gibbs' eyebrows rose. He turned to confront Amy. "You didn't tell me that!"

"Sorry, I promised to keep my mouth shut."

"Well, you didn't hear it from me, either," Reno said. "This is off-the-record, remember?" He expelled a long breath. "Engstrom was right. I should have had more sense. With all those newspeople in town, God knows what'd happen if this hits the fan."

"It will, sooner or later," Gibbs said. "You know it and I know it. And Engstrom, bless his little pointy boots, he knows it too."

Dick Reno shrugged. "If it happens, it happens. But don't forget your promise."

"Still loyal to the old uniform, eh?"

"To hell with the uniform! It's the town I'm thinking about. Last night was bad enough, but if the media people tie those murders in with this Bates business—"

Gibbs gestured quickly. "You don't have to draw a picture, believe me, I'm thinking the same thing. They're taping me for network news this afternoon, probably end up just running a couple of sound-bites, but I've got to figure a way to duck some of the questions. They're bound to bring up Bates, probably Claiborne too, and I'm willing to bet some smart-ass is going to try and tie little Terry Dowson's death in with the mess."

"Who knows?" Reno said. "Maybe there is a connection." He stared down at the weapon in his right hand. "I'm going back in and have another talk with Sandy."

"Think she did it?"

"I'll ask her."

As Dick Reno turned and moved away, Gibbs opened the car door for Amy. "Good thing that gun isn't loaded," he murmured.

Amy didn't reply. It wasn't until they were back on the dirt road that either of them spoke again. As they drove past the bordering trees to the right, Gibbs' profile was alternately sunlit and shadowed, but his expression remained unchanged.

"What's bothering you?" Amy said. "Is it the interview?"

Gibbs shook his head. "Interviews don't worry me. It's just that everything Dick Reno said is true. Salem had the witch-hunts, London had Jack the Ripper, and from now on Fairvale is stuck with Norman Bates." His grin was grim. "Strange, isn't it? All the time and effort Otto Remsbach spent trying to publicize that damn motel. He never realized the best way to promote it was his own death."

Amy frowned. "Maybe his partner had that idea."

"Possibly." Gibbs turned onto the county trunk. "But we both know his partner also has an alibi."

"They all have alibis," Amy said. "Including you and me."

Gibbs' grin returned. "You still claim you didn't do it?"

Amy nodded, but her reply didn't match his mood. "Stop clowning. If we eliminate Dick Reno and Sandy, who's left?"

"Just about everybody else in town," Gibbs said. "They all hate what's been happening here and I have a pretty strong hunch that if Remsbach had lived to go through with his plans there might have been some organized opposition. Of course, that wouldn't help anymore. It's no use trying to keep a low profile after last night. From now on the smartest thing to do is open a dozen new hotels and restaurants for the tourist trade."

"You just mentioned something about the possibility of organized opposition."

"I also said the possibility was past."

"You're being evasive. Aren't you going to give me any names?"

"You're being persistent. But let's just start with a few you already know. Irene Grovesmith, Reverend Archer, Bob Peterson, Dr. Rawson. And I've got a pretty fair hunch that you can throw in Sheriff Engstrom himself, just for good measure. Come to think of it, so far the only one we know in that bunch with a solid alibi is Grovesmith. You can scratch Irene, if you like. Personally, I wouldn't touch her with a ten-foot pole."

"Be serious."

"I am. Very." Gibbs took a deep breath. "We can't change the past, we can't anticipate the future. So why waste the present worrying about either one?"

"Hedonist."

"Pragmatist." Gibbs' grin returned. "Which reminds me, what are your present plans?"

Amy glanced at her watch. "It's one o'clock. How

long will it take me to get from the hotel to the State Hospital?"

"Twenty-five minutes. Half an hour at most. What time's your appointment with Dr. Steiner?"

"Three-thirty." Amy glanced ahead, noting that Gibbs was entering town now by the same route they'd left, and undoubtedly for the same reason; if he dropped her off at the rear of the hotel she could return to her room via the service elevator without detection. Pragmatism had its practical advantages, no doubt about that.

And she had a good two hours of free time. The thought that occurred to her was promptly voiced. "I wonder if they locked up the Bates place again?"

"You'd have to ask Pitkin about that. He and Remsbach would be the only ones who had keys."

"What about the people who'd been working out there? Didn't those two girls get in with somebody's duplicate?"

"After Terry Dowson was killed, Engstrom checked out alibis on all the workers and members of their families. While he was at it he picked up the extra keys. Far as I know they're still somewhere in the Sheriff's office, probably stashed away under the Kleenex box in Irene's right-hand desk drawer." He sobered. "Why did you ask? I hope you're not thinking of going out there?"

"Never mind the rhetorical question. You know damned well I've got to see the place for myself. I want to get there before those newshounds find out about what was in Remsbach's bed and start sniffing around the Bates property again." Amy reached for her bag on the seat beside her as they pulled up to the curb at the rear of the hotel. "Right now I have two hours to spare and according to the map book I'd be only a mile or so off the route to the State Hospital. Besides, it's broad daylight—"

Gibbs nodded. "The sun is bright, yes. But standing in the sunshine out there and trying to pick locks with your nail file isn't bright."

"What makes you so sure? Maybe the place hasn't been locked again."

"And if it is, maybe Pitkin will loan you a key. But if I were you I wouldn't count on it."

"I'm not. All I want is a chance to look around before there's a mob scene. One way or another, I've got to see it before I leave town."

"That figures." Gibbs nodded again. "I'd drive you over myself if it wasn't for that interview session coming up."

"Thanks, I know you would." Amy opened the door and swung her feet down to rest on the pavement. "And thanks for the breakfast and limo service." Emerging, she straightened and turned to close the door behind her.

"Amy?"

"Yes?"

"Promise me something. Don't risk going out there by yourself. I'll be free again tomorrow morning, but if you can't wait, at least get somebody else to come with you. Don't go there alone."

For a moment she hesitated, then nodded. "You're right, of course."

"That's better." The slam of the passenger-side door punctuated Gibbs' words. "By the way, what time do you expect to be back from seeing Steiner?"

"I don't know but my guess would be somewhere around six. Six-thirty at the latest."

"If you feel like it, give me a call at the office. Maybe we can have dinner together."

"Where?"

"They say Irene Grovesmith makes a terrific pizza."

The car moved forward and Amy turned away as it departed. As she made her way through the back entrance to the waiting service elevator she couldn't avoid a rueful reflection. What did she do to make herself attractive to older men?

Maybe just being younger was enough. But rightly

or wrongly, she was beginning to feel that Hank Gibbs' intentions involved sharing more than a pizza. And why was it that he seemed incapable of being serious whenever he became serious? It would probably take someone like Dr. Steiner to answer that question; she ought to remember to ask him when they talked.

But there was so much to talk about, so much to think about, far more than she had anticipated. A good thing she'd promised not to go out to the Bates place this afternoon; what she really should do during the next two hours was to organize her thoughts, recopy some of her random notes in chronological order, and set down a list of things she meant to ask Steiner about. There already was such a list, of course, but in view of last night's events and today's revelations, it would have to be both revised and expanded.

The upcoming meeting with Dr. Steiner would be crucial, particularly so because the other meeting she had counted on—the one with Adam Claiborne—would never take place. Nor would she meet again with Otto Remsbach.

Stepping out of the service elevator she fished the key from her purse and moved to the door of her room. Once again she hesitated before metal met metal; a ghostly Adam Claiborne peered over her shoulder and on the other side of the door Otto Remsbach lay bedded and waiting, ready to receive her in bloody embrace.

Amy forced herself to turn the thought aside before she turned the key. There was nothing behind her but a shadow, nothing more substantial awaiting on the bed in her room.

Closing and locking the door behind her, she put her purse down on the bureau and opened the top drawer. Now where had she left the big notebook?

And who was tapping, ever so softly, but ever so persistently, on the door?

"Miss Haines—"

The muffled voice that spoke her name answered her question.

Eric Dunstable. How could she have forgotten about him?

"I'll get the key."

Finding anything in that overloaded bag of hers was always a problem and this instance proved no exception. After her first and fruitless scrabblings she bowed to the inevitable and dumped the contents of her purse on the bedspread. The rest was easy.

Amy unlocked the door. "Here we go."

And here he came. It might have been a televised rerun of the other evening; the taller version of Toulouse-Lautrec hadn't grown an inch. He was still wearing the same clothing and, as far as Amy could determine, had slept in it as well. If he'd slept at all. And the right lens of his glasses was cracked at the base of its outer rim. Spectacle frames could not conceal the crescents of darkness under his eyes. Nor the twitch in the left one.

All this was apparent at a glance, and Amy did her best not to stare. "I've been trying to get in touch with you," she said.

Dunstable nodded. "Would you mind if I sat down?"

"Please do."

While he settled back in the armchair, Amy seated herself on the edge of the bed and began to restore the contents of her bag in their proper disarray. "Where have you been?" she said.

"Montrose. Rock Center. Selroy." Another twitch. "That's where I ended up last night; the Selroy Motor Lodge, because there was no way of getting back here again by bus until this morning. At first I'd planned to try hitching a ride, but then the storm came up and I decided against it, even though it meant spending extra money when I already had accommodations over here." Now the inevitable twitch was accompanied by a movement of beard-bordered lips suggesting a smile. "This was probably one of the most fortunate investments I've ever made."

Amy closed her bag. "How so?"

"It provided me with the necessary alibi for my whereabouts at the time of the murders."

"Then you've seen Engstrom."

"A couple of his deputies came by this morning just about ten minutes after I stepped off the bus." The smile disappeared and the twitch returned. "They probably phoned ahead to the Sheriff's Department here the moment I bought a ticket in Selroy. I gather my description has been rather widely circulated."

"But Engstrom accepted your explanation?"

"Not until he checked it out with the Selroy Motor Lodge." Sunlight from the window glittered against the cracked lens as Dunstable glanced up. "I understand you had some problems last night."

"That's a very polite way of phrasing it." Amy paused. "I was on the scene after Doris Huntley was murdered. But I didn't kill her, and at the time I wasn't even aware Otto Remsbach was dead."

"I believe you." Dunstable's left eyelid blinked in affirmation. "You don't have the aura."

"Aura?"

"Of evil." He leaned forward beyond the reach of the sunbeam's ray and his shadowed face was somber. "So many have that aura here. I could feel it at the church—"

Bedbug, Amy told herself. *He's as crazy as a bedbug.* But she didn't tell him that; you're supposed to humor the crazies.

She did her best. "The other night you said that if you attended the memorial services you'd be able to identify Terry Dowson's murderer."

"I was wrong." Again the affirmative twitch. "Because they were wrong. The auras, too many of them, too confusing; impossible to separate vessel from contents."

"I'm not following that." Amy frowned.

"The body is a vessel, its contents good or evil, most generally an admixture of both. During possession the aural emanation is pure evil. A contradiction in terms, of course, but it's difficult to explain."

"I know." At least she'd better pretend that she did. "But you still haven't told me what you were doing in all those places."

"Yesterday morning I hitched a ride to Montrose. In the afternoon I got over to Rock Center and then on to Selroy just after dinnertime. That's where I finally found it."

"What were you looking for?"

"Apparently something of a rarity in these parts. A Catholic church."

Amy nodded. "You wanted to talk to a priest."

"Not so. I wanted to steal some holy water." Dunstable leaned back, but the sun had shifted slightly, just enough so his face was still in shadow. "And I did, from the font they have near the exit." In the dimmer light the twitch was almost invisible. "A good thing I had a few minutes before they picked me up after I got back here. I more or less assumed that would happen so the first thing I did was empty the little cough syrup bottle of holy water into the glass in the bathroom. As I expected, they searched the place when they came and one of them named Al was still at it when his partner took me over to the Sheriff's office." Shadow and beard hid the smile but satisfaction sounded in his voice. "Naturally he didn't find anything, and he never noticed the water in the glass."

"I assume it has something to do with exorcism?"

Dunstable nodded. "You might call it the vital ingredient."

"Exactly how will you use it?"

"That all depends upon who or what I use it on."

"Which means you still feel that some form of possession is involved."

"More than ever, after what I've learned about last night." Once more the winking from the shadows accompanied the words. "Do you know that Dr. Claiborne died over at Baldwin Memorial Hospital just before those murders took place here in town?"

"I did hear something to that effect," Amy said. "But of course nobody has established the exact time when Remsbach and Doris Huntley were killed. Even an autopsy report will only be an educated guess."

"This isn't guesswork." Eric Dunstable's hoarse voice rose in reply. "And it isn't the first time this demonic entity has deserted the dead to possess the living."

Now he leaned into the light. "There's no way of telling just when and where the possession originated, but we do know that all those who came in contact with the entity were themselves possessed and died in turn. The phenomenon may have begun with Mrs. Bates herself rather than Norman."

Amy frowned. "You have nothing to support such a theory."

"Not entirely, but you can't dismiss the necrology. First Mrs. Bates, then her lover, Ed Considine. Next were Mary Crane and Arbogast, the insurance investigator. Then the two nuns, Sister Barbara and Sister Cupertine." His fingers rose and fell in accompanying enumeration. "After which came Norman himself. But it didn't stop there. There was that producer, Driscoll, out in Hollywood, and Vicinzi, the director. Now we've had Terry Dowson, Doris Huntley, and Otto Remsbach here. An even dozen."

As the list mounted Amy felt her own apprehension mounting with it. She knew the names, but somehow, up until this moment, she had never consciously realized the chain had so many links. And while possession might be a preposterous explanation, the linkage remained. The thought disturbed her and she strove for a light dismissal.

"Let's hope there's no more. Thirteen is an unlucky number."

"I don't believe in superstitions." Dunstable was actually serious, Amy realized. And, she mustn't forget, crazy as a bedbug. Except there was something about what he had said, or the way he said it, that continued to trouble her.

Eric Dunstable seemed aware of that, because now he attempted to relieve her mind. "Don't worry about the number," he said. "The entity has already passed to take over another."

"If that's the case, you're right back to square one," Amy said. "You still have to identify whoever is being possessed."

"Now the circumstances are different. This time I think it will be comparatively easy."

Amy's fingers pressed hard against the bedspread and the mattress beneath. "Aren't you going to tell me whom you suspect?"

"I'm not quite ready to do so yet."

"But when you are—"

"Exorcism."

"How?"

"By whatever method proves necessary." Dunstable stared at her. "Words banish. Water purifies. Fire cleanses."

His eye blinked.

·20·

SHERIFF Milt Engstrom parked his car a little way up and off the road.

And it was his own car, not the Department's. Anyone passing by wouldn't be apt to give it a second look and nobody would be trying to reach him on the squawk. In fact no one knew where he was and that's the way he wanted it.

His pointed boots moved soundlessly along the elbow at the right-hand side of the road, still silent as he crossed to the door.

It was only after he unlocked it and entered the office that his heels clicked against the floorboards.

"Hello, Norman," he said.

The figure on the pivot pedestal did not turn, nor did it reply.

"What's the matter?" Engstrom said. "You got wax in your ears?"

Just a little joke. A very little one, but right now he'd settle for whatever might lighten things up, even for a moment. Just too damn bad the power hadn't been turned on here; even in the shadows and with his back turned Engstrom didn't particularly care for Norman's looks.

Looks. Better case the room and bath, just to make sure. Floorboards creaked as he crossed to the door of number one. New lumber and old lumber; both creak the same. Engstrom wondered if the floorboards were silent when someone walked on them in the old motel. Had to be, of course. That's how Norman managed to sneak into the room and the bath beyond, just the way he was sneaking now.

Only he didn't have to sneak. There was no need, because for the first time since last night he was alone. No phones, no messages, nobody yapping questions. Which meant he didn't have to give any answers. That was one of the reasons why he was here, to get away from giving answers.

There were none to be found in the bedroom when Engstrom opened the door and switched on the flashlight he'd lifted from his waistband. Its beam traveled with him into the bathroom; no answers here, from the wax figure of the victim standing under the shower.

He wondered what Fatso Otto might have done about it if he'd lived. How long would it've taken him to pipe water out here and set his prices? Five bucks to use the john, ten bucks for a shower. Just the thing for the tourist trade. Nice conversation piece for the ladies when they got back home. Tell all your friends you used the bathroom in the Bates Motel. Give 'em a gift certificate. Get your picture taken with the dummy.

Engstrom shook his head. Come to think of it, Fatso Otto would never think of it. This was the kind of stuff Charlie Pitkin would try to pull; he was the brains and Otto was just the blubber.

Right now the coroner would be carving away at the blubber over at Baldwin Memorial. But where was the brains? Nobody at the office since noon, and at the house his daughter said he'd left right after lunch, she didn't know for where.

Lot of things she didn't know about dear old Daddy, or did she? How much was she onto some of those deals he had going for him up at the legislature, or even here at the Fairvale office? How much and how often did she cover for him?

Troubling questions, but there was another one which bothered him even more. How much did he really know about that girl? When you got right down to it, damned little except with the kind of gossip Irene Grovesmith brought back from the beauty parlor, which didn't count because Irene hated that girl almost as much as she hated this place. All the women seemed to hate it; Sandy Oliver, Marge Gifford in Doc Rawson's office, the waitresses, store clerks, even the girls in the steamy back room over at Qwik Dry Cleaners. Emma hated it too, and it was a good thing she was off visiting her sister Frances in Springfield this week. She'd missed all of the excitement and he'd missed all the static he would have gotten about how it served Otto Remsbach right, why didn't somebody stop him from building out there in the first place, why doesn't somebody just burn it down?

In his own mind Engstrom could almost hear her saying just that, but he couldn't picture her burning anything down. Some of those other women, yes, and some of the men too.

He retraced his steps to the office, flashlight fanning the silver bell on the counter and the figure facing the wall behind it. Certainly was some piece of work, that one. And so was the pivot mechanism in the pedestal. He'd already checked the battery setup that operated it when you pressed the bell on the counter and turned on the little strip of voice-tape. No clear print on the bell, and of course Banning's people couldn't get anything off the connecting wire that ran down behind the desk and into the base of the pedestal. Pretty cute the way they'd figured that one out, but then the outfit Charlie had hired did a lot more complicated things for some of those special effects in the movies.

Engstrom's lips tightened as he left the office. Don't look now, but your age is showing. They don't make movies anymore; it's all films. Got to keep up with the times.

And got to keep up with the present situation too. Switching off the flash, he started for the house. Where were all of those potential arsonists right now?

Irene was at the office handling calls and reporters, God help her; she wouldn't even have time to light a match. Sandy Oliver'd phoned in sick, so she was probably at home, but Doc Rawson's office hadn't heard from her. That's where Marge Gifford worked and she was on the job today. He'd talked to Pitkin's daughter less than an hour ago, out at the lake cottage. But where the hell was Amelia Haines?

Not in her room this morning, that's for sure, and nobody downstairs saw her leave. The lobby was like a

snake pit; if somebody talked to her on the house phone
the desk had been too busy to notice. She could even
have used the service elevator and sneaked out the back
way but her car hadn't been moved. He should have
checked again before coming out here, but you can't
think of everything.

Or everyone. The weirdo, Dunstable, there was no
excuse to hold him after checking out his alibi this
morning; he said he was going back to the hotel, but
Christ only knew where he was now. And He wasn't
talking to anyone, not even Reverend Archer, who'd
been asking for divine intervention to help destroy this
place. Maybe Archer would lose patience and act on his
own. Meanwhile, as of his wife's response to a noontime
call, the Reverend was not at home, she didn't know
when to expect him and couldn't say where he'd gone.

Homer was holding the fort at the *Fairvale Weekly
Herald* office but his boss was out. According to Homer,
Hank Gibbs was slated to tape an interview over at the
hotel sometime around four o'clock; TV and radio people had rented—and were taking turns using—the ban-
quet room, which was a fancy name for the place where
the Kiwanis Club held breakfast meetings every Friday
morning. Today the meeting had been called off, which
meant there were that many more prospective firebugs
on the loose. They hadn't been happy about Fatso Otto's
project from its beginning and now they'd be anxious to
see it end. Then there was Dick Reno to consider. Tall
man, short fuse. He didn't take kindly to being fired, but
you can't depend on someone who doesn't know enough
to keep his mouth shut. He'd sneaked off while he was
on duty last night; where could he have sneaked off to
now?

Again Engstrom's hand dipped to his waistband,
this time not to locate the flashlight but to reassure himself his revolver was ready before he opened the front
door of the Bates house. After considering all those

likely to have incendiary intentions it was possible that he might not be the first visitor here.

Sunlight hazy, clouds coming in from the west. More rain coming?

If so it didn't concern him; not at the moment, anyway. Truth to tell, a little rain this evening might be just the thing. Nothing like a good storm to put out fires. Unless, of course, the fire started before the rain did.

Once inside the house he closed the door quietly behind him. It was time to use the flashlight again. Here in the hall nothing seemed changed; a big sheet of plastic still covered the area where Terry Dowson's body had lain and the stained flooring beneath. Didn't look as though anyone had disturbed it since blood samples had been collected. Whole mess would have to be cleaned up sooner or later, but not right now. Maid's day off.

The flashbeam aided vision but it didn't help his hearing or other senses. As far as these were concerned, he'd have to depend on himself. Up until now all he heard was the sound of his own footsteps and all he smelled was a lingering trace of semiglossy paint. He didn't expect to be touching or tasting anything; then again, one never knows.

One never knows, but one had damn well better find out. Move slowly, softly, carefully. Upstairs first; switch the flash to your left hand and keep the right hand close to the holster. Dick Reno turned in his revolver this morning, but he had one of his own. How many more of those jokers on his list might have revolvers, target pistols, deer rifles, shotguns, or other weapons? For that matter, an ordinary butcher knife would do; it had done before, several times, and most efficiently.

Darkness hid his grim smile as he mounted the stairs, keeping the flash low so that its light wouldn't advertise his approach. Once on the upper landing he pointed his boots down the hall and made a slow-motion survey door by door, room by room, closet by closet. All clear.

Satisfied, he retraced his route down the hall and the stairs, then duplicated his efforts on the first floor. Nobody had been hiding under the bed up above, nobody lurked behind the furniture down here. The drapes in the parlor were less than floor-length and stirred only in response to his passage.

Funny thing, though; no pictures on the walls, upstairs or here below. Maybe they'd been ordered but hadn't arrived. Perhaps they'd come in at the last moment, too late for hanging. Only it was never too late for hanging, not in this state. Or framing, either.

Again the grim smile. Wonder what kind of pictures were supposed to go on the walls here—regular old-fashioned paintings or maybe blowup photos of Norman and his mother? Have to ask Charlie Pitkin the next time he saw him. *If* he saw him.

Hopefully that wouldn't be in the basement. Or the fruit cellar.

Boot tips teetered on the steps. Down and dirty. That's what they used to say in stud poker games when he was a kid. But this wasn't a game and he wasn't a kid anymore; just a grey-mustached man who had plans for living to a ripe old age. Should have sent somebody else out here in the first place, but with Reno gone he was left shorthanded. Besides, it would be too risky.

Either it was darker in the basement or his flashlight was starting to give out. That had happened here before, or was it just his imagination? In any case he'd come too far to turn back now. Now that he knew the basement was empty. Now that he had to look into the fruit cellar.

The door was slightly ajar.

Had it been that way before? He couldn't remember.

Point the flashlight forward. Pull out the revolver and point it too. Ease the door open very gently, very slowly, using the tip of the left boot. Now fan the beam in on—

Emptiness.

It was a relief, of course. A relief, but strange;

strange not to see Mother there, where she belonged. Should have had a pivot installed for her. Here, or in Otto Remsbach's bed.

This time the smile was not quite as grim. The tension was easing now that he could be sure—reasonably sure—the house hadn't been invaded. And wouldn't be, if he could prevent it. Eventually those news-media turkeys would be coming out here but all they were going to get was what they'd gotten the first time around; exterior shots of the house and the motel setup. If Captain Banning pitched in they wouldn't even get that much, but Banning's nose was out of joint because the Highway Patrol didn't get any exposure on the Remsbach case. He wasn't about to detail any round-the-clock surveillance here, not even on a drive-by basis.

Banning wasn't worrying about the media or about possible arson either. And when you came right down to it, why should he?

Coming right down to it was something to think about when coming right up the stairs again. Better check out the situation just to be on the safe side. In arson, matches are less important than motives.

Once more he reviewed the reasons that might motivate potential pyromaniacs. Only the people on his list weren't maniacs, he reminded himself, except perhaps for Eric Dunstable. Do demonologists start fires? It didn't matter; this character was weird enough or wired enough to do anything. Too bad the laws on substance abuse didn't allow for a test when they'd pulled Dunstable in; both times Engstrom could have sworn the guy was on something.

The girl who worked for Doc Rawson, that Marge, was into his sample supply; he knew because Doc had told him. Said he was going to dump her as soon as he could find himself another. But so far nothing serious had happened and just because she popped a few pills didn't necessarily tie in with a burning desire to get rid of this place.

It was the others who really wanted it destroyed, and for good reason.

Now, leaving the house, Engstrom regretted he couldn't share their feeling. As an officer of the law he was responsible for the protection of life and property. The way things had been going, there were bound to be noises about how well he'd performed the first part of his duties. But if on top of that he let somebody burn down this place after it had been featured on the nightly news—

Engstrom shook his head.

It was up to him to keep everyone from playing with fire.

If not, he'd end up on the nightly news himself.

· 21 ·

DR. Steiner was waiting for Amy in the lobby, and at first glance she thought he was one of the patients.

But patients in institutions of this sort were not likely to be wearing business suits nor moving freely about in wheelchairs without anyone in attendance. If anything more was necessary, his greeting offered confirmation.

"Miss Haines? I'm Nicholas Steiner."

His outstretched hand was cold but his smile was warm. His grip was weak, his voice strong. Contrasts or contradictions? Another question among many for which she'd be needing answers. Better try an easier one first.

"How did you recognize me, Dr. Steiner?"

"There've been descriptions." The smile brightened. "Besides we don't expect many visitors this late in the afternoon, particularly the kind who arrive carrying oversized notebooks under their arms." Again the frail hand extended. "Suppose we make a deal? I'll carry your purse and notebook on my lap and you wheel me back to my office."

"Fair enough." Amy stepped behind the chair and, following Steiner's directions, turned and propelled it past the reception desk. The white-capped, dark-faced woman behind it looked up and smiled at Dr. Steiner as they passed. "See you got yourself a new nurse," she said.

"That's right," Steiner said. "Don't report me to the union."

Amy steered the chair into the corridor beyond—the administrative area, she concluded, since most of the doors lining the route were open to reveal glimpses of office furniture or filing facilities.

"Hang a left here," Steiner told her.

Here was a modestly furnished but comfortably old-fashioned office; drapes instead of blinds, light incandescent rather than fluorescent, desk solid wood, not flimsy metal.

Amy wheeled Steiner up beside rather than behind it, across from the armchair in which she seated herself after retrieving purse and notebook. Extracting a pen from the former, she held it poised, flipping open the latter to an empty page.

"I was just thinking," she said. "This must be quite a switch for you. Usually you're the one who takes the notes."

Steiner's right hand loosened the folds of the scarf around his neck. "Usually I ask patients if they need some water before they start talking," he said. "There's a cooler over in that corner behind you, and a cup dispenser. If you don't mind—"

"Of course." Amy rose and obliged his request. As she settled back in the chair again he drank slowly, then placed the empty cup on the edge of the desk beside him.

"That's better," he murmured. "Throat's still a little uncomfortable."

Amy nodded. "I'll try not to ask too many questions."

"Ask as many questions as you wish. I'll try not to give too many answers."

"Suppose I start with an easy one." Amy gripped her pen. "What was Dr. Claiborne like?"

"You call that an easy question?" The accompanying chuckle held a hint of hoarseness; then the voice sobered. "Depends on which Dr. Claiborne we're talking about.

"The Adam Claiborne I knew—or thought I knew, as my associate here—was a caring and competent co-worker, a decent and highly intelligent man who was almost like a son to me.

"But he was also the son of Norman Bates." Steiner expelled his breath in a silent sigh. "I failed him. All those years after he came back, all those attempts to help. And I failed him."

"I'm sorry," Amy said. "It must be painful for you to talk about this."

"After what Adam did to me the other night, it's painful to talk, period." Steiner gestured hastily. "Don't take that as a hint. I want to talk. I *need* to. If this hadn't happened, if I could do what you've been doing—"

Amy leaned forward. "You think you'd be able to identify the murderer?"

"Somebody must. And soon."

"How would you go about it?"

Dr. Steiner shrugged. "Not the way Engstrom has, or Captain Banning. I've talked to them both and all they're interested in is clues, alibis, and motives. The problem is they have no clues, alibis can be faked, and motives can be concealed."

"Then where do you start?"

"The same place you did when you wrote your book about Bonnie Walton. You begin by constructing a profile of your subject."

"But I knew in advance that Bonnie Walton was the guilty party. She'd already been convicted of murder. And the profile of her I constructed in advance turned out to be wrong."

Steiner took another sip of water. "So you changed it, correcting errors on the basis of what you learned as you went along. And in the end it's my opinion you came pretty close to the truth."

"Thank you."

"Thank yourself for doing an honest and thorough piece of work." Steiner dropped his emptied paper cup into the waiting wastebasket beside the desk. "The point is, you probably never would have started the project if you hadn't already formed a profile of the subject in your own mind. Right or wrong, you needed to visualize an image as a point of departure. Then interviews helped you correct that image as you went along."

"Let's talk about the image of a possible suspect in this case. Do you have enough to create such a profile now?"

Steiner frowned. "Only in generalities, on the basis of what little I've learned."

As he spoke, Amy's pen raced to keep pace with his words.

"No need to repeat what we both know. Actually there are just a few points of special interest that I think haven't been given enough consideration.

"First off, in the murder of Terry Dowson. According to Captain Banning, Highway Patrol people couldn't locate tire tread marks anywhere nearby. They say the storm must have washed them away, but I don't think our suspect would have left it to chance. Because nothing else was left to chance; nothing turned up in the house that was of any use to the forensic lab. So far the same thing holds true for the murders of Doris Huntley and her lover.

"This doesn't establish whether the homicides were premeditated or the result of circumstance but it does indicate the culprit is someone capable of careful and logical action to conceal these crimes. And, subsequently, to conceal identity. Which leaves us with only one remaining clue."

Steiner paused for a moment and it was Amy's impatience that broke the silence. "Aren't you going to tell me what it is?"

Dr. Steiner nodded. "Let me put it in the form of a question. Why would anyone steal the wax figure of Norman's mother?"

Now it was Amy who paused. "Some kind of a psycho? Someone who thought he was Norman?"

"If by 'psycho' you mean 'psychopath' then such a possibility exists. This type of personality disorder does not involve irrationality or psychotic patterns of behavior."

"Then the murderer wouldn't necessarily believe himself to be Norman."

"But it could be someone who wanted us to think he had such a belief. If that's true, there's no reason the murderer couldn't be female."

"Or a fanatic." Amy turned a page in her notebook. "Of either sex." She raised the pen and strove to make her question seem casual. "Mind telling me the name of the patient who visited you from Fairvale today?"

"I've had several visitors." Steiner's reply was casual too. "Frankly, if any of them were patients it's my obligation not to reveal their identities."

Amy smiled. "That won't be necessary. I think I saw the last one going to his car as I drove in. Reverend Archer, wasn't it?"

"Archer was here, yes." The casual note was missing from Steiner's answer now. "Fact is he comes out on a regular basis to pay ministerial calls on some of our cases. That doesn't make him a patient."

"But fanaticism does."

Amy too was far from casual; both voice and stare were direct.

Steiner sighed. "You understand this is privileged information?"

Amy lowered her pen. "I promise you I won't write anything down."

"Not for the moment, anyway. But my hunch is that the press will dig up all this material and a lot more, long before your book sees publication." He hesitated. "I still don't know—"

"Neither do I," Amy said softly. "But I want to find out. Not just for the sake of the book, but because of my own involvement. In some ways I feel personally responsible for what happened last night."

"Your only responsibility was being in the wrong place at the wrong time." Steiner moved the wheelchair a few inches forward, his voice lowering. "Now about Archer. He and Norman Bates were friends. In high school, and after. Archer actually knew Norman's mother; he used to go out to the house frequently before she first began seeing Joe Considine."

"Her lover." Amy nodded.

"And Norman's enemy. Or so he thought." Steiner settled back in his chair. "That's when the trouble began. You and I both know what happened to Mrs. Bates and Considine, but at the time nobody suspected Norman. Apparently nobody had any reason to suspect him, except for Archer."

"He knew?"

"From what he's told me, Norman found out about his mother's affair with Considine. In his eyes she had betrayed him; his rage grew to a point where he was openly voicing threats against them both. That's when

Archer stopped seeing Norman and by the time Mrs. Bates and Considine died Archer was already off to the university. But ever since then he's carried guilt feelings about not speaking up.

"According to him, he never saw Norman again, which is not all that unusual when you consider Archer was away for eight years between the time he started university and his eventual return as an ordained minister of the gospel. By then Norman was already a recluse, except during the performance of his duties in running the motel.

"When they finally discovered what Norman had done over and above the call of duty, it was too late for Archer to do anything except condemn himself for not ever coming forward with his suspicions. I needn't tell you what the man has gone through in the years that followed."

"He hated Norman?"

Steiner shook his head. "He hated what Norman did to Fairvale and its reputation. He hated the notoriety he felt would follow Otto Remsbach's plans to rebuild the house and the Bates Motel as a tourist attraction."

"Enough for him to kill Remsbach?"

"Enough for him to make every effort that might prevent Remsbach's plans from going through." Dr. Steiner's brow furrowed to betoken the thought behind it. "I'd say he was highly motivated, determined, perhaps obsessed to the point of fanaticism—but I'd draw the line at describing him as murderous. What I saw this afternoon was a sorrowing and deeply disturbed man."

"Where was he last night?" Amy asked.

"He doesn't know." Steiner shrugged. "Amnesic fugue. Could be triggered by emotional distress. It happens."

"It happened to Norman." Amy paused. "Could Archer—"

Steiner gestured before she could continue. "We're talking about an elderly diabetic."

"I know this may sound foolish, but isn't there such a thing as maniacal strength?"

"Rubbish." Steiner's smile softened his reply. "You might as well suggest I got up out of this wheelchair and sneaked off to commit those murders myself."

"Anything is possible." Amy could smile too. "Adam Claiborne almost did you in with just one hand."

"True," Steiner said. "I should have been more cautious. I was supposed to have a male nurse standing by but he went to the washroom. You might call it a security leak."

He chuckled, then sobered. "Wasn't so funny at the time."

"What reason did Dr. Claiborne have for attacking you?"

Steiner's voice was very sober now. "Because of my own stupidity. I ought never to have gotten into a discussion about the Grand Opening plans for the Bates place."

Amy nodded. "You're saying he took all this personally?"

"Very." Steiner paused reflectively. "I should've remembered something he told me in one of our early sessions. 'Norman Bates will never die.' And in a way, of course, he didn't. Because there was a part of Claiborne therapy never reached; a part that still believed he was Norman."

"Maybe he was."

Dr. Steiner glanced up quickly. "You're not serious—"

"Eric Dunstable is."

"The self-styled demonologist?"

"I take it you know about him."

"Bits and pieces. Not enough." Steiner leaned forward. "I'd appreciate hearing more."

He listened intently as Amy recited her contacts with Dunstable from the first momentary meeting in Chicago up until their most recent encounter a few hours ago. "So according to his theory Norman did live on through Dr. Claiborne and has taken possession of someone else after his death."

"His theory?" Steiner's right hand rose in a gesture of dismissal. "Demonic possession is one of the oldest and most widespread concepts in human history."

"Does that mean you believe in it?"

"Quite the contrary. No amount of age or faith transforms fantasy into reality. Stop and think. There was a time, up until just a few centuries ago, when it was generally accepted that the mentally ill were possessed by demons. Today we're starting to believe there may be a physiological basis for certain types of schizophrenia— evil organisms instead of evil spirits. For all we know demons may turn out to be just molecules in a DNA chain."

"That's not what Dunstable believes," Amy said. "He's convinced that Norman lives on."

"And must be exorcised." Steiner frowned. "Did he mention any details about the ritual he had in mind?"

"Not directly." Amy tapped the point of her pen against the page beneath it. "I remember something he did say, though. 'Words banish. Water purifies. Fire cleanses.'"

"Mean anything to you?"

"He told me about stealing holy water from that church. My guess would be he needed it as part of the ceremony."

"That sounds logical." Steiner nodded. "And I assume that the words he refers to would be in the form of invocation and prayer. Fire probably involves the lighting of candles."

"He wasn't specific about that."

Dr. Steiner frowned. "Where is Eric Dunstable?"

"I don't know," Amy said.

But now, of course, she did.

· 22 ·

STEINER had a sandwich and coffee in his room.

The sandwich was hard to chew, the coffee difficult to swallow. The same applied to much of what he'd been thinking and hearing about this Bates business. Hard to chew over some of the facts, difficult to swallow some of the fantasies.

Or even to separate one from the other. He certainly didn't believe everything he'd heard. Some people aren't on speaking terms with the truth.

On the other hand, who was he to expect anything better? Most of us want more than we deserve. "Help— I'm drowning! Throw me a yacht!"

Perhaps he was being presumptuous. There was no reason to assume that those he'd spoken with could differentiate between the real and the false. The parade is endless, the crowds cheer, and the Emperor strides naked through the streets.

So much for rock-lyric philosophy.

If he really wanted to come to grips with this problem it might be necessary to invent a philosophy of his own. Or at least make use of what he'd developed over a lifetime of professional practice. Not that practice makes perfect; but the best course for him now was to be professional. In which case his philosophy was simple enough.

People wear masks to hide behind from others. Sometimes they wear masks to hide from themselves. And his job was to remove those masks.

Steiner pushed himself back, away from the food tray on the tabletop, away from the lamplight and into the shadows. Closing his eyes he evoked images behind the lowered lids.

Masks. Two masks—Comedy and Tragedy. Who wore them, and why? And which other disguises did they don, the people involved in this affair?

Hank Gibbs wore Comedy, Dick Reno's wife affected Tragedy. What did they conceal? He knew what was under Reverend Archer's mask of piety, but wasn't certain he could recognize the real Engstrom behind the false face of authority.

Dick Reno? He wore a half mask that only half concealed the bitterness beneath. And that ex-wife of his, Sandy Oliver; she too wore a domino, though it didn't prevent the violence in her eyes from blazing through.

Masks. Sometimes they slipped in moments of stress, sometimes they were ripped off in rage. Wearing them permanently was an art that few could master. But of course there were physical aids; cosmetics and cosmetic surgery, beards and mustaches for men, eyeglasses for both sexes.

He remembered Amy's description of Eric Dunstable. Beard, mustache, glasses—he had them all. Plus the twitch. Symbolic, of course. Demonologists wear death masks.

Now he wondered what lay under that particular mask. Was it too good to be true, or just too bad to be true?

And why was it being worn?

He slipped the forefinger of his right hand beneath the scarf to trace a gentle semicircle around his bruised and tender neck. *Nicholas Steiner, M.D.* Was the degree a mask in itself? Was he hiding something just like the others, Archer, Gibbs, Reno, Pitkin—

Charlie Pitkin. He'd forgotten about prim and proper Pitkin, with the corners of his mouth turned down even when he smiled. The mask of Tragedy. But in Pitkin's case, it wasn't a mask.

Then he knew.

· 23 ·

AMY left the hospital as darkness deepened in the parking lot and clouds converged overhead. The night air was chill and still; the calm before the storm.

But Amy wasn't calm, hadn't been since she'd realized what Eric Dunstable must have in mind. Or *had.* Perhaps by now she was already too late.

That's why she'd terminated her visit with Dr. Steiner so abruptly. She tried to appear calm then because there was no sense alarming him; all he could do was sit in his wheelchair and stew. But she made no effort to conceal her concern when she called Hank Gibbs from the hospital lobby.

"Has anything happened?" she said.

"I just finished my interview session. How did yours go?"

"That's not important now. Did any news come in? Anything about the Bates place?"

"Not to my knowledge. Why should there be?"

"Have you seen Eric Dunstable this afternoon?"

"No." Gibbs' voice conveyed concern. "Slow down, Amy. Tell me what this is all about."

She told him, but not slowly. Not slowly and not calmly because there wasn't time. "When Dunstable mentioned using fire in exorcism, I thought he was talking about lighting candles. But now it hit me—maybe he believes the demons came from the Bates place. And he's just flaky enough to exorcise them by burning it down. Or am I crazy too?"

"I don't think so," Gibbs said. "Did you call Engstrom?"

"Not yet. I was thinking about the fire department too."

"Let me ask Engstrom; maybe he can lean on them to take a run-by, just in case. I'll wait for you here at the office."

"No," Amy said. "I'm going out there now. Dunstable doesn't trust anyone but I think he'll listen to me."

"Stay away! Suppose something happens—"

"What kind of a question is that for a newspaperman to ask?"

"All right. I'll meet you there. Half an hour?"

"Okay." She prepared to hang up but the voice from the receiver forestalled her.

"One thing more," Gibbs said. "If by any chance you arrive ahead of me or Engstrom, for God's sake don't go looking for him alone."

"Right."

And that was it, or almost so. One of the reasons Amy used a notebook was because she couldn't recall conversations verbatim. Even her own past thoughts were paraphrased unless taken down at the moment of inception. Since she'd promised Dr. Steiner she wouldn't write during their meeting there were things he'd told her, things she'd told herself, that were already forgotten. What exactly had Steiner said about the psychological equivalents of demonic possession? And why had he said nothing at all when she described Eric Dunstable and the way he impressed her?

Never mind. Concentrate on trying to remember the route back to the freeway, getting dark now so better switch on the lights, make sure you're not on brights, should have had that damned air conditioner checked the other day, open the window and get a little air, here's the turnoff sign for the on-ramp, didn't realize rush-hour traffic was this heavy around here.

It's almost as bad as the expressway to O'Hare back home, bumper-to-bumper, just crawling. What's the matter with these people, where did they all come from, where are they going? Don't tell me there's some kind of accident up ahead.

Yes, that's got to be it, all those lights. And everyone trying to inch into the left lane. There it is, flares on the pavement, man in uniform swinging a flashlight. Brown uniform, different hat, not like one of Engstrom's people, must be Highway Patrol.

What happened here? Two cars piled on shoulder, white van behind, probably paramedics. That awful smell. Don't look, don't try to look, he's waving you on with the flashlight, keep going, keep your eyes on the road. Moving faster now, clearing up ahead. Get out of this mess, get away from that smell. Gasoline. Maybe one of the cars caught fire.

Was I right about Dunstable? I hope not.

Quit lying to yourself, part of you hopes not but part of you doesn't, that's why you want out from this damned crawl-along traffic because if anything did happen, if anything *is* happening, you don't want to miss it. This could be the big chance, the big break, hello Geraldo, good-bye to crummy apartments forever.

Really dark now. Turnoff ahead, not far, right fork or left? Why did you leave the county map at the hotel, dummy? Try to visualize it. Got to be left, right leads to the swamp, swamp leads to discovery of car, car leads to discovery of Mary Crane's corpse inside, corpse leads to shower, shower leads to motel room, motel room leads to Norman Bates waiting, waiting for someone to come down the side road in the storm then just as she was coming down that road now.

Then and now.

One and the same. Or almost the same. Then it was raining, now it was going to rain. Both times rain, the corpse was Crane's and she was Haines. Also an idiot for allowing herself to pollute her stream of consciousness this way.

No stream outside yet, not even a drizzle, just mist. Better clear the windshield. Blades squeak. Blades, swooping back and forth, up and down. Stop them, stop thinking like that, the windshield's clear and you've got to clear your mind of all that.

It wasn't easy, but Amy managed. Moving through the mist, feeling the tremor as she peered ahead. Was it fear, excitement, or just anticipation? Perhaps all three, plus a surge of anxiety when a curve in the road brought her destination into view.

The low outline of the motel loomed beyond and to the right. Behind it on the slope, the house raised its rooftop against a clouded sky. No lights shone from the windows of either structure, and there was no hint of flame.

Amy's sigh of relief was augmented as she caught sight of Hank Gibbs' car parked near the motel entrance. Then vision blurred as her windshield misted over again. It would be raining soon now.

As she turned into the driveway that circled past the entrance Amy signaled her arrival with the horn. Unnecessarily, of course, because he could see the headlights.

Or could he? The beam swept forward, moving across the car ahead and revealing no occupant.

Nobody behind the wheel. And no sign of anyone from the Sheriff's Department. Which meant Gibbs had come alone. Had he gone inside alone too?

Judging from their phone conversation, he'd expected she would arrive first, but neither of them could foresee her delay on the freeway. Still it was only logical he'd wait for her to get there before going in. Unless something had happened.

Amy braked, horn blasting as she halted.

Then she waited, motor running, windshield wipers working, apprehension mounting.

The wipers screeched. She leaned on the horn again, staring out into the mist that shrouded the empty windows and dark door of the motel. Nothing stirred except for a swirl of rising fog.

Now she glanced ahead, switching on the brights to bring the outline of the house into better focus against the foggy slope and solemn sky. Still no sign of light in the windows, no sign of life anywhere.

Once more Amy used the horn. If Gibbs had gone into the house for any reason he should still be able to hear the racket she was making; the sound of this horn was loud enough to wake the dead.

To wake the dead—

Abruptly Amy lifted her hand. Then she switched off the lights and wipers, cut the motor, dropped the car keys into her purse, opened the door, and stepped out into the mist-chilled night.

As she moved forward her voice rose. "Hank! Where are you?" Her cry brought no echo from the fog; no echo and no response.

Amy came up along the right-hand side of Gibbs' car, gazing through its windows, dreading what she might see.

Nothing.

Nothing except for the key still lodged in the ignition. What did that indicate—absentmindedness or sudden need for haste? And if the latter, where had he gone?

No answer. Nothing but silence. Dead silence.

Turning, she glanced again at the motel; its office windows dark, its door closed, or nearly so.

Nearly? Amy blinked, then stared again.

The office door was ajar.

Suppose that was the answer? Suppose Hank Gibbs had gone inside because *he* was there?

Amy started across the driveway, calling softly as she neared the door. "Hank—"

No response came.

But the door was ajar, her purse open, the cigarette lighter was in her right hand. The left zipped the purse shut, then pulled the door outward.

Beyond the threshold was the darkness, darkness that the glow of her lighter could pierce but not dispel. And if there was anything within that darkness, the lighter was scarcely an adequate weapon.

Fire cleanses.

Taking a deep breath, Amy thumbed the lighter, then hastily extinguished the flame. Because now she could smell the odor, just as she had on the freeway. But this time the reek of gasoline rose from within the room before her.

"Eric!"

Her shout rose; no sense in silence, no hope in hiding. The odor told her who it was and what he was doing; what he must have done when Hank surprised him.

"Eric—stop!"

But there was no stopping now for her as she moved into the silence and the shadows. Shadow of the reception desk, shadow of the wax figure on the pedestal, shadow on the floor.

Amy swerved just in time to avoid colliding with what lay there, sprawled facedown.

Her scream broke the silence. As she backed away against the countertop, her elbow struck the bell. Then everything seemed to happen at once.

The bell sounded.

She turned to face the counter.

From somewhere behind her a glimmer of light flashed across the open doorway.

The pivot revolved, revealing the figure atop the pedestal.

"Welcome to the Bates Motel," the taped voice said, and Norman faced Amy with a waxen grin of greeting.

But the knife came from behind her.

· 24 ·

THE knife that hurtled past Amy's head buried itself in the wall, but the revolver of the uniformed man in the doorway behind her found its target.

The uniformed man was the red-haired, skinny sheriff's deputy named Al.

Amy was properly grateful. Though, given a choice, she would have preferred that her rescuer had been Dick Reno.

But Reno had already made a choice of his own; he and Sandy Oliver were going to make another try of getting together, now that Engstrom was giving him back his badge. Amy didn't see him again. In retrospect it was probably just as well.

She did see Engstrom. But here retrospection failed her; he was just another figure in the nightmare following the events at the motel, the nightmare that included so many figures and seemed to linger for so many days. During that time everybody did their best to protect Amy from the media, though there was no way of keeping them from her entirely. And until the furor began to die down, leaving town was not the answer.

That was the real problem, of course; not enough answers.

Nothing from Charlie Pitkin, who split a whole bottle of sleeping pills between himself and his daughter the night after what took place at the motel.

None from Eric Dunstable, whose body Amy had almost literally stumbled over in the motel office.

None from Hank Gibbs.

Nor would there be.

He'd died from his bullet wound while still en route to Baldwin Memorial Hospital.

· 25 ·

GIBBS had covered his tracks well. And bringing them to light again wasn't all that easy. Despite the spectacular advances of criminology, forensic medicine, and computer science, in the end it came down to a matter of just plain hard digging.

The partnership between Otto Remsbach and Charlie Pitkin on the Bates project was fully confirmed by data in their respective files. But it took digging to establish the shadowy connection between Charlie Pitkin and Hank Gibbs.

At least that's what Sheriff Engstrom confided to Amy on the day before her departure.

"Gibbs didn't have anything down in writing," Engstrom said. "But he probably would have after Pitkin did a job on Remsbach's estate. That was no big deal; the will named Charlie as executor, and he'd made enough private loans to justify a takeover for repayment. The house, the business, the Bates property—Pitkin would have ended up with it all. Plus Hank Gibbs as a partner."

Amy's pen moved over her notebook page quickly. "But if there was nothing in writing—"

Engstrom shook his head. "Nothing about a partnership deal, no. But we found other things on paper. Memos in Gibbs' handwriting, locked away in Charlie Pitkin's files. Very detailed memos on how to set up the Bates project from the beginning. The two were thick as thieves."

"Stealing's one thing, murder is another," Amy said. "Do you really believe both of them were in on this?"

"That's something we'll probably never know for sure." Engstrom sat with crossed legs, the pointed tip of his right boot jabbing empty air. "But in view of the circumstances, it's likely they did plan the murder of Otto Remsbach together." Now the legs uncrossed. "Thing is, plans don't always work out. And that's when the trouble starts.

"We don't think anyone planned Terry Dowson's death. The way we see it, Gibbs went out there for only one reason—to get hold of that wax figure of Norman's mother."

Amy frowned. "Then you're assuming he already knew what he intended to do with it."

The sheriff shrugged. "There doesn't seem to be any other logical motive."

"Nothing he did seems logical to me," Amy said. "Killing that child—"

"Remember what I said about plans getting fouled up. Gibbs did his best; got himself an alibi, parked his car God knows where. And he was willing to lug that wax dummy a long way, most likely through wooded acreage, just to make certain nobody would see him. What he didn't count on was those two kids showing up.

"Nearest we can figure, they were already somewhere upstairs when Gibbs arrived; still don't know if he got a dupe key or found the door open. Maybe he heard the girls talking upstairs and took a chance on getting the dummy out before they came back down. My hunch is he was worried about having to handle the figure, and he had to hurry because his alibi would only cover him for so long.

"Anyhow he got the dummy. From what the other girl, Mick Sontag, told us about their movements, he could have taken the figure just before they came down the basement stairs. When Gibbs heard them he hid somewhere until they went into the fruit cellar.

"That gave him enough time to sneak back up, but not enough to get out before Mick came running upstairs. What he must have done was hide behind the front door. When she ran outside he waited to give her a chance of getting far enough away so as not to see him when he slipped out. That's probably what he was starting to do when Terry Dowson got upstairs. My guess is what happened then was panic, not plan."

Amy nodded. "The plan was only to kill Remsbach."

"Frankly, we have no way of knowing. We do know Doris Huntley slipped Pitkin a lot of information about Remsbach's deals, so she might have been killed intentionally to prevent any chance of her talking. On the other hand it's quite possible she died for the same reason Terry Dowson did; she just happened to be in the wrong place at the wrong time.

"Either way, Gibbs knew where he was going to be on the night of Remsbach's murder. He did go to Baldwin Memorial Hospital to provide himself with an alibi, but he counted on no one knowing the exact time of his arrival or departure. And no one did."

Amy added a line at the bottom of one page and finished her sentence on another. As she did so she glanced up toward the open doorway and outer office beyond. From behind the reception desk Irene Grovesmith nodded and smiled.

It was difficult for Amy to account for such a drastic change in attitude until she hit upon the reason. Irene must have seen her on the nightly news. Anybody who appears on prime-time television automatically becomes a celebrity, someone you smile at in hopes that they'll smile back.

Amy did so, but when she faced Engstrom again her expression changed. "We spent a lot of time together," she murmured. "I can see now what he was doing—trying to find out just how much I knew. Pretending to help by taking me around, while his real reason was to keep me from learning too much more on my own." The pen twisted between nervous fingers. "And all the while I thought it was because maybe he had a thing about me." Amy shook her head. "How could I have been such a fool?"

"One thing's for sure," Engstrom said. "You never should have gone out to the Bates property in the first place, even if you expected to meet Gibbs there. And when you saw his car parked and empty it should've been enough to signal that he'd set you up.

"Which, of course, he did—with the office door left ajar to get you inside."

"I just didn't stop and think," Amy said. "I was concerned about him."

"And he was concerned about you. When you reported seeing Dunstable and feeling he might torch the Bates place, Gibbs had no choice. If you'd guessed right he had to move fast, hoping he'd be in time to stop Dunstable from lighting a match.

"The problem was he had no way of preventing you from coming when you insisted. Even if he could, if something happened out there, Gibbs would have to explain why he lied to you when he promised he'd call us. Either way, he had to do two things—stop Dunstable and get rid of you."

Amy was adding to her notes. "I still can't believe it," she murmured. "Two cold-blooded murders—"

The Sheriff shrugged. "Remember Terry Dowson, Otto Remsbach, Doris Huntley. They say killing's pretty much like anything else people do. It gets easier as you go along."

No big deal. Amy heard the echo of Bonnie Walton's words when she'd interviewed her for the book. If true, there really should be a warning from the Surgeon General. *Warning: murder is habit-forming and can be injurious to your health.*

Gallows humor, that's what they used to call it. But there'd been nothing even remotely amusing about the deaths of those others, or her own close call. She met Engstrom's gaze. "You actually think Hank Gibbs went out there prepared to kill us both?"

"He didn't have many options. Looks like he arrived just in time to surprise Dunstable sprinkling that gasoline. Maybe he put up a struggle, maybe not, but we know how it ended. Then Gibbs had to deal with you. Again there's no telling, but our theory is he'd have burned the motel himself to get rid of the evidence."

"Meaning our bodies." Amy's shudder was involuntary. "Since no one knew I called him, he'd probably say something about just happening to be driving by and seeing the flames."

"Something like that," Engstrom said. "Burning the motel would get him off the hook. Rebuilding it could be expensive but at least he'd save the house." The Sheriff leaned forward. "Tell you something else. If things had worked out, I bet that wax dummy of Norman would have ended up in the fruit cellar instead of melting in the motel fire. There'd be plenty of time for Gibbs to risk moving it before leaving to call the fire department, since he didn't figure on any of us being around."

Amy looked up from her notepad. "Why did you send someone?"

"You can thank your friend Steiner for that. If he hadn't figured things out and called us, Al wouldn't have been coming by to check on the place and give you a hand."

Amy frowned. "Dr. Steiner didn't know I was going there."

"True. But from what you told him, he had a pretty good idea about Gibbs showing up sooner or later."

"What made Steiner so sure?"

"Who knows?" Engstrom shrugged. "Maybe you'd better ask him about that."

And on the day before leaving town, she did.

This time Dr. Steiner greeted her in his office. And there he answered her question.

"Masks," he said. "After we talked the other day I got to thinking about how we hide behind them, and what they symbolize in our society. The most commonplace extremes, of course, represent Comedy and Tragedy, and I found them on the faces of various people you and I discussed. All but Charlie Pitkin. Tragedy, for him, was not a mask."

Amy's notebook was open, her pen at the ready. "What do you mean?"

Dr. Steiner shook his head. "I'd rather you didn't write it down. And please, if you use this information, no attribution."

"I promise." Amy flipped the notebook shut with the tip of her pen. "Was he one of your outpatients too?"

"That's right."

"Then perhaps you don't have to say anything. From what Sheriff Engstrom told me about the double suicide, I think I can guess the rest. The burden of such a relationship must have been unbearable for them both."

"He was doing his best to fight it," Steiner said. "But after what happened the other night, it was too much. He undoubtedly realized that once his involvement became known he couldn't hope to shield himself or his daughter from the investigation that was bound to follow."

Amy nodded. "Then he knew about Hank Gibbs."

"I don't think so. That's why he went into trauma. Granted, Pitkin was far from a model of rectitude, but he'd never knowingly act as an accessory to homicide." Steiner sighed. "I just wish he had come to me before—"

His visitor frowned. "It doesn't add up," she said. "This sad man with his sad secret, giving Otto Remsbach all those way-out funny ideas."

"That's how I knew," Dr. Steiner said. "I can't recall seeing him smile or say anything indicating he might have the slightest sense of humor. But Hank Gibbs always wore the mask of Comedy."

"Were you aware Hank and Pitkin were secret partners?" Amy said.

"I knew they were close and I assumed it was some kind of business deal. But until this notion about the masks came to me I didn't guess it must have to do with Remsbach's plans to turn the Bates property into a tourist attraction. Then everything seemed to fall into place—the relationship between the two, Gibbs feeding Pitkin ideas to pass on to Remsbach, the motivation behind the murders—"

"The Sheriff thinks the little girl's murder wasn't premeditated, and they're not certain about Doris Huntley. But he's sure about Hank Gibbs planning to kill Remsbach."

"That's why he needed the wax figure of Norman's mother, because he wanted it to be found with Remsbach's body in the bed."

Amy's frown returned. "You think he did this as some sort of a sick joke?"

"Quite the reverse. Putting that dummy beside Remsbach's corpse was serious business. You couldn't buy that kind of publicity."

"But that's insane!"

"Technically speaking, no. By both clinical and legal definitions, Hank Gibbs was in full possession of his faculties, aware of what he was doing, and realized the consequences. His *rationale* was psychopathic, not psychotic. Within the context of later events, getting rid of Eric Dunstable and attempting to get rid of you was logical procedure."

Amy shook her head. "As I remember it, a psychopath is someone without empathy, someone who can't identify with others. But Hank was always so helpful, so friendly—"

"Friendly with everyone, but no friends of his own. A loner in a job that demands interaction with just about everyone."

"Then why didn't he get out?"

"Perhaps he liked being a big frog in a little pond. Or maybe he hoped he could find a way to jump and make a splash in a bigger pond." Steiner smiled. "Just like you."

"I didn't realize it was that obvious." Amy paused. "All right, it's true—I think most writers want the reward of fame and fortune, and I'm no exception. But I wouldn't kill for it."

"You're not a psychopath." Steiner smiled again. "I know it's all guesswork on my part now, pretty much like coming up with an autopsy report without ever having had a chance to dissect the actual corpse. But I think I knew Hank Gibbs as well as he allowed anyone to know him. And to coin a phrase, actions speak louder than words.

"If you stop and consider, everything Gibbs did fueled media attention, in a society where such attention is essential for material success. That's what he wanted out of life, and nothing else mattered, even if it meant taking the lives of others."

"It's hard for me to accept," Amy said. "He seemed like such a caring person."

"And so he was." Dr. Steiner nodded. "But only for himself. If you're looking for the bitterness and the cruelty, it's there, in his humor. He used it both as a shield and a weapon. His self-deprecation served as both." Steiner's chuckle rasped faintly. "I ought to know. I've had the same tendencies at times."

"You mustn't let me overtire you," Amy said.

"That's no problem. If there is anything else I can do to help—"

"You've already done more than your share," Amy said. "I only wish I knew of some way to repay you for all your kindness."

"Don't worry about that. Just go write the book. And when you do, remember to tell about the demons."

"Eric Dunstable's demons?"

"No." Steiner shook his head. "The demons that possessed Hank Gibbs and continue to possess so many others. Greed. Avarice. The real demons that are taking over this world."

"I won't forget." Amy rose, smiling.

"Let me make a suggestion," Steiner said. "When you're finished, maybe you can write another book, about life in the asylum."

"Here?"

"No." Steiner gestured toward the window. "Out there."